THE ALMOST QUEEN

ALYS MURRAY

Sword and Silk Books
105 Viewpoint Circle Pell City, AL 35128
Visit our website at SwordandSilkBooks.com

To request permissions contact the publisher at
admin@swordandsilkbooks.com.

First Edition: October 2021

The characters and events in this book are fictitious. Any similarity to real
persons, living or dead, is coincidental and not intended by the author.

Ebook: 978-1-736430-5-7

To anyone who never saw themselves in the pages of fairy tales or wearing crowns in the movies.
This story is for you.

PROLOGUE

The Royal Academy of Aulen, with its prestigious pedigree and nearly thousand-year history of schooling the children of the kingdom's most elite, had never hosted a witch-child before. And every day since Ellara Wist had arrived at their hallowed halls, the school and everyone inside of it seemed to go out of their way to remind her they didn't want to.

Getting into the Royal Academy had taken no less than a handful of small miracles and a mountain of deceit, but her acceptance letter allowed her travel permission past the border of Outerland. By the time she'd arrived at the imposing gates surrounding the school and everyone realized that Ellara Wist *wasn't*, in fact, a humble farmer's daughter with an exceptional I.Q., but a witch who'd duped every barrier separating her from an education, it was too late to send her back without some kind of scandal. After all, her scores on the written entrance exam broke records, *and* they'd already awarded her the scholarship. The Regents of the Academy feared witch unrest in Outerland if they returned her, so she remained.

Back then, she had been so sure that if she kept her head down, everyone would outgrow the scary stories they were probably told about her kind. They would learn to see past her green skin, dotted with dark freckles. They would know *her*, not the lies everyone told about witches.

But a year had passed. And no one was growing. No one was changing. No one saw her.

"Someone left horned snakes in the search drawers again. You can fish those out, can't you?"

"Of course. I'll be happy to get them." She beamed up at her usual library companion, a tight-curled, tight-smiling girl named Cendris, from her place behind the carved Thrisall desk where she spent most of her free time re-cataloguing books and repairing broken leather spines.

"I'm sure you will. I guess you would like them, wouldn't you? You know what they say about birds of a feather. Or, should I say, scales of a feather?"

Cendris disappeared with a twittering laugh before Ellara could inform her that her made-up expression didn't even make any sense, leaving her alone in the great, yawning library.

Her work-study job as a library assistant may have been a way of hiding her away so the rest of the school only had to look at her during lectures, but Ellara couldn't help but love the stacks of books towering toward the sky. Nor could she help but feel like the building's two wings—which moved out from the atrium where her desk was situated—were reaching out to embrace her. As prestigious as the school was, as renowned as it was for educating future rulers, most of the students were more interested in coupling off or training for the upcoming war everyone couldn't stop whispering about than actually studying, which left her alone with her books more often than not.

When she wrote home to her mother and her sisters and everyone in their village who would undoubtedly huddle around to hear her news, she spoke of the weather and the beauty of the architecture and the challenging aspects of the finer points of the advanced arithmetic they taught her. She never spoke of the loneliness. Or of the solace she found in books. An almanac of the stars over Aulen couldn't judge her. A compendium of the history of Aulenian queens didn't laugh at her green skin or poke at her dark freckles. Her favorite characters never left horned snakes for her to wrangle. Humans, on the other hand, weren't so kind. And now that she'd been around them for so long, she didn't believe any of them were capable of it.

Whistling one of her mother's favorite folk songs, she reached for a pair of scaled gloves she kept in the bottom drawer of her desk for just such an occasion. After her first pair had gone "missing," only to end up on the hands of a statue of a witch being tortured by King Yavul, the mastermind behind the banishment that sent Ellara's kind to Outerland, she kept them locked away for safekeeping.

After the snakes had been wrangled, she wasn't in a rush to return to the dormitories. She never was. If she thought she could get away with sleeping under her desk and only resurfacing for meals and lectures, she would have at least attempted it. So, as she made her way through the south wing, she strolled through the moonlight pouring in through the wide, brass-hung windows. During the day, sunlight baked the room, but at night, it was the perfect place to see the moon dancing with its reflection in the river. Here, Ellara could see it all, everything about this place that she actually liked: the gates in the distance, the dark water, the flicker-bugs that danced over the meadows, the dragon's cave at the base of the river, a human-shaped shadow wrestling a much larger, dragon-shaped shadow, the stars that—

Wait. Human? Dragon? The human and the dragon weren't usual at all. Or, more precisely, the dragon was a fixture near the River Gate, where it would occasionally poke its head out and prey on small birds who wandered into its watery path, but humans never went anywhere near the dragon, much less tried to wrestle the thing.

Pressing her nose against the glass, she glanced across the

shadowed landscape, desperate for even the slightest hint that someone else was out there, someone who could save the body currently fighting the dragon. She could see no one. As the rest of the academy's dormitories were on the other side of the vast library, she could be almost certain no one could see them, either.

Fates, you've got to be kidding me, she thought, her wrists pricking painfully as magic crackled between her fingertips. The trouble with being a witch of the light meant that her magic didn't give her much room to ignore the suffering; her magic itself *wanted* to help. She'd been in control of her magic most of her life, but light magic crackled as it came to life, sparking between her fingers, as if reminding her she could do some good.

She didn't need reminding. The binders on her wrists—two heavy cuffs like bracelets, given to her by the Academy Regents when she arrived here—bound her magic. She could use it, but every time it sparked to life, the binders burned into her skin. It was supposed to be a deterrent, and after the first time she'd burned herself while absent-mindedly using her magic to make up her bed in the morning, she had been sufficiently deterred.

But if she wanted her magic to stop pricking, she at least had to *try* to help the shadowy figure. Or, she at least had to see that he was alright. The humans may not have done the same for her, but she wasn't like them.

Gathering up her skirts, she dropped the scale gloves and took off out of the library. The tall grass separating her favorite building from the lake whipped around her calves, and the bend in the river grew larger and larger in front of her.

The moon was full tonight. Thank the Fates for that. It meant that the closer she came to the bank of the river, the easier it was to see and take stock of the situation.

Unfortunately, it also meant she had a perfectly clear view and a spotlight when the dragon sunk his teeth into the gut of his victim.

All at once, a few things became clear to her as time slowed and energy whipped through her body, electrifying her every nerve ending. The victim was a man, bloodied and bruised. One of the dragon's teeth—the one diving between the victim's ribcage—was broken. The sword and half of the tooth were lying, discarded, a small distance away, being lapped at by the quiet river.

And the victim held something small in his hands. Something moving.

A duckling?

Ellara's stomach sunk as her spirits soared. She *had* to save this man. No matter what it did to her, he didn't deserve to die like this.

And, if she couldn't manage that, perhaps she could at least save the duckling.

Bracing herself for the pain, she pressed her palm out towards the dragon and began screaming a curse her mother taught her, the words strangling her throat as her wrists burned. Light flooded the bend in the river, brighter than the moon, and the entranced dragon retreated, dropping his human prey to the wet sand below.

The world spun. The pain was so strong. But the duckling in the man's hand quacked and scurried off as the body laid there, slack on the ground, and she knew she couldn't run away to lick her wounds.

Body shaking, she stumbled towards him. *Still breathing. Good start.* Hands out again, each finger trembling and twitching, she pressed into the bloody wound, letting the heat seep into her flesh and the red dye her skin.

The spell was ancient, as old as magic itself, her mother used to say, and it whispered from her tongue before she registered that she'd done so. Inch by inch, she moved her fingers out of the wound as the magic stitched his body back together.

And when it was done, when she'd absorbed his pain and taken even more from her binders, enough to haze the moon and shake her vision, he groaned back to life.

Even a bloodied mess, she recognized him. Tarran of the Rosson House, a noble family with more wealth and power than anyone in Outerland could dream of having. He wasn't so handsome now, but she'd certainly eyed him in the halls before. He was the noble prince type she read about in her stories, and she'd never seen him without a smile.

Until now, of course.

"What were you doing?" she hissed, letting her anger fuel her and cover up the weakness in her voice. "Were you *trying* to get yourself killed?"

"Training..." he coughed. "I was training."

So, the youngest prince of Rosson House was a liar and an idiot. Interesting. His hand, which had held the duckling, clenched and unclenched, and she leaned back against a nearby rock to survey him. Besides, in lectures, none of the humans had ever let her get this close to them before. She wanted to take advantage of the opportunity.

"Training against the River Gate dragon? I'm sure your house would be very happy if their son came home as an ash heap."

"I'm sure they wouldn't care. One less son to worry about," he said without a trace of humor.

"Well, I'm sorry I disappointed them, then."

Brown-green eyes snapped open and met hers. They widened until they dominated his entire face and gave away his confusion.

"You. You're...you're the witch."

"I just can't stop disappointing people today, can I?"

For a few blissful moments, she'd been able to talk to someone like she used to talk to her friends back home, with ease and wit and without prejudice. But Terran, a full foot taller and strong from his military training, inched back from her, stopping only when the heels of his hands touched water.

He hated her. She'd saved his life and still, he hated her. Ellara knew she shouldn't have expected anything more from a human. They were all the same. But still...disappointment soured everything.

"They said you can't do magic," he snapped accusingly.

"I can. It's just..." With a practiced strength, she pulled the tight binders slightly down her skin to reveal new burn marks. Raw. Bloody. She hissed as the cold wind hit them. "It's just very, very painful."

Maybe it was her wry smile or the sight of his blood on her hands, but something shifted in his eyes, something definite and real. It wasn't a trick of the moon or her perspective; he changed.

"You need to see the healers," he said.

"They won't help. They never do."

His dark brows knit together. "You knew it would hurt and that you wouldn't get any help after and you still did this?"

"You're alive, aren't you?"

"Yes," he scoffed, blowing past her little joke. "But why did you do it?"

If she were a more cautious person, she wouldn't have answered him. She would have disappeared into the night and forgotten all about him and the dragon and the duckling. After all, if she told him the truth, maybe he'd tell his friends, and they'd use it against her, put themselves in fake danger so she'd hurt herself trying to save them.

But she wasn't cautious. These humans, they were all too safe, too protective of their feelings. They played games with one another and tossed everyone who wasn't like them aside. They didn't care. But she wouldn't be the evil witch they believed her to be, not even if it meant putting herself in harm's way.

And apparently, away from the trappings of school and the eyes of other humans, he didn't want to be the rotten human she thought him to be, either.

"Because you're a prince who fought a dragon to save the life of a little baby duck." She shrugged and pushed herself to stand. "I don't know. I suppose I thought you were being heroic. There isn't enough of that around here." When he said nothing, just stared at her as if she were an ancient rune he couldn't decipher, she took her leave, calling back to him over her shoulder. "Make sure you drink something strong before you go to sleep tonight. Even my magic can't save you from the pain you'll feel in the morning."

The grass crunched beneath the heels of her boots for one step. Two steps. Five steps. And then—

"My lady. Wait."

Every sinew in her body froze. *My lady?* No one at the academy even called her by her *name*, much less by a title as genteel as *my lady*. Her chest flushed, blossoming warmth fighting against the cold. He caught up, stepping in front of her to offer a small silver circle. It glinted in the moonlight.

"Please have this."

They'd played a dozen tricks on her this way, playing nice just before doing something cruel, like pushing her out of a tower. But he did something they didn't. He didn't flinch when their skin touched. Holding up the circle of metal, she inspected it. A crown twisted with flowers and axes. Some words in ancient Aulenian.

"Pretty," she muttered.

He breathed a laugh. The sound sparked something inside of her. It felt like magic, but it didn't activate her binders.

"It's a token. They're used to symbolize debts. You saved my life tonight. So, if you should ever need me to save yours, I will be there."

"That's very kind. Thank you."

She blinked, still staring down at the token, rubbing her thumb over the engraving. The prince of a royal house just gave her—a witch—a debt. After months of being ignored and hated, it meant a great deal to her.

Not that she would let him know that, of course.

"But I don't think I'll ever need saving."

CHAPTER ONE

War. It may have been over, but Ellara could still smell it in the air. The people in the cloistered walls of High Court were celebrating down below the window of her prison cell, but her bones told her this wasn't the end.

She'd seen this entire act before. Over the last eight years of blood and destruction, half a dozen men threw themselves on the throne of Aulen and declared themselves king, only for another army or horde to open a front in the fighting and tear the new monarch down. Too many peace treaties had been written and broken. Too many alliances made and destroyed by infighting or greed or incompetence. This wasn't the first time someone fancied himself the new ruler, and it certainly wasn't the first time she'd seen the inside of a jail cell.

Which meant that she knew how to escape. And since she didn't have any interest in being in High Court when the next army arrived ready for a fight, she'd have to do it again.

She paced the steps of her cell, letting the frayed hem of her battle gown dance in the slender space between the wall and the skin of her calf. Five steps north. Five steps south. It didn't give her very much room to work with, but she'd worked greater miracles with less room. The real problem would be fitting through the slender slat in the wall they had the audacity to call a window.

Swinging her arms around her chest once, twice, then three times, she let her powers flow through her, awakening her muscles after hours of being curled in a passed-out ball on the floor. The aches and stiffness didn't surprise her. After all, this was how the so-called ends of war usually went: she'd be in the middle of a battle, wielding an axe and spells like extensions of her own body, shortly before some weak-kneed man would surrender their campaign. As a witch, she was always one of the first to be taken into custody. The leaders of Aulen—and all the factions that made it up—feared they'd never catch her if they didn't take her by surprise, which was probably correct. And when she woke from the darkness of whatever misery they'd put her through, it was always in a cell.

And the stupid fools *never* remembered to place binders on her.

"Idiots," she muttered, smile twitching upward.

Hands pressing out towards the wall, she sent a wave of magic through it, closing her eyes tight against the flying debris of stone and timber that her power disturbed. A few pieces cut into her skin, but pain that small barely registered. Eight years of war erased most of her ability to register anything less than a dagger to the stomach. Below, the voices of the singing crowd turned to screams.

If a falling brick had hurt a passerby, then she didn't have much time. Everyone would look up at her.

Well, better make the show worth their attention.

The sun hit her skin and flooded it with warmth as she stepped onto the edge of the now human-sized hole in the wall, which framed her body like a misshapen stone portrait case. She braced herself with one hand when she saw just how far down she would have to travel. Still, she braved a look at the crowds below, relishing their gawping mouths and the scandalized hands that flew to heaving bosoms.

"People of Aulen," Ellara called over the din with a voice of false enthusiasm, holding up her fist as if riling them up for battle. "Your leaders are cowards and fools. Escape while you still can!" She smirked and released her hold on the wall, shrugging slightly. "I know I will."

For a split second, she allowed herself a smile of triumph, a breath of air in which to soak in their shock. But as soon as she heard the shouts of guards and the metallic *sling* of swords being torn from their sheaths, her body snapped into action and she screamed one last message.

"Freedom for Outerland!"

Jump.

Her mind revolted against the command, but her body obeyed. She swung out over the crowd, groping for the wire-connected flags strung over the street. The momentum pushed her across the cord until she landed with a *thud* on a rooftop.

Below, the guards were beside themselves trying to head her off, running around like half-awake mousing cats. Shouts followed her every step across the rooftops of High Court, but they mixed together into little more than a cacophony of distant sound, the voices of frightened masses who could never capture her.

It might have been easier to stay in her cell and manipulate her way out with magic, to use a few spells on the weak-minded guards and slip out of a side door before anyone with any real power knew where she was going. But if the guards weren't so easily persuadable, she might have found herself on the executioner's block or in some kind of retribution camp, and neither of those scenarios was acceptable. She *had* to get home. She had to return to Outerland. The only reason she'd left home all those years ago was to fight for the freedom of her people. She couldn't do that from a cell or a hole in the ground.

Pressing her body faster, and still faster, she leapt from one housing block to the next. Her heart and her feet pounded out a steady rhythm, one that drowned out everything else, except the sound of loosing arrows from behind aiming straight for her back.

Her hands clenched the air blindly for her axe. They must have taken it from her, and she missed its familiar weight in her grasp. At least with that, she could defeat anyone who dared try to stand between her and escape.

But the lack of an axe didn't matter. Because up ahead, she caught sight of the high stone walls of High Court, the defenses that had kept so many armies at bay for so long. Blood still stained the parapets, but the guards at the nearest sentry post dozed off soundly against one another, clearly exhausted from a night of drinking. The green grasses of the plains beyond the city-state's walls called to her, whispering promises and congratulations. She was *free*. She was getting out. None of these half-witted guards could catch her. She'd be halfway home before any of them even realized they'd lost her.

At least, that's what she thought. Until the arrow pierced through the fabric of her bodice and the soft green skin of her back. The stab of pain broke her concentration. She lost her footing. Any magic she'd been collecting for the final jump over the wall shattered. And the flint through her back sent her toppling, toppling, toppling down towards the unforgiving stone street below.

She woke. Panic filled her. This time, she hadn't woken up back in a jail cell. She'd woken up on her back, bound and swaying through the air. Things weren't going according to her usual prison break plans, but her mind was hazy, and the ground kept moving beneath her, which made her thought's immediate jump towards a second escape rather difficult. She couldn't come up with a plan when she couldn't even remember how to open her eyes, much less figure out where she was. Men below her carried her on a four-board; they walked on slightly unsteady feet. The constant swaying wasn't doing much to help her orient herself.

"You alright?"

A gruff voice from above her seemed to address her directly, each word sending shards of ale-scented spittle in her direction.

"That depends," she replied, testing her fingers with small twitches of magic. Each twitch rewarded her with a sharp sting around her wrists. They'd remembered the binders this time. Damn.

"On what?"

"On where you're taking me."

This must have been extremely amusing to her captor because he released a wave of belly laughs and a new shower of spit. Her first rule of being captured was to never show weakness, to wrap herself in a cocoon of bravado and confidence, even if they were false, but she couldn't help but flinch as a small piece of something—wet, half-chewed meat?—landed on her cheek.

"We're taking you for execution, of course. Your little insurrectionist's speech counts as treason. *Freedom for Outerland.* What a load of nonsense. Your little green legs will be dangling from a noose in no time at all."

Ellara must have suddenly remembered how to open her eyes because they snapped wide open. *Execution.* She'd gotten close to it during the last years of the war, but it had never been explained to her in such simple terms. Her death was always more implied than commanded. The word itself had never been used like a cold, unforgiving fact.

She was taken through what appeared to be dark, windowless catacombs on some kind of stretcher. They'd gone to a lot of trouble to string their little prize up, latching her arms to her body and her body to the board below her back with heavy leather straps. A cold metal circlet tightly choked her neck. Another binder, like the ones on her wrists. A heavy one. Even the little magic it would take to get out of the leather trappings would be enough to kill her with that thing on.

Maybe she could talk her way out. A risky proposition—maybe even a stupid one, without her magic—but she had to try. She couldn't die here in High Court, not like this, not without saving Outerland. She hadn't spent eight years fighting a war to die as nothing more in their eyes than a little witch.

"Say, I've been out of it for a while," she intoned, glancing up at the burly man carrying the head-end of the board, the man who she assumed spoke to her earlier. A curly black beard obscured most of her view of him. Pity. She had always been good at reading faces. "What's this I hear about the end of the war?"

"Oh, don't give me that, little witch. You know very well what's happened. You were there."

The truth was more complicated than that. Sure, she'd technically been on the battlefield when they'd lost. But after so many years and so many campaigns and so much blood, she'd stopped seeing the colors of the banners. She stopped seeing the faces of those fighting unless they were on her side. She couldn't have told him who they'd been battling against, even if it meant saving her life.

"The last thing I remember, I was in a prison cell. Before that, I was on a battlefield listening to the sounds of war. I don't know who—"

But that's when she saw it. Lifting her head as much as she could manage, she saw it all. The banners hung on the walls. The crests on their uniforms. The buckle on one of her leather bindings. The rotting heads of her former leaders were lined along the floor of this catacomb, their faces still drawn in the terror at the moment of their murder.

The brand carved into each of their faces was the same as those on the banners, the uniforms, the buckles. It was the same emblem on the coin she'd sewn into the breast of her jacket. The same one Tarran, the noble human she'd saved, had given her almost ten years ago.

Someone from Tarran's house had won the war. And they had *really* won the war. That much she could tell from the severed heads screaming silently at her from their places on the floor. The heads of the men she'd fought alongside in battle. The heads of the men who'd promised the witches their freedom if they fought for their cause.

She'd saved that coin forever. She'd never used it, even when it could have meant a less painful prison break, a safer escape from the clutches of her enemies.

But if she didn't take this gamble, they would execute her. She was willing to make this bet if it meant it might save her life.

"You can't execute me," she exclaimed, the words slipping from her lips like a deathbed declaration.

"Oh, yeah?" He chuckled again, as arrogant as she'd been during her failed escape. "And why is that?"

"Because I'm under the protection of Lord Tarran. A member of *your* new royal house."

The caravan carrying her halted. Her conversation partner tripped. The room held its collective breath, and Ellara did everything in her power to keep the terror out of her eyes. This was the moment that would decide her life, which sat in the hands of the half-drunk executioner carrying her to the hanging block and hung on the ten-year-old word of a man whose family had apparently killed half of Aulen to get the throne.

"I believe you'll refer to him as *King*, little witch."

"...What?"

They couldn't actually be saying what she thought she was hearing.

"That's *King* Terran to you. "

"King... King Terran?"

15

"Yes. Ruler of Aulen."

Her mind had always been faster than her magic, her axe, or her feet. With this new information—Terran, the soft-eyed human boy she'd caught trying to save a duckling from a dragon all those years ago—had won the war. Of all the bloodthirsty, cruel men who had tried to conquer his enemies and capture their armies, *he'd* been the one to succeed. Her stomach dropped to the cold stone floor, and the blood rushed out of her face. If there had been any hope in him all those years ago, his winning the war meant it was surely gone by now.

But a debt was still a debt. And she could only hope that even a king would honor it. If he didn't, her life and the lives of everyone in Outerland would be forfeited.

"Well, your new king owes me a debt. And I would like to collect."

CHAPTER TWO

"Your Majesty?"

It took every ounce of Terran's willpower to keep from shuddering at the sound of those two words. He'd heard them countless times, of course, directed at the various men who had made themselves king over the years, but to hear them directed towards himself...the sound was downright sickening.

"Yes?"

The throne room of High Court had been mercifully empty for ten minutes—ten entire minutes in which Terran could be alone—and with this newest intrusion, he desperately wished for that silence once more. In the silence, in the stillness, no one looked to him for answers. Answers he didn't have.

Elias, his Warden and now his official royal protector, stood in the doorway, hands on his sword, eyes scanning the room for any signs of danger. A side effect of eight years of battle and death. When his gaze settled upon the awkward set of Terran's shoulders and his fractured posture, his golden brow furrowed.

"Is there something wrong with your throne, Majesty?"

There wasn't any regal way of informing him that sitting on that throne made him feel as if he were sitting upon the bones of thousands of slaughtered men, no way of explaining that without denigrating the sacrifices it took to get the crown upon his head and his family's banners flying above the castle towers.

"Just fancied a walk. Isn't a king entitled to a walk?"

"Of course," he said, a sardonic smile tugging at his lips as he stepped further into the broad, circular chamber, his silver armor glinting in the sunlight. "Just thought you'd be saving your strength. There's much to be done."

Yes, there *was* much to be done. No one told him that winning the throne would mean winning a host of administrative duties along with it. Picking the color for royal cushions and selecting silverware for the first royal banquet was the last thing on his mind, yet it seemed to be the only thing on which anyone in this castle was interested in hearing his opinion.

"And I'm sure you're bringing even more glorious tasks for me to complete?"

"You appointed me as your royal Warden, not your royal friend. If you had wanted me here for drinking ale and singing war songs, you should have given me a cushier job. One that didn't require I wear this ridiculous display-" he gestured to his armor, which a poor stable boy had no doubt spent all morning polishing to a mirror-shine- "every time I leave my rooms."

A smirk tugged at Tarran's lips. The battlefield had turned him from a boy with delusions of dragon-slaying grandeur into a war-shocked man. Every time he closed his eyes, he saw the horrors of the dead. Every time he tried to sleep, he heard their screams. But Elias understood that. *That*, not his perfect armor, was the reason he'd chosen him as Warden. Tarran didn't believe that war made friends out of any men and he'd lost all of his own brothers in the fighting, but if there was ever a man he'd consider his closest ally, it was Elias.

"Get on with it, then."

"Right. There are three things that require your immediate attention."

"Let me guess: tablecloths, colors for the coronation banners, and where to bury the heads of the dead kings?"

"I'm glad they didn't select you based on your guessing abilities."

"Just tell me what they want."

"In short? A queen, an heir, and...well, there's also this small matter of the witches."

Those issues scrambled in his head. A queen...Impossible. An heir? Out of the question. But the witches...he could handle a conversation about the witches. At least that was something vaguely political, something that challenged his expertise and said something about what kind of king he would be.

Pity, then, that he had absolutely no idea what to do with the witches.

His mind flashed momentarily to the witch who'd saved his life all those years ago and the scar he still bore from that night. What a stupid boy he'd been back then, trying to save an innocent creature from the mouth of a monster. If the last eight years taught him anything, it was that stupid decisions like that only ended in more death and suffering.

"Let's start with Outerland, then," he said.

"Your Majesty," Elias tutted, shaking his head. "You can't avoid the queen and progeny question forever."

The war ended less than a week ago. Only six days ago he'd been kneeling in a field of bodies and blood. It had been such a short time since they'd first placed the Aulenian crown upon his head. But already, the people called for his future to be secured. He almost couldn't believe it. Almost.

He understood their desire for a semblance of normalcy after all the years of fighting. And, if he had been in their position instead of the king, he probably also would have wanted some kind of distraction. A wedding meant gowns and feasts and polished, bloodless armor and dancing and all the joys of life the war had denied them.

If it weren't *his* wedding they were after, he would have agreed with them.

"I'm not avoiding the question. Just prioritizing."

"Of course."

"Now, what's all this to do with Outerland, then?"

But before Elias could open his mouth to answer, the doors of the throne room smashed open, disturbing a candelabra and sending the Warden and the king reaching for their swords.

"Stop everything!" A voice boomed, loud enough to rattle jewels in the chandelier above Tarran's head. "Stop everything at once!"

The door swung open to reveal the speaker—Viceroy Agis— along with a posse of lesser nobles and their partners, all bedecked in their finest courtly attire. They curtseyed and bowed to him before taking their places in the room, arranging themselves in groups of card players or embroiderers and setting themselves in the perfect spots to collect gossip. Though none of them dared to look Terran in the eye, he felt their gaze upon him.

And thus, the quiet, confidential meeting between a man and his friend ended, and a meeting between a king and his court began. Terran arranged his face in what he hoped was something approaching regality. This public performance was for his brothers, his sisters, his friends he'd lost on his way to ending the war and becoming king. He hadn't wanted it, but now that he had it, he'd be damned if he didn't honor their memory with every decision he made and every word he spoke. He would carry them with him, more precious and more important than the crown weighing down upon his brow.

"Viceroy Agis," he said, turning his back on the red-faced man to take his place on the throne. "I didn't expect to see you so soon."

"Well, my boy, that was your first mistake. Thinking that you could keep me alive *and* at arms' length. Oh, no. When I heard the matter of the Outerlands was being discussed, I knew I couldn't be kept away for a second longer."

The man stalked towards the throne, only to be stopped dead in his tracks when Elias drew his sword and blocked his path, the Yarian steel glinting in the sun like a set of poisoned dragon scales.

"My lord, I believe you'll find he's no longer *my boy* to you, but *Your Majesty*. Or have you forgotten that *your king* was the one who spared your life and allowed you to keep your position?"

The movements in the room stilled for a brief second as that reminder hung in the air. Everyone said Terran had been a fool to not slaughter everyone who'd ever before held power. But that was what the old kings had done. That was how his six brothers died. And he knew better than to repeat the mistakes of his predecessors.

Besides...he'd seen enough death for a thousand lifetimes. As long as he was on the throne, he wouldn't stomach any more.

"No, no, no," Agis said, scrambling to his knees, his self-preservation instincts rising above his pride. "My apologies, Your Majesty. I only have the good of Aulen at heart."

Lie. The man made himself rich off bribes from witches desperate to escape their banishment, and he fed his own hatred of them through regular raids and beatings. He was a cruel, opportunistic man who would have his voice heard. Luckily for Terran, his wasn't the only voice in the room.

"Let's convene, then," he said, raising his voice slightly so the nobles of the Royal Council could excuse themselves from their card games and embroidery to assemble at the foot of the throne. "I'll have all of the counsel you'll be gracious enough to give me."

"You are most magnanimous, Your Majesty," Agis said, dumping himself into the chair provided to him by an overeager servant.

Eager for the business of running the nation to begin, the members of the council presented themselves in a half-moon of heavily embroidered chairs around him, their eyes shifting back and forth as if they were more ready to jump back into war than maintain peace. Everyone wanted the weddings and feasts to begin—until they realized that their chosen man wasn't sitting on the throne.

Terran didn't blame them for their shiftiness and uncertainty. Eight years of conflict and deep hatred wasn't a simple thing to toss aside. He hated half of the people staring up at him now and disliked most of the others. But the voices of his family called to him, urging him to save Aulen. He had to. It was the only way he'd put their ghosts to rest.

"Now," he said, leaning forward to engage each of them, hoping it was enough to at least build some sense of camaraderie between them. "Will someone explain—"

Agis raised his walking stick. "I'll be good enough to explain the situation, Your Majesty."

"Of course he will," Isla, one councilor with long, fiery hair and an attitude to match, sniffed. "Not as if he doesn't have enough interest in Outerland."

"Oh," he said, jumping from his chair, encroaching on her space at the other end of the half-moon arrangement. "So when it comes to discussing trade routes along the Etrurian Sea, you won't have a whisper of an opinion?"

"I'll say plenty to you if you take one step closer to me," she growled.

Children. Absolute children.

"And *I* will have plenty to say if you all don't conduct yourselves in a manner befitting the running of this nation," Terran bellowed, before softening slightly and turning to his Warden. "Now, Elias. Will you do the honors?"

"Yes. The issue is this: the witches of Outerland had no *official* alliances during the war. They couldn't, of course. They were, after all, still banished. However, a large and significant faction managed to escape or overstay their leave to remain in Aulen and banded together, supporting first Igor of House Dubron and then Refel of House Tier."

"Crafty witches."

If they were so crafty, they wouldn't have been on the losing side, Terran wanted to say. But he held back. Snappy retorts weren't going to get him anywhere. His sisters always warned him against his quick tongue. It would get him into trouble one day, they said. And they were probably right. He just couldn't let *today* be that day.

"They supported them because those houses promised an end to the banishment."

"And our new king doesn't."

That wasn't entirely true. His family and his house didn't support the witches returning to the fold of society; he'd heard everyone from his youngest sister to his eldest grandfather curse them all, though he wasn't sure they'd ever met one in person.

But Terran...Terran wasn't so sure. Every time he thought he hated them, his thoughts returned to that night at the Academy, when that witch burned through her skin to save his life, the life of a man who'd never once looked her in the eye or given her half a thought, and who, after that night, pretended as if she didn't exist. She'd had no reason to save him, yet she did. That had to say something about the witches, that they might not be the monsters everyone assumed they were.

He didn't voice his uncertainty out loud. After all, his house had been in charge of the campaign that won the war. He'd gotten his crown because of the loyalties to his house and the victory they secured. He also suspected that they had finally fallen in line behind him because they thought he might be easy to manipulate. He couldn't go back on his promises and loyalties so easily. With a slight look in the man's direction, he allowed Elias to speak for him.

"It's for this reason that we are all here today. News of your reign has not come with great celebration in Outerland and there is talk of rebellion."

"Oh, please." One of the councilors whose name he could never remember rolled her eyes and snickered. Elias shot her a silencing scowl, and she recoiled in her seat.

"With our armies decimated and every defensive barrier between here and the witch country destroyed...It isn't too far a leap to think that they might at least attempt some kind of desperate bid for their freedom."

"So, we free them and risk the wrath of our people, or we keep them contained and risk the wrath of some of the most powerful creatures on earth," Terran muttered.

"Most powerful creatures on earth?" Agis scoffed. "Let me throw one of my dragons at them and see how powerful they are. They wouldn't last ten seconds."

Before anyone could ask the man how the witches fighting in the war had managed to get past his ever-so-fearsome dragons, Madame Bovere cleared her throat, drawing the entire room's attention towards her. She was a regal older woman, who Terran couldn't help but respect despite the fact that their families had exchanged terrible blows over the last eight years. While some women of the courts and noble houses were throwing other women in front of themselves like shields, Madame Bovere had opened her castle at Pyne Mount as a sanctuary, holding her own contingent of soldiers to protect the castle—and the women inside, regardless of what house or lineage they came from—for the duration of the war. While mothers were auctioning off their daughters to the highest bidder in exchange for protection, Madame Bovere sold her jewels and furs to provide for women who needed sanctuary. Her round face bore scars that proved how she'd defended them with her own life. She'd lost her sons to the wars, but not her dignity. There were countless women alongside him and against on the battlefield, but he'd never been as terrified or awed of a warrior as he was of Madame Bovere. So, when she spoke, he listened.

"I don't believe that this is the most pressing matter."

"Yes?" Agis harrumphed, falling back into his chair, glancing at his male compatriots as if seeking their support against her. "And what is, pray tell?"

"Your Majesty, you haven't even begun searching for a queen, much less begun the process of producing an heir. You've no surviving brothers or sisters. The matter of an heir is at stake, and if there's to be an insurrection of witches, then that matter is quite clearly the most important. If you die with no progeny, then you'll have single-handedly plunged us into another war."

The truth of her statement shot through him like a poisoned arrow.

"Lack of an heir won't be a problem if the witches steal the throne," Isla snapped.

Agis leapt to his feet, walking stick flying. "Over my dead body!"

"It may well come to that."

An explosion of discussion, threats, and thinly veiled insults followed, but in the cloud of violence and rhetoric, Madame Bovere waited patiently, staring at Terran as if he were taking slightly too long to pour her a cup of tea. Her direct attention choked him.

"Your Majesty," she finally said, cutting through the din. "What are your thoughts?"

"My thoughts..."

He didn't have any thoughts. Or, more precisely, he had too *many* thoughts, and they all waged war on the battlefield of his mind. The room focused once again on him.

"I think we must—"

Slam! The great doors swung open, disturbing the courtiers sitting nearby, sending them flying like a pack of shooed birds, and a small porter in a hastily thrown-on uniform bent over, struggling for each huffing breath that now echoed through the vast chamber.

"Your Majesty!"

"We are in the middle of a council meeting!" Agis's walking stick, which he stabbed into the ground with each word, punctuated his shrill voice.

"I beg your pardon, councilors, Your Majesty." He bowed deeply, almost tripping over himself in the process. "But there is a matter of great importance that requires your attention."

"And what is that?"

The young boy wearing the colors of Terran's house couldn't have been over fourteen, but he'd already learned the art of discretion. "I believe you may want to learn of it in private."

"Very well, then."

No one breathed too loudly or made even the slightest sound as he descended from the throne and followed the young boy out of the room. But as soon as the doors shut behind him and the guards outside of the door stood at attention, the sounds of their heated discussions and speculation followed him down High Court's intricate web of corridors.

He didn't pry the child for any information until they arrived at the doorway to his private library instead of the doorway to his public offices. Most unusual.

"What, precisely, am I walking into?" he muttered, glancing down at the boy.

"I think you'd just better see for yourself. Oh, and I was meant to give you this."

Slightly dirty fingers plucked something from his pocket and held it up towards the king for inspection. It took all his strength not to stagger back at the sight.

"My token?" he asked, taking it from him.

"They were going to execute her, but she says you're in her debt. She gave this to the jailer as proof."

And just like a shooting star, the boy vanished, leaving Terran alone before the doorway to his private chambers. He held the coin in his hands, rubbing it with the pad of his thumb. The grooves of his family's design had been worn down, but he still recognized every flower and every thorn, the same ones carved into the steel of his armor's breastplate and his sword's hilt.

The token was the first one he'd ever given. And the only one. Once the war started, he didn't want to be indebted to anyone.

Only one person could be on the other side of that door.

CHAPTER THREE

T he door behind her opened, then shut. Sturdy steps struck the wooden floor below. A strong, calm voice spoke out, sending a storm of shivers straight down her spine.

"I'd like to be alone with the prisoner."

Without so much as a word, the eight guards who had been standing at each of the octagonal room's corners paraded out.

She didn't have to turn around to know who she was dealing with. Something in his voice—that deep, aged beyond its years, sound—resonated with something inside of her, stirring from her basest levels with recognition. He didn't sound like the seventeen-year-old boy he had been when she'd sung magic into his body and saved his life, but it was him all the same. Somehow, she just knew. Maybe it was magic, maybe it was something else, something unexplainable, but either way, when he spoke again, he only confirmed it.

"Aren't you going to rise and bow to your king?"

"I would, Your Majesty. But they've chained me to the chair."

Her lips tugged at her own gallows humor, a coping mechanism she'd developed after too many near-misses with death. But with Aulen's new king still firmly behind her, hot tears welled up in her eyes, thankfully not overflowing. The taut air between them grew increasingly hard to breathe as the silent seconds ticked by and she had time to think of all the ways this one interaction—this one hope—could go terribly, terribly wrong. In this room, with this man she hadn't seen in ten years, whose character she didn't know beyond one chance encounter, she would have to argue not only for her own fate, but the fate of Outerland and everyone in it. Ever since she escaped the Academy to take up arms, she'd fancied herself an impenetrable warrior. She lived each day and fought each battle and trudged through war because they were all obstacles to getting what she needed: freedom for her people. She didn't allow pressure or fear factoring into her calculations.

But now...when her joke was met with silence, when she couldn't look into his eyes and figure him out, when she had no idea if he would slaughter her and every other witch just because he had the power to do so, when she knew everything his house threatened to do to her people, the weight of eight years of dead bodies and compromises threatened to crush her.

She swallowed. Hard. And tuned into the sound of his irregular breathing. That settled her, at least a bit. He was as uncertain as she was.

"I've never met a king before," she said, voice smaller than she could ever remember hearing it. She sounded like the girl she had been back at the Academy. "I guess I imagined it would have been...not like this."

Another joke he didn't answer with laughter.

"Who are you?" he asked.

"Didn't they give you—"

"They gave me a token, yes. But..."

There it was. The uncertainty she heard in the pattern of his breathing seeped into his words. They wavered in a way she'd never heard a king's voice waver. All the men she'd followed, everyone who assured her they would be a ruler one day, had never let themselves falter, at least not where she could see it.

A small ripple of calm disturbed her rioting heart. At least in this moment, he wasn't like the others.

The sturdy steps that carried him into the room softened, as if he were moving around her but trying not to disturb any creaking floorboards. As if he were as afraid of her as she was of him.

But then he stepped into view, placing himself between the weathered desk—one which looked like it had been carved out of a wrecked ship or a slightly charred cottage—and she knew the truth. It wasn't possible for him to be as scared of her as she was of him.

Because he wasn't just scary. He was terrifying.

The man stood nearly a foot taller than her, and witches were a naturally tall breed. Even beneath regal garb of thick brocade and golden thread, she could see his body was thick with the muscles of a warrior. Most of his bare skin, from his hands to his neck to his cheeks, bore some scar or mark of battles survived, battles won. He drew his mouth into a hard, unflinching line and the long, dark hair that had looked almost handsome in his youth now cast dark shadows over his face. The golden crown upon his head only heightened the effect; it was so incongruous to the rest of his appearance, it only made the rest of him darker, less like the weak, wounded boy she'd met all those lifetimes ago.

And his eyes. Those brown eyes that she still saw in her memory. They were...conflicted. There was light there, a flicker of promise, but it was like a candle lit beneath the surface of a frozen lake. She couldn't tell if the fire would die out or melt the ice.

Free and defiant, she could probably take him. But bound and at his mercy, she wasn't so sure.

"Let me have a look at you."

Her breath caught in her throat as he took a step forward, leaning in until she could count the stars in a constellation of freckles near his right eye. What he was looking for, she couldn't begin to guess. When he stepped away, face still impassive, the knot in his neck bobbed as he extended his hands palm-up.

"And your wrists?"

The binders clung to her, dragging her down, but she fought their heft and offered them up for his inspection. With the metal around her neck still snugly in place—or because he foolishly believed she wouldn't hurt him and escape if she had the chance—he released the brackets from her hands and placed them on the desk behind him, out of sight.

She was in a spell. It crackled in the air between them, something unspeakable, as his ringed and scarred fingers ran across the scars of her wrists, proof of the deed she'd committed when they were little more than children. Another shiver passed through her as invisible, imagined shots of lightning shot from his fingertips up through her arms.

"So," he said, glancing up at her from beneath thick, dark eyelashes. "It is you."

That could have meant so many things, both good and bad. But his tone was so flat, his eyes so shaded, that she didn't have the faintest clue how he meant it. Another smile tugged at her lips, and she hoped he saw it as some kind of peace offering.

"I'm afraid so."

He released her wrists. They instantly felt cold from the loss of his warmth. She tried not to shiver.

"I'd heard rumors about witches fighting for Tier and Dubron. But I never thought you would be one of them."

That wasn't a promising shift in the conversation. Well, if she was going to die, she might as well die fighting, as much as she could with her magic taken from her and her body still chained to an obnoxiously overstuffed armchair.

"You never thought I would want my people to have freedom?"

Tearing his attention from her, he stalked to the farthest end of the room, choosing instead to stare out of a fogged window.

"I never thought you would kill so many people for it," he snapped. "I've seen some of your kind fight. It's like watching death itself walk through the battlefield."

"And how many people did you kill for that crown, Your Majesty?"

"I..." He trailed off, and she knew she'd hit him in an unhealed wound. The thought didn't bring her much comfort. "We aren't talking about my crown. We're talking about you. And your treason against the nation." Breaking away from the window, he stalked behind his desk, where the decree for her death had been placed, awaiting his signature and seal. "What's this? *Freedom for Outerland. Your leaders are cowards and fools.* Surely you didn't know *I* was king when you said that."

"I didn't. It doesn't mean I wouldn't have said it, anyway."

Was that a smirk she saw threatening to tug at his cheeks? Maybe he hated her. Maybe falling in with Tier and Dubron was enough to stoke his bloodlust. But maybe there was an equal part of him that liked this sparring. Ellara could barely keep up over the pounding of her own heart, but she clung to the hope— vain though it might have been—that maybe, just maybe, he was as tired of war as she was. Maybe, just maybe, diplomacy would win the day. And her life.

The chair behind his desk screeched painfully as he dragged it out and placed himself in it to further examine the document.

"You were in prison," he read, glancing at her over the edge of the parchment.

"Yes."

"And you failed in your escape?"

"I don't think it takes a king's intellect to realize I wouldn't be sitting here if I had been successful."

In wartime captures, it was common to keep the prisoner blindfolded. Thank the Fates no one had bothered to blindfold her today, because she would have missed all his little tells—the slight shift in his posture or the double-blink that gave him away.

"I don't remember you being this impertinent when we were at school."

"And I don't remember you being so tall." She shrugged as best as she could with the chains still trapping her. "I guess things change."

"You know the penalty for crimes against the king is death. And the penalty for an escape attempt is the same."

"Yes, but—"

"But what?"

Another tell. His eyes flashed, clutching at her with their directness. But *what* they were telling her, she couldn't quite guess.

"I have a proposition for you. That's why I used the token." When he didn't respond, she closed her eyes and took two long, deep breaths, thinking of everyone in Outerland who counted on her. Everyone she could save. "I need you...and I think you might just need me, too."

"You don't know anything about me," he said, carefully avoiding her gaze.

"I know that a king's position would be *much* safer if he used witchcraft to his advantage."

There. Her biggest gamble. Out in the air between them. She couldn't take it back, and he couldn't pretend he hadn't heard it. If merely saying the words *freedom for Outerland* came to some kind of crime against the king, then surely suggesting that he use magic was enough to have her executed this minute.

"Witchcraft is illegal."

"Only if the king says it is. And besides, the king *is* the law. If he does it, then it can't be *against* the law, can it?"

"What is your proposition, then?"

Her estimation of him swung between two poles: he hadn't yet hurt her, and there were those soft, hidden edges to his gazes that made her question how a man with eyes like that could ever have become king. But, at the same time, he didn't so much as balk at her suggestion of using magic.

Which meant he hadn't been made king by accident. He wanted to be there. And what was more, he wanted to *stay* there.

"Let me be your sorceress. Anything you want, I could make real. The other kings were fallible because they forgot one thing about Aulen: everyone is afraid of magic. But if *you* controlled it, or some part of it, then you could do what none of the other six kings during the war did: you could actually keep the crown. You'd be a king no one could depose. Not even with a million armies."

This was the same language she'd used when arguing the witches' case to the houses of Tier and Dubron, to the skeptical men who'd raised their eyebrows at the thought of having witches in their midst. And, in truth, she hated every single word she spoke. Promising magic to humans who'd wanted her dead for having it made her skin crawl. But humans were a little like dragons. If she could distract them with something shiny like a few spells, maybe she could capture the treasure of her own freedom.

"And what is my end of this bargain?" he asked, leaning forward, elbows on his desk.

"Well, I'll have to be alive to be any good to you."

"I figured your life was a given. What *else* will you be expecting of me?"

His voice broke slightly, a hint of indecision. He wasn't playing a game with her; he was asking to begin a negotiation.

"I want freedom for Outerland. Freedom for all the witches. No more bowing and scraping to Agis. No more bribes, beatings, or banishment. I fought through the wars to secure our lives and I want to see that through."

The damned chains kept her from leaning forward, from grabbing his chin and forcing him to look into her eyes to see everything that the future could be. She *needed* him to buy into this. Sure, she was selling herself to a kingdom and a House that hated her and everything she was. She'd never see her family again. She'd never enjoy the freedom she fought for. But it would be worth it if her suffering was *for* something other than just saving her own neck.

"There would be revolution. I could never keep my crown."

"You could if the witches were on your side."

"How did that work out for Tier and Dubron?"

Tier and Dubron were led by stupid men who hadn't given her *enough* power. As much as they wanted her as an ally, they were afraid of her, too, which meant she was always waylaid, always fighting with one metaphorical hand tied behind her back. Not to mention that she was always fighting on promises that one day they would make good on their word to free her people. It wasn't enough.

But this time, she would have enough.

"They each had maybe six or seven free witches on their side. Can you imagine if every witch in Outerland came to your defense? If you let me deliver them to your cause, no one but the Fates themselves could take you off the throne."

CHAPTER FOUR

Terran's mouth fell open slightly. It wasn't regal, but he couldn't help it. If the legends and whispers were true, then witches never invoked the Fates unless they meant every word of what they were saying. It was to the witches what a token was to the humans, an unbreakable bond.

Which turned his thoughts to the reason she was here, the unbreakable bond he'd made with her when she saved his life. He could either free her and be known as the king who freed a war criminal, or he could be the man who broke the vow he'd made when rescued from death's door.

As it turned out, being king was an endless grappling with that one question, one that had been so simple before the war. What kind of man was he going to be?

He took far too long to respond. Another move not befitting of his station. When it seemed he wouldn't respond at all, she slumped back into her chair, rattling the chains across her body as she went limp, defeated. Her green skin couldn't exactly lose color, but the tint softened in such a way that it seemed she'd gone cold and resigned.

He'd never seen her on the battlefield, but if the way she fought him with her words, while thoroughly defenseless, was any indication, he was glad he hadn't. Now, however, she looked so small, so broken. Her battle gown, which once must have been made from the strongest of leathers and built for endurance, now frayed. Her shoulders collapsed in towards her chest. Even the dusting of freckles across her high cheekbones seemed to wilt. And something occurred to him.

"I don't think I've ever spoken this long to a witch in my entire life."

"I'm sorry to hear that. We're really not so bad once you get to know us. *I'm* not so bad when you get to know me."

He didn't need to get to know her to know she wasn't so bad. He had the scar across his belly and his own life to prove it. During the war, his closest brother, Drex, told him if he ever became king, Drex wouldn't need the advice of his Wardens or viceroys or the experts they called in. He'd just need his own intuition to guide him.

Instinct had guided Drex into a trap laid by House Toris, and he'd been slaughtered and strung up before he could even call out for help. But as his mind argued over everything his family believed about the witches—that they were treacherous, dangerous, and didn't belong anywhere near humans—and his past with this one, his brother's words rushed back to him.

Drex had gotten himself killed with his instincts. Terran knew doing the same might lead to a similar result. But his family's bodies were rotting, and the only person he could trust was himself. Even if it killed him one day.

For the first time, he allowed his posture to match hers, leaning back in his chair instead of perching on the edge of it. He couldn't remember the last time he'd reclined like this, but he almost moaned from relief. He felt as if someone had cut his strings.

"You don't want to destroy Aulen, do you?" he asked, more to himself than to her.

To his surprise, she didn't rush to agree. She hesitated, bit her pink lower lip, and then spoke without looking at him.

"That's not such an easy question to answer."

"Why not?"

Another hesitation. Her hands, as much as they could with her upper arms bound to the chair, were wringing themselves repeatedly as she mentally deliberated something. To trust him?

"Because part of me does. Part of me does want to tear this place down, brick by brick. And part of me does want to kill you right now where you sit. Part of me wants to see Aulen lost to history," she whispered.

He didn't know it was possible to hold so many conflicting ideas at once. He *hated* hearing that she hated him, but also felt a twisted sense of pride that she not only trusted him with that information but also that she didn't seem to give a damn what he thought of it, even though he held her life in his hands.

"Part of me hates you and your kind for what you've done to me and mine. Part of me wants to destroy every system you've built and melt down every coin you've made from our suffering and send you all out into the wilderness of Outerland where you'd never survive."

Seconds passed—then a full minute—while he waited for her to finish, to wave her hand and tell him she didn't really mean it. When it didn't come, he coaxed her.

"...I hope there's another part to you."

'There is," she said. The sigh that followed sounded nearly painful, like she was giving him a secret she thought she'd never part with. The chains rattled as she sank lower in her chair despite them. He tried to follow her gaze as it moved from his face, but she was staring off somewhere he couldn't see, somewhere in her own mind. He contented himself with watching the light from the nearby windows play against her skin. "There is another part of me that could not raise my hand to hurt another human if my life depended on it. I don't know if your report mentioned this, but I didn't harm a soul during my escape attempt."

"So, if I put you in a ring and told you the only way to your freedom was a match to the death with a dozen humans, what would you do?"

"...I'm just...*so tired*, Your Majesty. Aren't you?"

The question caught him off guard. One thing he'd learned about being king: when people asked you questions, they rarely wanted an actual answer. They wanted diplomacy or to hear their own opinions parroted back. But she waited for him to consider his reply rather than storming ahead to make her next point.

It was disarming. And it forced him to answer honestly.

"Yes. Yes, I am." Too honest. He deflected. "But I don't think making you my sorceress is going to make any difference in the matter."

"Your Majesty," she began, the words hanging on her lips like tears threatening to fall. "Please reconsider."

For a long while, they stared in silence, and he took her in, knowing she was doing the same to him. Now that he wasn't at her magical mercy or dying from a dragon's bite, he had time to examine her properly. But with every passing second, he realized he wasn't so much sizing her up as he was drinking her in. Even shrunken down in her chair and locked with chains, she was a larger-than-life figure, with a thick, curving body that spoke to a wartime diet of mead and whatever filling foods she could find. She was touchable, with enough of her to hold on to. Her impossibly black eyes contrasted with her smooth, green skin, the mark of her kind. Her black hair was tied up in broken braids streaked with thick, white tresses. Her freckles challenged him to come closer and see just how many stars there were in her face-bound constellation. Her lips were the soft pink of the sky, just gasping out the last of its late-afternoon sunset.

Even battle-worn and prison-dirty, ready for execution, she was strikingly beautiful in her own way.

But it wasn't her beauty that held him, it was everything else.

The scars of battle. The heavy softness of her gaze. The callouses on her hands. The set of her shoulders and the way she spoke to him as if they were the only two people in the entire kingdom who spoke the same language. They had been on opposite sides of the war, but at least she was fighting *for* something instead of for the flimsy circlet of gold resting upon his head. Ellara of Outerland had principles, and she stood by them, something he couldn't say for anyone he'd carried a sword beside for the last eight years. She was the kind of person he'd never before dreamed existed.

The kind of woman he'd always envisioned falling in love with.

The thought choked him. A plan began forming in his head, swirling in dangerous, undecipherable smoke signals, teasing him with possibilities. He, of course, couldn't fall in love with her. But if they were as alike as he felt, if the sudden affinity he felt for her was real and not some trick of magic or his lonesome imagination, then perhaps...Perhaps they could save themselves —and the kingdom—from more misery.

It was possible that both Agis and Madame Bovere were right. Finding a wife and solving the Outerland problem were of equal importance and required equal solutions.

"I think I have a better idea."

"I'm listening," she said, perking up against the chair at her back.

"...Have you ever given any thought to being queen?"

"Queen of what?"

"Aulen."

"Not all of us are entitled to such fantasies, Your Majesty."

He froze. Of course she'd never done the play-acting of him and his brothers. They'd all pretended—in games as children and in conversations with soldiers and ministers—that they were kings. Maybe she'd weathered the same war he had, but her aspirations hadn't been as lofty. Everyone else with a sword wanted a throne and a crown. She just wanted to live free with her family and those she loved. Bowing his head in a sign of deference, he shot her an apologetic look before letting his body get carried away with the energy of his words, each one animating him more than the last.

"I need a wife and an heir. You and your people need freedom. And we need some way of uniting humans and witches once and for all. No more war. No more bloodshed. No more banishments and cruelty. A fresh start."

She blinked, black eyes betraying no emotion other than skeptical shock. Not that he blamed her for that.

"You want *me* to marry *you*."

"A marriage of convenience, of course. Purely political. After we have an heir and the future of Aulen and Outerland is secure, we can do whatever we'd like."

The words rushed from his lips in a giant heap, falling at her feet without ceremony. The last thing either of them needed was for her to believe he'd been carrying a secret torch for her since that night with the dragon.

Something briefly twisted in her face.

"Your family would hang you if they could hear you talk like that."

"Yes, well, my family went and got themselves killed, so thankfully, they aren't around to hang me."

"I'm afraid I can't negotiate any further tied up like this." When he hesitated, his mind flashing through a portfolio of old nightmares and prejudices, she coughed. "If we're going to be married, you can't keep me chained up. You'll have to trust me."

Approaching her like an animal trapped in a cage, he crossed the library with slow, hesitant steps before using the key on his desk to unlock her.

"See. I'm not going to hurt you."

"I know."

He said it so quickly, so easily, that it even surprised him. But once the declaration was out, he couldn't take it back. And he didn't want to, either. He trusted her, even though the voices of dead friends and family members screamed at him not to. But after he'd let those voices talk him into becoming king, he wanted to do something—*anything*—on his own.

His casual reply must have spooked her, too, because she stared up at him from under dark, heavy lashes with wide eyes.

"Really?"

"You wouldn't have saved me all those years ago if you were the monster they said you were."

"And you wouldn't have saved me now if you were the monster they said *you* were."

"Then you'll be my queen?"

As he extended one hand to her, he also extended his hope. Maybe she wouldn't ever love him. Maybe they'd be married solely for the kingdom's sake. But perhaps, if he was lucky, he'd finally have another friend. After losing so many, after becoming so desperately lonely, he could use all the friends he could get.

Her mouth opened and closed once, as if she were going to correct him on the distinction, amending *my queen* with *the queen* or *queen of Aulen*, but thankfully she didn't. Instead, her lips drifted up into a half-smile, and she placed her hand in his, letting him pull her to her feet.

Standing at her full height, she was so close he could count the lines on her perfect lips. They were close enough to kiss or kill each other, and for the first time since he was nineteen and the dreaded war began, he had the deep, unsettling urge to take the kissing option instead of the alternative.

"Yes," she breathed, her words like soft bird wings against his cheek, her hand still spreading warmth through his own. "I think I will."

Was it possible she heard his heart hammering in his chest like he was about to charge a legion single-handedly? And when had they gotten so close?

"I beg your pardon, Your Majesty—"

Before the Warden could finish his sentence or fully enter the private library, Ellara managed to fly halfway across the room, settling herself near a bookshelf as if they hadn't been close enough to...what would they have done if Elias hadn't walked in?

"What is this?"

Sometimes it frightened Terran how easy it was to slip between being himself and being the king. Straightening up, he acknowledged Elias' bow with a tip of his head.

"Elias. Meet Ellara. Ellara, this is my Warden. Elias."

Free of her chains, she moved forward with her skirts in hand, ready to curtsy. But the delicate fingers clenched into fists when the Warden barely glanced in her direction, tossing a careless greeting her way.

"Pleasure."

"If everyone in High Court is as warm and generous as you are, then the pleasure is all mine."

The king's urge to laugh at her quick snipe was quelled by the flicker of rage he felt when Elias ignored her entirely, pulling Terran in close to speak to him in confidence.

"I wasn't informed we had a prisoner in the royal wing of the palace," Elias practically hissed, eyes darting back and forth, clearly watching the witch for any signs of trouble.

"We don't. Ellara isn't a prisoner here. She's a *guest*."

He pressed the final word for emphasis, hoping his Warden would understand, or at least hold off judgment until everything had been revealed. Ellara, for her part, stared out the window as her hands rubbed the raw skin of her wrists.

A shot of guilt raced through him. If he hadn't met her all those years ago, he would have hated her and all of her kind just as much as Elias did now.

"Your Majesty." The Warden cleared his throat, drawing his attention away from the woman basking in afternoon light pouring through the stained-glass, the reds and blues playing against her green skin, pulling out the contrast with her freckles. "Things have significantly deteriorated in the throne room. I suggest you return at once."

"What's happened?"

"They've begun to plan a bride pageant in your honor."

Without waiting for Ellara—or Terran, for that matter—Elias began a steady march out of the library and towards the throne room, hand at his sword. Offering an arm, Terran escorted his would-be bride a few steps behind their guardian.

"Oh, they don't need to bother," he said, sharing a conspiratorial glance with Ellara, who wore the weary expression of a seasick sailor.

"Of course not. Because you'll never be married. I've heard it all before."

"No. Because it's all settled. I plan to be married by the solstice next month."

"Oh, really? To whom?"

"Ellara."

A clatter of armor signaled the abrupt ending of his militaristic march. Breaking every protocol, he ripped Terran into an alcove by the edge of his tunic, leaving Ellara alone in the halls. Pressed into the stone passageway, the shadows cast dark lines across Elias' somber face.

"You can't be serious."

"Of course I'm serious. When have you ever heard me joke about marriage?"

"They'll *kill* you," he hissed.

"They may try."

"Yes," he barked out, huffing a sarcastic laugh, "and they have armies."

"Of course. But now, I have a witch."

"Have you completely lost your head? A witch as our queen?"

"Don't be so dramatic. She's going to bring the witches of Outerland to our side. She's going to ensure that the viceroys and vicereines fall in line."

"And if she doesn't?"

"Then we'll just kill her."

CHAPTER FIVE

The corridor's cold marble seeped through the thick, snow-ready winter fighting gown that Ellara had barely taken off in months, chilling her already cold blood.

Then we'll just kill her.

Her stomach tightened. Her throat constricted. She attempted to conjure up some rational explanation, some reason why the man who tenderly touched her and told her she wasn't a monster would be so willing to kick her aside if she didn't give him exactly what he wanted. She counted to ten. Frontwards first, then backwards. She barely felt the men as they returned to her, peeled her off the wall and guided her towards the center of High Court. She couldn't hear them speaking over the din of her one single, consuming thought:

Not if I kill you first.

For the moment, it didn't matter that she'd been tossed on the winds all day, desperately trying to right her sails. She'd been captured, injured, re-captured, sentenced to death, met with an old schoolmate who happened to be king, cashed in on a life-debt, had her death sentence revoked, fought to free her people, almost believed the best in someone, and now, she was walking into the throne room of High Court, the most sacred and high meeting place of the ruling classes of Aulen on the arm of a *king*. None of that mattered. Rage clouded her every thought.

Such a small betrayal, his whispered promise to Elias. Such a stupid belief, her thinking even for a moment he was any different.

It shouldn't have mattered. He was a means to an end. She'd done with him what eight years of battle hadn't. She'd gotten close to winning the freedom of her people. The barriers around Outerland would be broken and the witches would finally have the lives they always deserved. So why did it bother her? Why did replaying his voice in her mind stab at her heart like a sword-blow?

She didn't want to look too closely at it. Clinging to her rage was easier than examining why it was there. Besides, rage had gotten her through the war. Why wouldn't it get her through the rest of her life, too?

Elias pressed open the twin doors to the throne room, revealing the bickering court within. At the sound of his herald of the king's arrival, human faces turned, one by one, and dropped their collective jaws at the sight of her. A witch not bound and chained but holding tightly to the arm of their king.

The silence cut her almost as deeply as their enraged stares. She'd had human blades plunged into her gut that pained her less.

"My lords and ladies, I'm pleased to announce that we can adjourn this council." He squeezed her arm tighter, pulling her to his side. Ellara wished, for the first time in her life, that she had the power to divine human thoughts; she couldn't tell if he was playing for the crowd or if he subconsciously wanted her closer. "Please meet your future queen, Ellara Wist of Outerland."

"What?"

"Your Majesty—"

"You can't be serious."

Raising a single hand, he called for silence, and a silence he was granted. Even she didn't have that kind of power. Her insides burned. This man told her they were on the same side, that they'd both been tired of war and struggling. And he was willing to play his court and her against one another to keep his power, willing to indulge in a bit of bloodlust if it got him what he wanted.

Every fiber of her being burned to hate him, but he held the key to the future. Without him, she was just a witch who'd hang at dawn. With him, she was the queen who'd liberate Outerland. She tried to smile, but by the way the people recoiled at the sight, it must have looked more like she was baring her teeth.

"With this marriage, I hope to make an alliance with the witches of Outerland, one that might secure their support of Aulen in exchange for their freedom."

"She's bewitched him!"

Ellara stiffened. "I haven't done anything like that."

"Did it just *speak* to me?"

A ripple of scandalized whispers broke through the crowd, but if the king heard, he didn't acknowledge them. Instead, he led Ellara to the throne. The throne of Aulen, the throne of kings, the throne carved from the extinct ash trees of Outerland. But instead of taking the seat himself, he released her arm and placed her in it instead, once again deaf to the gasps behind him.

Ellara sank down, every eye in the room bearing into her very soul, as the late afternoon sun shone through the upper windows of the room, casting her in a golden haze.

"Ellara. If you will bow your head."

There was a response on the tip of her tongue, something about bowing to no man, but it died as the metal of his sword slid against his sheath. He placed it on her left shoulder, the cold blade whispering against the green flesh at the base of her neck. She stilled completely, holding her breath. She'd never been this close to a sword without death being a close threat.

Over the king's shoulders, the courtiers stood in shocked

awe, some clinging to each other, others clutching their glasses of alcohol so tightly she feared the glass would shatter in their hands.

"Ellara." That voice of his, which dug deep into her chest and vibrated her insides, temporarily silenced the anger she wanted to hurl in his direction. "Will you protect the realm of Aulen and all of its territories, serve your king, and bring honor to yourself and your people?"

"I will."

The sword slid from her neck down to her heart before tapping the tops of each of her hands: a symbolic gesture meaning she'd give Aulen her life, her soul, and her deeds. But what the oath—and the people in witness—didn't realize was that when asked to vow to her people, she wasn't talking about the people of Aulen. She was talking about *her* people. And she would give them everything she had.

"Then rise, Lady Ellara, Lady and Vicereine of Outerland."

Lady knocked all of them into action again, and with a spray of words and broken whisky flutes, they stormed the throne, stopped from approaching her only by the king's sword, which he swung straight at their chests.

"This is *preposterous*," one of the older men shouted. She recognized him from paintings—and less than flattering caricatures—hung around Outerland. Viceroy Agis. She knew she wouldn't have any luck swaying him, so she turned to the others.

"I only want to help."

"Yes, help destroy all humans everywhere. That thing," he pointed to her, "will be an end to us, mark my words."

Blood roared in her ears as she crossed the king's defensive line to approach her accuser.

"It'll be the end of *you* if you don't stop calling me *thing* and *it,* my lord."

The king pulled her back, shielding her from the crowd, turning his back to them. "What are you doing?"

"Trying to make them understand."

"By threatening them?"

"I *have* to threaten them. You haven't given me back my magic, so I can't do anything else."

In the noise and chaos of the humans threatening to push in on her, and with his threat against her life still ringing in her ears, she didn't allow herself to believe that the spark in his eyes had been something between respect and laughter. Even if she'd wanted to, Agis stepped forward, robes and overlong sleeves rippling with his every movement, giving him the appearance of a particularly aggressive turkey.

"Your Majesty," he said, lowering his voice. "I think we must take her away immediately. She's clearly clouding your judgement—"

"You're questioning your king?"

"I am questioning the intentions of one of *them*."

"I am speaking with a clear mind and voice and you *will* hear me. *Lady* Ellara will be my wife, your queen, and the mother of your future rulers, and that is—"

"But if she *is* bound—" one of the women piped up, voice caught between hunger and terror.

"I am bound. I couldn't use magic on you even if I wanted to."

And Fates, do I want to.

"Then it must stay bound. I, for one, won't be manipulated by some little—"

"I won't give up my magic."

"We don't even know what it can do," the same slender woman shouted, voice rising in pitch.

"I could show you if you let me out of this thing," Ellara said, gaze tripping between the king and his subjects. It was then she realized he'd dropped his sword, stepping aside to survey both her and the crowd at once. Another flare of betrayal. He'd made an oath to her and now was considering revoking it in the face of this blistering mob?

"And what of Outerland? You don't *really* intend on freeing them, do you? Out into the world with the rest of us? We just spoke of avoiding an invasion, and now you want to welcome it?"

"You can't free them," Agis declared. "As Warden of Outerland, I can tell you right now they aren't fit for polite society."

"Hear, hear!"

The king's distance inflamed her, but she'd never once stepped away from a fight. Her instincts carried her, pressing her forward even when her spirit wanted to retreat.

"Then give them a trial."

"Oh? What kind of trial?" one courtier, a stately older woman in high-collared black garb, asked. She stood at the back of the crowd, a glass of dark liquor swirling in her hands. At least she didn't seem disgusted at the very sight of Ellara.

"I'll be queen, won't I? A queen has got to have a court of her own, advisors and a Warden."

"Yes, but if you are to be queen, and I sincerely doubt that if I have anything to say about it," Agis tutted, "then you'll be given a group of proper *Aulen* ladies to furnish your court."

"I could have a mixed court," she said, "turning free the witches and bringing some of them here. If they don't prove their worth, that they're as worthy as you are to live here, then you can send us all back."

"*All* of you?" Agis asked, the words a challenge.

"Yes," she agreed, weighing the potential shame of becoming the banished Queen of Aulen against the hope of a future for the witches. "All of us. Even me."

"No," Agis snapped. "I won't serve a queen who—"

"And in exchange..." Her body fought the words, the ones she knew she had to say if she had any hope of winning them over. "I won't touch my magic until you're satisfied. I'll wear the binders. You'll know how you feel about the Outerlanders is sincere and not my manipulation. I'd be practically human."

"Practically human isn't human at all," one woman sniffed.

King Terran took up his sword once more, leveling it in the woman's direction. If the negotiation had been a test, then apparently, she'd passed. The cost burned at the skin on her neck and wrists, but she held her mother's face in her mind. A few months without her magic would mean her freedom.

"I'll remind you that you're speaking to your future queen," the king threatened.

"Yes, Your Majesty."

For a long while, the room sunk into a muttering, quiet deliberation. When it became clear that the king wouldn't hear Agis in confidence, the man stormed out of the room. It was the woman in black, with her glass of dark liquor, who eventually broke the quiet.

"I think you're offering too much, dear. But I agree to the terms, and I suggest everyone else do the same. Not that it matters, of course." She downed her drink, the inky liquid sliding out of the glass in one go. Then her gaze leveled at him. "Your Majesty, will you accept the terms and avert another war?"

"Yes. I accept your terms, Lady Ellara."

"Then it's settled." She poured another glass and lifted it, offering the smallest of smiles to Ellara. "To our future queen and the future of Aulen."

No one, not even Ellara, joined her in the toast.

THAT NIGHT, ELLARA RETIRED TO BED WITHOUT SUPPER AND without speaking to anyone besides the poor, frightened page who guided her to the quarters just beyond the king's. He apologized until his face went nearly blue about the condition of the rooms—Aulen hadn't had a queen in this room in nearly six years, so the occasional cursory cleanings left plenty of spider webs and stuffy sheets behind—but she waved him off, sending him away without even asking him to make a fire in the stone fireplace. Away from all the humans and their chatter, their sidelong stares and their whispers, she wanted nothing more than to relieve herself of her dress, creep beneath the bedclothes, and slip into a long and dreamless sleep.

But, by the clock hand hanging over the mantlepiece, taunting her from across the room, that had been four hours ago, and sleep hadn't come. Her mind wouldn't obey her, wouldn't quiet down long enough to rest.

There wasn't any shortage of things to think about. She'd have to make a list of the witches she'd require for her court. She needed to meet with human women as well and decide which of them she'd want in her inner circle; the power brokers of Aulen would be even more suspicious if they found out she was only keeping witch counsel. A new bed would be necessary; this one was far too comfortable. She remembered the words and the glowers of the humans who hated her, who called her names and cursed her. But none of that actually prevented her from sleeping.

It was the embroidery on her bed clothes and on the curtains hanging over her bed. These were the queen's quarters, and a sea of stars had been stitched in silver, darkness-defying thread in the blue drapery. How many women had slept in this bed before her? What were their lives like? Their kings? The answers to those questions were as elusive as sleep, but with every imagined queen and her past, she thought of her own future.

This was *her* bed. *She* would be queen. This was her palace. And...the man who said he would kill her if she wasn't useful was to be her husband. This was the reality of her new life, a reality that shot an arrow straight through her stomach.

She couldn't live like this. She couldn't give her life to a country that hated her *and* a man who wouldn't mind her dead.

But betraying her bond was impossible. Not when she could save so many.

No. She'd just... have to make them love her. All of them, including the king.

And when hour four finally turned into that fifth hour, she

slipped out of her room, drawing the blanket and her candle close to her, and decided to explore her new home.

Home. What a strange and foreign word. Trying to fit High Court into her understanding of home was like trying to fit into a gown two sizes too small. Impossible. Outerland was nothing like this place. Her childhood home had been rural and humble, but warm and embracing. This place...She shivered. It was cold. And halfway between a portrait of a king holding a witch's head and a statue of a winged human, she found something else she would never have found there.

"Your Majesty!"

Her candlelight caught him tucked in a small alcove, his forehead pressed to the stone and his eyes closed, his breath coming in fast, short exertions, each one more labored than the last, though he didn't appear to have been doing anything particularly athletic. Her heart bent towards him in concern, a fact she *hated*. He didn't deserve her feelings. This was a political alliance, a convenient truce called until one of them decided that war wasn't so bad after all and killed the other.

"Lady Ellara."

His eyes shot open and widened at the sight of her. He evacuated his alcove in a rush, straightening to his full height and trying to look as if he hadn't just been cowering alone in a dark corner.

Without his crown, he didn't look so intimidating. And the far-off, desperate look in his eye paired with his attempts at addressing her like a fellow courtier only made him seem less regal than ever.

"I don't like the sound of that," she said, shaking her head. Though he'd given her a title, she never intended to be called Lady of Outerland. No one wanted to be the ruler of a prison, no matter how beautiful the prison was. Or how much she missed it. "Just Ellara is fine."

"Terran is fine, too, then."

Terran. Even back at school, she'd had to call the humans by their titles. Being given his name, his actual name, was so raw and vulnerable she almost forgot his promise to Elias.

She almost forgot her promise to herself.

"Would you like to take a walk?" she asked. It was a leap of faith, a chance she had to take if she was going to survive this life. He blinked.

"A walk?"

"Yes. The night is…I'm so…I could use the company."

The moment of silence that followed caught her between two extremes: the fear that he would dismiss her and the fear that he wouldn't. That she'd be trapped in this life with no one to save her.

"I'm afraid I'm engaged in other matters. Another time, perhaps."

"Yes. Another time."

And then he was gone, disappearing into the shadows left by the small flickering light of her candle. Maybe he didn't mean it, but she had. If it was the last thing she did, she'd convince the king she was too valuable an asset to kill. And too good a wife to ignore.

CHAPTER SIX

A s it turned out, Elias had been right when he told him that his future wife was dangerous. He'd just been wrong about how. Ellara was not a danger because she was a witch. She was not a danger to the kingdom. She was a danger to him. She was dangerous because of everything else.

It was everything *else* that made her terrifying. She'd been trying for days now to corner him, to spend time with him away from the gawking faces and whispering lips of the court, just the two of them, but he'd always make an excuse before she could. The struggle between them—between his resistance and her insistence—was seeping into his dreams, his nightmares, and the waking hours when he should have been devoted to his duties.

And since there were only a few people in High Court he knew he could trust, he turned to the only one he knew would understand his current position.

"So, you've come to me for help."

Madame Bovere walked beside him through the Arching Gardens—a rooftop display of flowers and greenery that could be seen all the way from the edge of High Court's farthest sentry posts—her face halfway between amusement and concern. Rumor had it she took walks here often, and he'd cornered her after he'd turned down what seemed like Ellara's eleventh request for a trip to the King's Forest. Unfortunately for him, Lady Bovere wasn't the type to take quiet strolls about the garden. In fact, the intricately carved shrubbery wasn't shaped by any of the palace staff, but from her own swordplay practicing against the greenery. Today, she seemed delighted to have a partner, asking him to draw his sword before she'd indulge him in conversation.

They lifted their swords. Counted to three. And began.

"I don't know what to do with her," he said, defending against a front thrust. For an older woman, she was shockingly spry, matching him blow-for-blow. "She's an absolute mystery."

"Have you tried speaking to her? I generally find talking to be the best way to learn about someone."

"Don't be ridiculous, Madame Bovere." For the first time, he pressed forward, forcing her up onto a stone bench where she teetered with every strike. "I need your help, not be made fun of."

"I can't help if I don't know the problem."

"I just told you the problem," he snapped.

"If your problem is, *I don't know the stranger I asked to be my wife and queen and the mother of my future children*, then I've just told you the solution. Speak to her. Listen to what she has to say. Until her friends from the Outerlands arrive, there's no one else here who can tell you the slightest thing about her."

With a swish of her skirts, she distracted him just long enough to jump off the bench and sweep down a row of flower bushes, presenting the tip of her sword to him in a challenge. He struggled to keep up.

"But what if *you* got to know her and reported back to me?"

"I've a terrible face for spying. I can be read like a book."

That wasn't entirely true, as she feinted left and struck right, slicing the sleeve of his tunic.

"Well, *I* certainly can't do it."

"Get to know your own wife?" she asked, pressing him backwards, his shuffling retreat against the stone walkway between the garden beds a humiliation. When she cornered him against the edge of a fountain, locking her sword against his, he fought for breath. And for clarity.

"Yes. She's...I just can't."

Taking a step back, she allowed him to reset the fight, even bowing so he might make the first attack.

"Your Majesty, why did you choose her?"

The clanking of swords underscoring their conversation did nothing to quiet the arguments raging in his head, the same ones he'd been having with himself day after day now.

"I chose her because an alliance with the witches will be beneficial to all of us. Their collective power could protect my reign for the rest of my lifetime, and if our children are half as powerful as she is, then the future is secure even after I'm gone. I needed a wife. She needed her freedom. Everything seemed to fall into place."

It even *sounded* like a lie, and with a raise of her eyebrows and a shrug of her free shoulder, Lady Bovere made it clear that she heard it as such.

"So it was political, then. You had a witch at your mercy, and you decided to blackmail her into a convenient political alliance."

"Yes."

Just as he thought he had her cornered, she swirled out of reach, forcing him to chase after her.

"Imagine if another witch—any other witch—were in her place. Would we still have a Lady of Outerland and a future queen in our midst?"

"Of course not."

"And why is that?"

He scanned the horizons for spies or eavesdroppers, knowing full well that no one could have hidden themselves in the garden. The break in his concentration awarded the lady another strike, this time cutting a thin line up the left leg of his trousers. Like her words, her blows were deliberate and precise, too precious to break his skin.

"Do I have your confidence?"

"Of course. I swear it."

It wasn't a secret he'd ever told another soul. None of his family had taken this story to their graves. None of his friends were buried in battlefield graveyards with this story stuck somewhere in their dead memories. Once he told her, it would no longer be his own private recollection, a story he told himself to remind him of the good in the world. But if anyone would understand, he had to believe it was Lady Bovere. In a war of dishonor, she'd been most honorable. If he couldn't trust her, then he couldn't trust anyone.

"When I was a boy, she saved my life."

The lady's steps faltered, but she recovered with a half-hearted strike that he barely had the strength to repel. His mind was elsewhere, back at that lake, back in the library, back in the swirling sea of Ellara's eyes.

"She scarred herself to save me from a dragon at school. And...I see in her a kind of kindred spirit. Do you know what she said to me when I was interrogating her? She said she was so tired. Tired of war. Tired of fighting. Tired of bloodshed. I just thought...If I have to be king, then that's the kind of queen I want beside me. One who shares my vision for the future. One who has fire and compassion and bravery and the ability to deliberate." His mind was running without his permission, but he couldn't find the strength to fend off Lady Bovere's blows *and* his own thoughts. "I felt like such a fool that day, when she took over negotiations with the court. I should have helped her, should have said more or come to her defense, but I was struck. I couldn't do anything but watch her. She was magnificent. More of a queen than I could ever be a king, and I'm already crowned."

Another blow landed, glancing off his armor's chest plate. He almost laughed at the image. If he wasn't careful, Ellara would become a threat to his heart. And he couldn't have that. He wouldn't allow it.

"And so, you see why it's impossible, why I need your help to, I don't know, keep her at arm's length."

They re-set and tried another pattern of intricate footwork in half-distracted silence. He'd never considered the lady to have an easily readable face, but now, he could see something cooking up behind her dark eyes.

"Does she know you feel this way about her?"

"I don't feel any way about her," he rushed, threatened by her question and her sword, which kept swinging closer and closer to his neck. This wasn't his most brilliant idea, sword fighting with the matriarch of a former enemy's house. "I'm just stating facts about her."

"It seems to *me*, an impartial and outside observer, that your heart is running away from you."

His heart? No. A heart was a luxury he couldn't afford, one that would see a king ruined and his legacy tarnished. He hadn't lost everything to have his crown stolen from him because of something as distracting and taxing as a heart. The strength rippling in his arms slackened, and he turned towards the defensive, letting her approach and fight.

"Lady Bovere, you went through it. You know what kind of people we became during the war. How could I ever ask someone to feel anything for me after what I've done? How could I allow myself to feel anything after what I've done?"

"Well, perhaps it would be at least a bit easier if she didn't think you were going to kill her."

"*What?*"

In the years since he'd finished his swordsman's training at the Academy, he'd never dropped his sword. Not once. But all the same, his sword—killer of kings, slayer of enemies—clattered to the ground, landing uselessly at Lady Bovere's slippered feet. For a brief moment, he caught his own reflection in the steel. Dark circles hovered under his eyes, and in the warped perspective of the reflective surface, he looked more like a little boy playing royal dress-up than an actual ruler. Even after all the compromises he'd made to wear the crown, he still didn't feel much like a king either.

"Rumor around the castle is that you're going to have her executed if she's not useful." Lady Bovere took his sword in her own hand and angled both blades at him, their points threatening his throat. Then, as if she'd just been testing how it felt, she tossed the sword back to him, carrying on casually as if she hadn't been an inch from murdering a defenseless king. Terran had to hand it to the woman: he never knew exactly what she was doing, which direction she was going to duck. "It's part of the reason the court eventually settled down. They're just waiting for the day you kill her. And if I've heard it and someone like Agis has heard it, then you can bet that your almost wife has heard it."

Tired of the fighting, he sheathed his sword. Wracking his brain, he sorted through the last week, trying to understand how in the world she'd gotten that impression. Why would he ask her to be his queen if he was going to kill her? What advantage would such a scheme net him? Realization dawned on him. Elias. The man who wouldn't defend Ellara against the mob of courtiers who'd threatened her that day in the throne room, who wouldn't walk in step with her, but always two steps behind, as if it terrified him she'd suddenly murder them all.

"I told Elias that, but I didn't mean it," he said, sinking to the edge of a stone-walled garden.

Madame Bovere sheathed her sword, but stood over him, holding his gaze with strict, maternal eyes. "A king should say what he means."

"I was trying to placate him."

A weak defense, and they both knew it. He'd told Elias what he wanted to hear because he couldn't have his Warden revolting before he'd even been king a month. He'd bowed to the pressures of his ally instead of listening to his own conscience. The mistake of a weak man. Suddenly, Ellara's desperation to be close to him, to spend time with him, made infinitely more sense. She was trying to endear herself to him, to make herself valuable enough that he wouldn't slaughter her as she thought he would. His stomach turned.

"I see. Well, it looks like you've gotten everything you wanted, then. A quiet court and a wife who's in no danger of falling in love with you."

"Yes." When she put it that way...he had gotten what he wanted. What he *needed*. Such a shame that no one told the throbbing ache of guilt stabbing right through the center of his chest. "Good. Yes."

Madame Bovere raised one severe eyebrow, as if she knew more than he did about his own life. "Unless that's not actually what you want?"

Though he opened his mouth to call her impertinent and out of bounds, the insults died in his throat at the arrival of a page who stood at attention at the top of the garden staircase.

"Your Majesty, the exiles have arrived."

Perfect timing. Ellara would be so distracted by her people and the wedding preparations, perhaps she'd forget all about him. Perhaps she wouldn't even have an opportunity to speak to him until the ceremony.

"Thank you for your council, my lady."

"Just..." Madame Bovere's hand fiddled with the handle of her sword, a blossoming golden rose. "Think on what I've said. Maybe you don't want a wife who thinks she's dancing on the edge of a sword. You never know when she might pick it up and turn it on you."

Her words followed him down the stairs and into his chambers, where he changed out of the ripped clothing and into something suitable for greeting their newest guests. He'd lost his mock battles with Lady Bovere, and if he was being honest with himself, he'd lost their conversational battle, too. Ego bruised, he tried to console himself by saying he'd have won both if Ellara hadn't so thoroughly scrambled his mind, but he knew he was lying to himself.

CHAPTER SEVEN

I n her time in the palace, Ellara did her best to make herself useful, to get into contact with as many humans as she could to let them see the real her instead of the rumored Ellara that the courtiers were always whispering about (*Her teeth are filed into sharp fangs. She threatened to eat our children if we didn't give her the crown. I heard she can kill us all with one lightning bolt. Did you hear that her skin is actually made of scales? That's how she gets the green color*). As it turned out, planning a royal wedding and a queen's coronation was no small feat. Though the regents and viceroys assumed she'd be content to sit back and let them plan everything, she made it clear that was not the case. She elbowed into every meeting and session she could, giving her input on everything from the menu of the week-long wedding feast to the color of the banners hanging in the High Court public square to which little girls of the court would be allowed to help her down the aisle.

She also helped herself to the library, where she poured over the Aulenian texts that had been impossible to get in the Outerland. Every minute in that library reminded her of calm, cool nights at the Academy, when she'd bury herself in a story and get lost in the pages, back before everything turned to chaos. This time, though, she didn't reach for the fairy tales or the novels of love and defiance, but for the histories and stories of Aulen's former queens.

Queens murdering their kings were more common than she'd originally thought. There must have been something in the High Court water that turned all the women homicidal, but if their husbands were anything like her future one, she could relate to their struggle.

The man was an infuriating mess of contradictions, a man so political and deceptive she didn't understand who he truly was. And it was possible she never would. But the not knowing drove her mad, keeping her awake at night and seeping into her everyday thoughts. Getting to know him was no use. Now that he had her in on the marriage plot, she was practically invisible to him. Every time she tried to get him alone, he conjured some new, outlandish excuse for avoiding her.

It made her plot to have him see the real her infuriatingly difficult. She'd tried everything, even resorting to human tactics. She'd tried dropping handkerchiefs, so he'd have to pick them up and hand them back to her, their fingers "accidentally" brushing against one another's in the process. On one occasion, she "accidentally" placed her hand on his knee during dinner. She attempted to engage him in conversation at least half a dozen times, but always ended up being referred to a stuffy old man in a stuffy old office, getting a lecture on the finer points of her made-up question instead of locked in conversation with the man who held her fate in his hands.

If only she had some magic. Just a bit. Just enough to turn his head, to force him to look her in the eye without being able to look away or leave the room. How did humans ever fall in love if they couldn't even slightly tip the scales in their favor?

Not that she wanted to fall in love with him. He was still a human. Still from a house that threatened to slaughter her people. On the battlefield, some of them had actually succeeded. Any time her mind broached thoughts of a romantic marriage, one where they'd exchange hearts and be the just, love-driven rulers she'd read about in her fairy tales, the cold, pragmatic side of her remembered that this was just a different kind of battlefield. Their marriage couldn't be romantic. The more she cared about him, the more clouded her judgment would become.

No, she just needed to make him fall in love with her. With *his* judgment clouded, it would be all the easier to convince him to let her out of the ridiculous binders, keep her alive, and increase her people's rights. For days now, letters and missives had been slowly trickling in from the borders around Outerland, where the witches were testing the waters of their newfound freedom. The quiet resolve in those letters flooded her with hope. Dangerous hope, but hope she couldn't shake.

"Good morning, Lady Ellara."

At the steps to the High Court's central chamber, where guests and dignitaries alike were welcomed by their king, Ellara had been bouncing on the balls of her feet, only to be instantly stilled by the greeting. Only one person in the entire palace called her *Lady Ellara*. The one man who'd promised to call her by her real name. She curtseyed deeply, eyeing the man in full dress armor from under her thick lashes. A small contingent of personal guards followed behind him, but beyond that, no one else had bothered presenting themselves to the newest members of the court. Every so often, a ripple in the curtains of the palace's upper rooms would catch her eye, and she knew they were watching, but none of them had the guts to show up themselves.

"Your Majesty." She tipped her head. "Thank you for coming to meet my people."

The gratitude wasn't necessary, but she assumed that all humans liked their egos stroked. To her surprise, he bowed his head, shaking it so some stray strands of ebony hair fell into his eyes. Her heart stuttered in her chest; with the afternoon sun peeking through the clouds, he looked almost golden.

"Well, they're my people now, too, aren't they?"

She gestured to the empty receiving circle. Not even those who had been loyal to witch-supporting houses materialized. "Not to speak ill of your court, but I think you're the only one who sees it that way."

"Then I'm glad I'm king and not them."

Without giving her time to think through what he'd just said, he took his place beside her on the steps and stared out into the arch of the gates, staring down the great hill leading from the walled city below to the palace above. Her fingers itched to reach out and grab his hand, to take hold of something that would tether her to the ground. She'd trained her face to hide the excitement ravaging her chest, but inside, she could barely control herself.

Then, the tops of a series of carriages—in Outerland design, all black from the twilight trees they'd built them from and designed with red etchings—appeared down below, and a wave of nausea rolled up her throat.

"Here they come," she whispered, feeling the heat of Terran's stare.

"Your hands are shaking," he whispered back.

"I haven't seen them in years. Not since before the war broke out."

"And you're afraid?"

"No," she exclaimed, expelling a laugh of a breath. "I'm excited. I've never been this excited in my life. You have no idea what it's like to operate in a world that's not yours, under someone else's rules, having no one who understands you. No one who even tries."

She aimed the dig directly at him, pinning the blame squarely on his shoulders. *Come on. Fight me. Defend your honor. Or...say you're sorry and that you'll try. Give me anything but silence, Terran. Please.*

Her prayers went unanswered. The man said nothing, holding onto his silence like a shield against her.

Well. If the humans murdered her as they all seemed to want to, at least there would be people to mourn for her at her funeral. The carriages pulled into the circular courtyard, halting before the king and Ellara. A group of guardsmen jogged to the doors, moving to open them.

"Ellara! Get me out of here!"

Too late. No sooner had the men reached for the handles than the door on the second one flew off, forcing everyone below to dive out of the way to avoid flying wood shards. A glimmer of frustrated magic followed the spell, and when it settled, Ellara's heart soared.

"Briony!"

Her friend since the cradle posed for a split second in the door-shaped hole in her carriage before clattering down, her wild and unruly body gesticulating and flopping with no regard for etiquette and decorum. Ellara's smile threatened to break her face. At least Briony hadn't changed.

"In the flesh! Can you believe it? They wouldn't even let us fly here. Of all the nerve, forcing me to be cooped up in that thing for days. Humans." She scoffed and dragged Ellara into a hug which she was more than happy to return. "Absolutely inconsiderate. Absolutely rude. Disrespectful, even."

"Apologies for the poor travel conditions," Terran said, stepping forward to greet the newest green addition to court. Despite all the pomp and deference that usually greeted the man wearing the kingdom's crown, Briony couldn't have cared less, not bothering to curtsy or avert her eyes.

"Oh, so you're the one who's in charge here? This was all your doing?"

"Briony," Ellara muttered in what she hoped was a discrete tone. "This is King Terran. My future husband."

"Hm." The witch looked him up and down from head to toe, taking in every inch before dismissing him with a wave of her hand. "I see. Frankly, Ellara, I think you can do better." She turned back to the other carriages, which still hadn't been opened. "Ladies, what are you doing back there? I'm sure the humans can carry our things to our rooms. Now scoot."

Within seconds, a group of familiar faces stood at the base of the steps, each face filled with a mixture of trepidation and excitement. These were Ellara's friends, the ones she'd held onto when she left for the Academy, and she'd specifically requested each of them to join her court. She needed people she could trust, but more importantly, she needed people who would keep her sane in the madness of this place. Even after scraping her brain, she couldn't remember the last time she'd smiled as much as she had since Briony's arrival.

"Your Majesty, I'd like to introduce you to the beginnings of my court. This is Briony, Lucita, Ava, Reeta, and—"

Her stomach dropped. Her smile disappeared.

"Where's my mother?" she asked Briony, whose face similarly smoothed.

"I wanted to tell you in private."

Not good enough. The muscles in Ellara's face tightened. "Where is my mother?"

"She's leading a walking party. The witches...they don't feel safe going into the human world alone, so they're in groups. Your mother wanted to be here, but she couldn't leave anyone without a leader and protector. You know how she is."

The world, which had seemed so bright and full of promise a moment ago, dimmed at the news. That stupid, lovable woman. Terran leaned forward, his lips close enough to Ellara's ear that she could feel his breath tickle her skin.

"That's very noble."

"Yes, your king-ness. We know it's noble," Briony snapped before shooting Ellara a *can you believe this is the man you're going to marry* look, one Ellara didn't respond to. She struggled to make sense of the news. Her mother wouldn't be at her wedding? Her mother wouldn't be in her court? Her mother wouldn't be here to sew magic into her wedding dress or stroke her hair and tell her everything would be alright? Ellara had done fine without the woman for years, but now that she'd basically been ripped out of her hands...she felt like a little girl again, completely lost.

"My mother isn't coming?"

"She'll be here. Eventually."

The grief snapped into frustration. "She could have been in a palace, but instead, she's put herself into *more* danger?"

"Well, you could have been safe in Outerland, but *you* put *yourself* in more danger, so..." Briony shrugged, unapologetic. "At least you both come by it honestly."

Curtain rustles from the palace apartment windows above them reminded her this wasn't the place to have this discussion where everyone could see them.

"Come on." She waved at her friends, ready to make a beeline for her rooms and spend the rest of the day locked inside. But a firm hand stopped her. The hand of Elias, who stared down at her through an armored helmet with shadowed eyes.

"Lady Ellara, the king hasn't inspected or approved your court."

"I can choose my own court."

"That's not how it works."

Grinding her teeth, she turned her gaze back to Terran, imploring him with every thought to assert his power, to remind his Warden that he'd agreed she could choose her own court, to tell him that the queen's business wasn't any of his. *Fight for me*, she begged. But he didn't. Instead, he merely bowed his head and waved them on.

"You may go with my blessing."

"His *blessing*? What was that about?"

While the other women from Outerland split off to rest in their new rooms, Briony stuck close to Ellara, returning to the royal residence to stalk around the bedroom like a wild animal. Ellara, for her part, only stared at the ceiling blankly, counting the cracks in the painted images of the heavens above her.

"Briony, there's so much going on here that I can't even begin to describe it all to you."

"Well, try!"

She didn't try to control what came next. After weeks of having no one to talk to, the relief of having someone in her corner opened the floodgates of her mind, and one anxiety after another poured out of her.

"The fate of all witches and possibly all the kingdom rests upon my shoulders. I'm going to marry a man who sometimes seems like a ruthless politician bent on keeping his power, but sometimes seems like he could be a good person. He also told someone that he was going to kill me if I didn't give him what he wanted, so I've been desperately trying to get him to like me and prove myself invaluable so I can keep my position and my head and fight for everyone in Outerland, but he won't give me the time of day and seems bent on never speaking to me unless he's giving an order or exchanging basic pleasantries. Also, no one here likes me, and even if the king didn't say he might kill me, I think everyone *else* is looking for the chance."

There was silence. Briony's feet stopped their frantic pacing. And suddenly, Ellara felt something cold and glassy in her hand.

"First of all, here. Have this."

"What is it? A potion?"

"No, it's twilight tree whisky. Drink it all."

She threw it back in one gulp.

...And immediately regretted the decision. The liquid burned all the way to her stomach.

"I don't think getting drunk will help."

"No, but it will calm you down, which is what you need right now." She waited a minute before continuing, plucking the glass out of Ellara's hand and refilling it. "Better?"

"A little."

"Good." She returned the glass and Ellara took a sip. "Now, we have to take things one at a time, and I suggest we start with your future husband. He's really..." Her lips curled as if *she'd* just taken a swig of the bitter whiskey. "He's really *something*, isn't he?"

And he was. Something intriguing. Something infuriating. Something terrifying. Something alluring. Something handsome. Something strong. Every *something* that he was, was enough to tear her apart from the inside out.

"Oh, no. I don't like that look."

"We knew each other at school," Ellara said, fiddling with the frilly edges of her wrap. "That's all."

It *was* all. Seeing her fellow witches here in the castle had strengthened her resolve. She wouldn't love him. Wouldn't feel anything for him. Wouldn't allow herself to develop a softness for him no matter what. He was a means to an end. This entire marriage was.

Briony collapsed into bed beside her, sending Ellara back to their childhood days when they would lay in the fields together and daydream about what they would do if they ever got out of Outerland. Strangely enough, their childhood daydreaming never led them to the palace with one of them as the future queen.

"I think I have a plan that might get him to notice you."

"Really?"

"Well... it's the beginning of a plan. Do you trust me?"

CHAPTER EIGHT

The night before his wedding, Terran couldn't sleep. Not that this was particularly noteworthy. Sleep brought nightmares, so he generally tried to avoid sleep at all costs unless he got his hands on a sleeping draught that would assure him he wouldn't dream at all. A night with little sleep was, for Terran, more of a regularity than a cause for alarm.

But he'd wanted to be well-rested for his nuptials. The entire court, their families, the witches of Outerland, *and* the common people were all invited to attend in some capacity. The last thing he needed or wanted was anyone seeing heavy bags under his eyes and thinking he wasn't happy to be marrying Ellara. No one needed to know the truth about the growing knot in the pit of his stomach, the one that stretched painfully every time he so much as got a glance at her.

As much as he tried to tell himself he didn't know how to feel anymore, with every passing day and every sidelong glance and every whisper around court about her and her compatriots, he knew it wasn't true. He *did* have feelings. He just didn't want them.

And that was what kept him up the night before his wedding: the threat of falling in love with his own wife. That, and thoughts of holding her in his arms tonight.

He fought for control of his mind as he pulled himself out of bed and allowed his staff to begin the preparations for the wedding. But until the moment they entered Central Hall for the wedding breakfast, until the moment he saw her there, hidden from view behind a thick Moonlace veil, he'd never quite gotten control.

Unfortunately, seeing her in all her wedding morning glory—her curves pressing against the smooth lines of her golden-stitched gown—only tightened the muscles in his stomach and sent his heart off to the races. He desperately wanted to rip the veil away from her face and see all of her.

But, of course, a king couldn't behave like that. And even if a king could, Terran certainly couldn't. Marriage would bring prox-imity and...the duties of a husband. He couldn't afford to let his control slip, not even for a moment. Tearing away her veil and watching the sun catch the silver flecks in her eyes would only lead to him doing something stupid like kissing her or falling in love with her.

The music of bards and the antics of jesters, who took special care to keep far out of the reach of the new court of witches, swept away the usual royal pleasantries. They'd been making mischief all morning, tipping wine glasses into the laps of cruel men or opening the windows so birds could swoop down and snap up sweet pastries from the delicate, oh-so refined ladies.

He filled his mouth with watered down wine to keep from laughing. It wouldn't do to be seen encouraging the witches, no matter how much he appreciated the breath of fresh air they brought to his table. To her credit, Ellara followed his lead, biting back any humor she found in the court's shocked expressions and indignant huffs, and he remembered his conversation with Lady Bovere. Against all odds and his own aspirations, he had picked the perfect woman to become his queen. Beyond the political trappings, she was someone in whom he could place his trust. She was defiant and cunning, clever and compassionate, independent and strong. Years of battle had both hardened her on the outside and softened her on the inside, a quality he couldn't help but admire. She'd been able to adapt to this new world, while he felt more and more like he was being pressed and squeezed into it.

He respected her. And as long as he could ignore everything *else* he felt about her, he was nearly certain they'd have a long and —if not happy—comfortable reign together.

"Your Majesty."

Her small voice brushed the veil away from her lips. Grateful she called him by his title instead of his real name—that would have been too much for him, too intimate—he leaned in closer, just enough to smell the hill flower perfume on her skin. It dizzied him. He gripped the arm of his chair to keep himself from floating away on the scent.

"Yes?"

"I was hoping you and I could take a walk today. Just the two of us."

There was something brittle about her tone. A test. One he couldn't pass.

Jaw clenching, he swallowed hard. Why hadn't he seen this coming? Ever since the witches arrived, he'd been able to avoid her, brushing her off onto a member of her new court whenever she approached him for time alone. But now, here in front of Aulen's most powerful and influential families and dignitaries, she had him cornered.

"Why?"

Not exactly his most tactful response, but she breathed a laugh. Fates, he wanted to see her face, now more than ever.

"Because I wanted to speak to you before we're husband and wife," she said, flat and toneless.

"You're speaking to me right now."

"We're going to be married at sundown. Don't you want to get to know me? At all?"

All the responses in his head ran dry when his eyes drifted down to her lap, where she twisted and wrung her hands. A nervous habit of hers. He recognized it from even their brief interactions.

"Don't think I haven't noticed that you've been ignoring me," she continued.

"I have not."

You're going to make a terrible king if you can't make a lie sound better than that.

"A king is busy, but he's not too busy to see his future wife for a few minutes a day. Not too busy to talk to her about sea-trade or go for a ride when the weather is perfect. I'm not a fool, Your Majesty."

"I never said you were."

"You never had to."

His conversation with Lady Bovere swam to the forefront of his mind. When she'd told him that everyone heard of his assurances that he'd kill the witch if she proved less than useful, he'd understood Ellara's sudden desire to be close to him as pragmatic, her motives as cold and calculating as everyone else's in this palace. But...could it have been that he'd just hurt her feelings? Was she hurt by his refusals to get close to her?

It was the only thing that explained the wringing of her hands and the cracks in her voice.

He wanted to reach down and take her hands in his own and still them, to smooth over the brokenness he might have caused. An impossibility.

"I'm afraid a walk is out of the question," he said, returning to his breakfast.

"I see." She reached for a honeyed-sweet pastry and picked it apart, un-swirling the perfect circles of golden dough before lifting it beneath her veil to pop a bite into her mouth while keeping her face hidden from view. Though he wanted to unravel the mysteries of her emotions, he thanked the Fates for her veil. As far as the wandering attention of the court was concerned, the two were just having a casual conversation over breakfast. Terran made sure his face gave nothing away. "Then may I ask you something?"

"Yes."

"Are you ashamed of having a wife like me?"

A clatter disrupted the meal as he dropped his knife to the table, then down to the floor. A steward rushed to bring him a new one, and he waited until the small man hurried away before returning to their hushed conversation.

"What are you talking about?"

"You never talk to me. Never see me. Let others decide my fate and speak to me like I am nothing but a nuisance."

His mind flashed to the memory of her staring at him for help when Elias demanded her court be approved, help he couldn't provide. How was he supposed to maintain control of the court and the kingdom if he lost the trust of his Warden so soon?

"You seem to hate me, and I need to know if that is going to be the kind of life I have to look forward to."

There it was, in plain language. She was afraid of a lifetime of loneliness, of being ignored. He couldn't answer those fears with anything comforting.

"Lady Ellara, we agreed to make a political alliance—"

"And when the alliance isn't convenient for you anymore? Are you going to kill me like everyone else says you will? I am not looking for love. Only the assurance that you won't be rid of me the second it is convenient."

"I wouldn't do that."

She scoffed, shaking her head as if he'd just greatly disappointed her. "Why wouldn't you? All humans kill what they hate. It wouldn't surprise me if that included queens and wives, especially ones you're ashamed to be seen with."

A reply bubbled to his lips, but he swallowed it as a bard called for the attention of the room.

"My lords and ladies, if you will oblige me, please join me in singing a rousing chorus of our nation's song."

Music and bawdy voices filled the room, drowning out everything else. The song was a familiar one to him. Months ago, it hadn't been the national song, but the song of his house. Now, with him on the throne, it became the song of the nation, chosen to inflict unity upon even those who didn't want it. In this tune, he heard the voices of his brother around a campfire; he heard his mother's soft, off-key notes. He heard the ghosts of the past, all urging him to change the future. He took a chance and spoke what was in his heart—saying something he hadn't realized he even felt—while knowing full well that his Lady Ellara wouldn't be able to hear a word of it.

"I'm glad you're going to be my wife. I don't know if I could do this without you."

THE WEDDING SUIT WAS TOO TIGHT. THE SILK AROUND HIS neck threatened to choke him. Elias, who had followed him throughout his wedding preparations, filled the room with so much talk of politics and tension that Terran half-wondered if it was the suit or the conversation that made the air thick and hard to breathe.

"And there's been some restlessness in the outer regions, near the borders. It seems that the witches have taken you up on your offer of freedom."

"Good," he said with a nod, the word coming out before he could stop it.

"Good? Civil unrest is good? Free witches are good?"

"Perhaps."

His mind returned to that afternoon when Ellara's court arrived at the palace. The way they threw their arms around one another and held on for dear life, the way they talked about their friends leaving Outerland in groups for fear of their safety, how her mother remained behind to help bring more of their kind to the wider world. There was joy in their faces and hope in their words, even when everyone seemed to hate them and despise their presence. That touch of sympathy he'd had for them—the one planted by Ellara all of those years ago when she saved him —had been slowly melting him down into someone his parents would have been disappointed to know, someone who believed in their cause. He gave the diplomatic answer because this was Elias, a man he'd trusted with his safety and the day-to-day running of his reign, but in his heart, he was beginning to believe that the answer to his sarcastic question was actually *yes*.

"Your Majesty." Elias gripped him by the shoulders, the scar over his eye twitching as he frowned. "There's still time. You don't have to marry that *thing*. We can send them—"

Thing. Terran's skin burned at the word, but he gently pressed his advisor aside and returned to the looking glass so he could re-tie the leather laces at the base of his neck.

"Elias. We have a wedding to get to, so if you have anything else to say, I do hope you'll get on with it."

"But you don't *have* to. If you've come to your senses, I have a contingency plan that will—"

"This is a political game. We all have our parts to play and this marriage is mine."

Another diplomatic answer that concealed the truth. As terrified as he was of marriage, of giving himself over to someone else and trusting them completely, he wanted it. And he wanted it with Ellara, dangerous as she was.

"Yes. Of course. I understand the pressure you must be under." Clearing his throat, Elias took up sentry at the side of the mirror, making himself an unavoidable image right off center of Terran's line of sight. "But I have done some of my own work for you, sir. And I think you might find it useful."

"What's that?"

"First-" his voice dipped down to scandalously low levels, low enough that the servants bustling around in the next room, preparing the king's chambers for a night with his new bride, wouldn't be able to overhear- "I have engaged the attentions of several ladies of the court who would be willing to, let's say, offer you discreet entertainments. They're even willing to meet with you tonight once you've finished with—"

"I'm not taking a mistress. And even if I was, I wouldn't start on my own wedding night."

Strange as the idea was, considering the spinning wheel of marriage and infidelity that had taken over Aulen's highest families during the years of the war, Terran had always seen marriage as sacred. The marriage may have been political, but he could never fathom taking someone when he'd made a vow to someone else. Terran didn't break promises.

"You can't possibly want to bed that thing."

The waves of uncontrolled desire that took over his body every time he thought of sharing tonight with her begged to differ. Terran changed the subject.

"What *else* have you done for me, then?"

Elias reached into a bag hanging from his waist and pulled out a sheathed weapon, which he handed over. Terran pulled the dagger out of its leather case, heart skipping at the sight of the beautifully constructed tool of death.

"A blade," he intoned.

"A Witch-Killer," Elias said, the words landing like punches. "They're notoriously hard to kill, witches. I think that's why yours managed to slip through the war so easily. But poisoned blades forged in the Jaret Mountains do the trick."

"And what would I want with this?"

"What we spoke of in the corridor." Elias was as nonchalant as if they were talking about the weather. He spoke of this intimate violence as they used to speak of military campaigns, pretending that it was all a game instead of a bloody sea of consequences. "Once you're married, she's outlived her usefulness. You can say she was... Oh, I don't know. Murdered by a rival house hoping to rekindle the flames of the war. I still have some of the banners from our victories over House Trevil; we can plant those with her corpse. Then, believing that a mutual enemy murdered *their* queen and believing that you'll keep your dead wife's promise to free them, the witches will rise to your side. Band together to be the greatest fighting force this world has ever known. Then, if they get restless, we can trap them so they cannot turn on us. Our mines in the north can manufacture those binders at a rate of almost two hundred a day."

"You'd want to enslave the entire witch population to bulk up our armies?"

"Isn't that what you wanted? An army of witches?"

It was what Ellara had offered, and the idea was alluring.

"Yes, but—"

"Then I don't see the problem in gutting the little green frog if it will help you to that end."

Terran's free hand clenched into a fist. He stared at himself in the mirror, fighting for control. He couldn't deck his Warden for his wife, not when that wife was a witch whose place here was precious at best, at least for the next few hours. He had to play the part. The politician. The king. The ruler and master of whatever game they were all playing.

"Elias," he said through gritted teeth.

"Yes?"

"Thank you for your wise counsel."

"That's what I live for, Your Majesty."

"Now get out."

The man opened his mouth to speak but decided better of it and left the room, closing the door behind him. Alone at last, Terran sank to the small divan tucked away in his dressing room, practically collapsing onto the overstuffed pillows as conflict battled on inside of him. The jeweled handle of the knife beckoned him, filling his swimming head with reminders of Ellara's own words. *If you had an army of witches, not even the Fates them-*

selves could take you from your throne. So much death and loss had led him to the throne. If he did as Elias said, he could make their sacrifice worth it. Maybe, then, all the deaths of his house would be glorified in some eternal reign over Aulen. And if she was gone, he'd never have to worry about his feelings ever again. His transformation into King Terran the Terrible would be complete.

It was exhausting, trying to hold on to this throne and his heart at the same time. He wasn't sure he had the strength.

A timid knock on his door disrupted his thoughts. The jeweled blade dropped to the floor with a clatter.

"Enter," he said.

A tiny page entered, clutching a folded paper in his shaking hands.

"Your Majesty," he said, voice quivering. "I'm not sure how to tell you this."

"What is it?"

A pause. Terran's exhausted mind couldn't even imagine the possible answers.

"The witch has fled the castle."

He blinked.

"What? No. That can't..." *Fled?* "No, you're mistaken. You've just lost her."

"She left a note."

The boy practically threw it into the king's hands, then took a judicious four steps back as the man poured over the rushed, curling script.

Your Majesty,

I cannot sell my life to a man who will not love me. But I have kept my end of the bargain. Briony and my court will remain to facilitate the release of the witches and to ensure their loyalty to you and your house. Should you ever have need of me, you can find me near the Etrurian Sea. Then again, if a walk was out of the question, I can imagine a trip to the seaside is simply impossible. I thank you for honoring your life-debt to me, and I am sorry I could not have been of more use to you.

Yours in the Name of the Fates,

Ellara.

"Your Majesty?" the boy asked, breaking up the pace of Terran's ninth reading of the short missive. "What are your orders?"

Terran reached for the discarded blade and attached it to his belt, then folded the letter and tucked it into the shirt-waist pocket over his heart.

"Tell my Warden I'm going to find my wife."

CHAPTER NINE

E llara was not stupid. She was soft, yes. She had too much emotion and spent too much time and effort trying to conceal it, but she was not a fool. She knew how to play games and, more importantly, she was good at winning them.

She had to be, if she wanted to survive this.

I am glad you're going to be my wife. That small admission, whispered when he probably thought she couldn't hear him, rang in her ears as she rode out of High Court. It followed her through forests and across glens, over giggling brooks and arguing rivers. Her heart told her he was being truthful, that there was more to him than his actions and what she saw on the surface, the performance he put on for the court and their watchful, vengeful eyes.

And she was going to use that to her advantage. This was Ellara's plan—play the heart-torn little woman, desperate for love, and ensnare him in a romantic trap. If he had *some* affection for her, some softness, it was something she could cultivate and then use. If she made him devoted to her, then she would have a powerful ally. Then maybe she would live long enough to see the *real* end to the war. The war her people had been fighting for too long. For their freedom.

There was a human saying she'd heard before. *Absence makes the heart grow fonder.* Now, she was going to put it to the test.

This wasn't about love. At least, it wasn't about *her* love. It was about playing the frightened damsel so he would fall in love with her. Love that she would use to get what she wanted.

A risky gambit. But one she had to make.

As she rode towards the Etrurian Sea, she tried not to think about what she'd left behind. The more she thought about it, the worse her outlook became. When she'd fled her own wedding day, not a single person tried to stop her. Not the high-born ladies who'd seen her slipping out towards the stables. Not the grooms or the stable boy who saddled her horse and helped her ride out of the keep. And not a single person who saw the royal stitching on her gown and her green skin flying as far away as possible cared enough about her to try and get her to stay. Why on earth would she think the king would be any different? Perhaps she'd been foolish to think he would ride out here like some noble knight to rescue her. Perhaps he wasn't the would-have-been hero she thought he fancied himself.

She tried to put thoughts of him out of her head and focus on the life ahead of her. For the first time, she was free. There were no humans to impress. No wars to win. Just a boundless tomorrow that offered her infinite possibilities, possibilities she'd never even considered before.

Maybe she would fail in this quest to earn his favor and own him mind, body, and soul. Maybe she would build a house in the trees near the sea and sell incantations. Take a lover. Make friends with the sirens in the sea and feed her lover to them once she was bored with him.

Maybe she would open a school for young witches. Terrify the local humans. Invite a few older witches to teach with her and live as a happy spinster with a thousand children who weren't her own.

Maybe she'd find some human man who could love her—powers and all—and they'd dance in the sprays of high tide, kissing at sunset and swimming naked through the ice-clear water.

She just wished that every time she thought of lovers and love, her mind didn't conjure images of Terran. She couldn't allow her feelings to complicate this plan of hers.

These daydreams followed her for hours as she and her mare moved beyond the walled cities surrounding High Court and into the forests that would lead her to the distant sea. When the sun began to set through the trees of Evervale Forest, Ellara finally allowed herself—and her poor horse—a walking rest.

A rest she instantly regretted when an arrowhead arced across the fabric of her traveling gown at her left shoulder, just nicking the top layer of skin.

Without a second thought, she urged her mare on, pushing her faster and faster without looking back. Stupid. She'd known this forest was full of bandits. Why had she thought she could just walk through? Rookie mistake. Keeping her eyes on the road ahead, she pressed onward. At the edge of the forest, there was a village where she could take shelter and tend to the wound. No robber or brigand would dare enter a village like that, not if they took to shooting at innocent women from sniper's points in the dense treetops.

"Ellara!"

That voice. Another rookie mistake. She'd gotten so caught up in her own thoughts and fears that she hadn't listened to the road she'd left behind. She'd been so concerned with possible snipers in the trees that she hadn't listened for the sounds of horse hooves gaining on her. She didn't slow down. She couldn't. Even if he *hadn't* been shooting arrows at her, there was no way she could face him.

The hoof-fall behind her was louder and faster. Only one set. He hadn't brought an army, thankfully, but he *was* gaining on her.

Her poor, tired mare was near the point of exhaustion, but Ellara leaned into the wind and prayed that she could lose him.

Another arrow whizzed past her ear.

"Ellara!" He called again, that regal voice shaking her to her core. She tried not to imagine his furious eyes staring her down or the rippling muscles of his legs holding onto his horse as he held his bow and arrow aloft. "Don't make me shoot you again!"

Whatever she'd been expecting him to say, that wasn't it. Barking a laugh, she barely turned her head over her shoulder, glimpsing him just a few yards behind her, looking every bit the warrior-king he was. The wind caught his hair and sweat made his swordsman's practice tunic cling to his chest, outlining the defined shape of his powerful body.

"You wouldn't dare!"

He loosed another arrow. This one landed in the solid back end of her leather saddle, piercing through the top layer of her skirt draped upon it.

"How's that for daring?"

"It'd be more daring if you were a better shot!"

"I'm missing you on purpose!"

"Coward!"

The smartest thing he could do now was kill her. After all, it was what everyone wanted from him, wasn't it? They wanted her gone, even if it meant seeing her run away on her wedding day. If their king killed her with his own arrows, all the better. Her heart twisted in her chest. To think that she ever believed this man would be anything but another one of them, a power-hungry human bent on slaughtering her kind and holding onto his crown. She regretted ever looking for the best in him.

All of a sudden, a flash of white passed in her peripheral vision, and her mare reared back, nearly bucking her, before settling. Terran had cut her off. He and his white steed stood firmly in the middle of the only path leading away from High Court.

"Ellara, please stop!"

He was out of breath and the directive struck her more as a plea than a kingly command.

"Why?"

"Because." He paused, and when he couldn't come up with anything better, he spluttered, "I'm your king and I command it!"

Bad reason. I've killed kings before.

"You'll have to do better than that."

If she couldn't get past him on horseback, she'd walk around. Ripping the arrow pinning her skirts to the saddle, she dismounted and steeled herself. Once on foot, she grabbed her mare's reins, not bothering to pick the hem of her wedding gown out of the mucky road.

To her surprise, he didn't keep his advantage. Following her lead, he dismounted and kept close behind her.

"Because I want to talk to you, and this is childish!"

A flare of injustice exploded in her chest. She spun on him, squaring off as if they were about to do battle. This man told her he was as tired of war as she was, then attacked her and tried to call her childish? No. "*You* are the one slinging arrows! A bit drastic, don't you think?"

"*You* ran away on our wedding day! Isn't *that* a bit drastic?"

"No. If the choice is running away or staying to be killed by my husband, then I've clearly made the right choice."

His answer was immediate. She couldn't decide if that was a good thing or a bad thing.

"I'm not going to kill you."

"Tell that to my bleeding arm!"

With a sigh, Terran tied his horse to the low branch of a nearby tree, then approached her once more, offering something in his outstretched hand. Ellara didn't immediately take it.

"Here."

"What's this?"

"A poisoned blade."

He offered it again, and this time, she took it for inspection.

Her own horrified reflection stared back at her in the intricately carved face of Jaretian steel, which bore the words of a death sentence.

"A Witch-Killer," she read, her mouth filling with the metallic taste of blood. She blinked away a rush of emotion before braving a glance up at Terran, who stared down at her with an unreadable expression. "Why are you giving me this?"

"Because it's the only one in the kingdom. And if you have it, then you know you're safe. I would never hurt you."

The temptation to trace the blade's beautiful edge with her fingers was almost too great. She retired it to her saddle bag. If he was telling the truth, then half of her reason for leaving was faulty. *If* he was telling the truth.

She sniffed. "I'm bleeding because of you."

Pulling off his gloves, he dipped his head. There were those shadows again, the ones of a man she'd never met, one who was softer and warmer than the king who currently ruled over Aulen. She wanted that man to step out of the shadows. "You're right. My aim isn't great. I meant to graze your shirt. I'm terribly sorry." He extended his hands to her, almost as if offering an embrace. "May I?"

"Fine."

Even the tepid, begrudging agreement was good enough for him. Without waiting for her to change her mind, he ripped the bottom of his own tunic clean off, tore it in half, and then reached into the pouch at the front of his saddle for a decanter of water, which he used to wet one half of the cloth, keeping the other half dry. From the corner of her eye, careful to give him as little attention as possible and not to let him catch her looking, she followed as he moved with an easy, natural grace.

His fingers touched her now bare skin. And she completely forgot about the wound. He couldn't have been a witch, but there was magic in his hands. He cleaned the cut, carefully working through her pain, before moving in with the bandage. After days of encouraging his touch, only to be ignored or avoided, this sudden contact thrilled her down to her bones, plucking her body's strings like a tightly tuned instrument. Only a few touches, and already she wanted more.

She shivered. And caught him looking at her.

"You're good at that," she responded, knowing it wasn't any kind of explanation.

"Thank you. My mother always said I had dainty fingers."

His lips tipped into a wry smile.

"She was wrong. Your hands are very strong. It's what makes you so good at this."

The words were out of her mouth before she could think better of them. Was cringing at her own words better than shivering at his touch? She hoped so.

"Thank you. There. All stitched up." But even though he'd finished his task, he didn't immediately retreat from her. Instead, his fingers trailed down her arm and found her hand, which he took in his own. Oh, the delicious feeling of his sword-roughened hands upon hers. "Will you come back to the palace with me?"

Her heart clenched. She took her hand back.

"I can't marry you," she said, rubbing her palm, which wouldn't stop craving his electric touch. "I can't."

"Why not?"

All the stupid sparks between them weren't enough to erase the way he'd treated her. The threat of being murdered by her future husband was only *half* of the reason she'd run away. The other half? Well, that was what the plan was for. To play the lovelorn maiden long enough for him to develop an affection for her. This was her chance. She took it.

"I've already told you. I can't marry a man who won't love me."

"Oh...I was hoping..." He cleared his throat and went to work, returning his makeshift medical supplies to his saddle pouch. "I had hoped that wasn't the truth."

"No, It's the truth," she lied.

Terran shifted on the balls of his feet. She almost felt sorry for him. Almost.

"I didn't know that love meant so much to you."

"I didn't either. But..." What a stupid girl she'd been when she made the deal, thinking her heart was completely hardened. This felt infinitely harder than any army she'd ever faced. "I don't just want an end to the wars, Terran. It isn't enough. I need love, too. At least, I need the possibility of it."

"I can't give you that."

"Then I can't be your wife."

He returned to her, his face open and honest. There wasn't a touch of politician Terran anywhere to be found.

"But what if I could try?"

Was her plan to win his favor already working? "Try?"

"Yes." He hummed for a moment as he broke his hold on her and began pacing. "We can postpone the wedding. Get married when you're comfortable. Take outings and walks and work on the business of running a nation together. And when the time is right, I'll ask again if you'll marry me and I hope you'll say yes." Her heart skipped. "I don't know if I can love you. Or anyone. But I can try."

The look on his face was nearly enough to tear her apart, but she remained steadfast. A little heartbreak for the prince left open just enough room for her to wedge her way into that heart. She pushed her luck a little, revisiting a belief she'd lost during the war. "Everyone is capable of love," she whispered.

"I hope you're right about that."

"Why don't you think you can?"

"Maybe that's something you'll have to discover during our courtship." Another smile, the kind she wanted to bottle up and store for a rainy day. It was so unpracticed, so rare, that she couldn't help the thrill of delight that filled her at its appearance. *She* was the one who made him smile like that. He reached for her hand. "Do we have a deal?"

Deal. The word soured her. A deal could be broken. Betrayed. She needed more than a deal.

"Let's not call it a deal."

"No, you're right. May I..." This time, when he reached for her hand, he did so as if to kiss it. "May I court you, then?"

Her eyes rolled back for a moment as she savored the sensation of his lips upon her skin. But then, that same skin turned to ice as a realization dawned on her. There was rustling in the trees. There were whispers in the distance. The forest had, all at once, gone too quiet and too loud.

"Well, Terran. My answer is yes. But I don't know if we'll have the chance."

"Why not?"

"Because we're about to be kidnapped by a gang of thieves."

CHAPTER TEN

He didn't know what he regretted more: stopping his future wife in the middle of a thieves' forest or promising to try to love her. They'd been kidnapped and tied up back at the thieves' camp, where they would probably be slaughtered or auctioned off to pirates or ransomed. That was bad enough. But then, he'd promised the most dangerous woman to his heart that he would *try* to fall in love with her, something that, even if it was possible, he couldn't allow himself to do.

Worse still, he couldn't allow her to fall in love with him.

But how could he have said no to her? When she'd spoken of wanting closeness with him, when her lonely eyes shone and he felt her sadness radiating through the air between them, his heart spoke for him, offering her a compromise. He couldn't imagine anyone else as his queen. He'd meant it when he said he wanted her at his side, that he couldn't do it without her. And now, he was in danger of losing that stupid heart of his.

On the bright side, the thieves would probably cut it out before he would lose it to his future wife.

The being captured and brought to the thieves' lair portion of the event was a surprisingly civil affair. Terran was used to battlefield captures that always ended in blood and gore, but these men merely held them at arrow point, tied them up, and pulled them up into the trees, where they were led through a construction of treetop buildings and bridges. It was an entire city in the sky, a patchwork village of treehouses and rope walkways.

Terran would have been impressed if it wasn't the place he'd probably be killed.

When they finally reached their destination, they were tossed, unceremoniously, to the ground in a wide central square, which was essentially a plank-work deck floating between five of the strongest and tallest trees Terran had ever seen. To think that something like this was not only in his kingdom, but so close to his own palace, and he hadn't known about it...It turned his stomach more than the thought of dying already did. He and Ellara had been situated back-to-back in the center of the deck as their captors muttered to themselves and poured glasses of strong-smelling fruit liquors from hand-carved casks littered along the edges of the square. With the thieves fully distracted, Terran took the opportunity to vent his frustration that was threatening to boil over into rage.

"Was this how you thought running away would go?"

"Yes, but I was alone with the thieves and they were all much more attractive than this," she said wryly.

"Oh, I'm so glad you're able to find the humor in all of this."

"Of course I am."

"And why is that?"

Behind him, Ellara fidgeted until she found his hand. Her fingers, contorted in an unnatural position, reached for his, and the warmth of her skin was almost enough to reassure him. Almost. He swallowed hard against the sensation and tried as best as he could to focus on the dangerous situation at hand, something Ellara didn't seem interested in doing.

"Because, in my dream, the thieves also tied the knots much, much tighter."

"What?" Terran hissed.

Before she could answer, one man in an ill-fitting doublet strode forward, swaggering with a blade in one hand and a goblet of sickly sweet-smelling liquor in the other.

"Just follow my lead," she whispered.

Terran bit the inside of his mouth as regret washed over him. They'd had precious seconds to come up with an escape plan, and he'd used them to snark at her about her escape from the castle. A completely understandable escape, given how he'd treated her.

"Well, well, well," the thief said as he approached, swinging his sword on the edge of his finger by the hilt, surprisingly deft for someone deep into his first mug of something strong. "Who do we have here? A lovely couple out on a little pleasure ride?"

Another man behind him, a tall, spindly thing Terran would have pegged for a tall blade of grass before he ever guessed he was a fearsome thief, snorted. "Don't be daft. She's a witch. I wouldn't touch that with your—"

"Who's in charge here?" Terran asked, adopting the king's voice he'd stolen from all of his brothers, a tone that usually granted him instant regard from anyone who heard it.

Ellara removed her fingers from his, using hers to pinch him. "I thought you were going to follow *my* lead."

"You're taking too long."

"Fine," she sighed. "Your funeral."

He didn't like the sound of that. But before he could question her any further, the tip of the thief's blade dug into the soft hollow of his neck. Even a breath more of pressure would have been enough to draw blood. The man leaned in close enough for Terran to count the broken blood vessels in his right eye.

"Who's asking?"

"Just a humble merchant," he said, spitting out the first lie that came to mind. "This witch stole from me and—"

"He's King Terran."

"What?"

"*What?*"

Every eye—except for Terran's—was now on Ellara, who leaned against him as if he were a reclining chair instead of her betrothed. Every single nerve ending in Terran's body lit aflame as her words sunk in. She'd just revealed his identity to a band of thieves.

"You're bluffing," the leader said, his eyes focused on her, but his blade still very much focused on Terran.

"He's wearing the king's signet. Third finger. Left hand."

Her voice was as smooth and casual as if they were politely discussing the weather or a particularly droll courtier's weekend activities. Maybe it was that quiet confidence that forced the thief to drop his sword with an unflattering *thump* and rip off Terran's glove in search of the ring. Once he'd removed the ring, he retreated to his group, who stared upon it with a mixture of awe and concern.

"What are you doing?" Terran hissed, careful to keep his voice down even as he wanted to scream at her to stop whatever she was attempting.

"Do you trust me?"

"Not right now. No."

If Ellara had some kind of defensive statement, she didn't make it.

"It's real," the thief said, holding it up so the gold could sparkle in the sunlight pouring through the gaps in the trees. Terran kept the thing at such a polished sparkle, he was surprised the reflective light wasn't enough to blind someone.

Ellara huffed, apparently indignant at having been questioned. "I know it is."

"He's the king, alright," one lout from the group called, nodding his head as if he'd known all along. "I'd recognize that face anywhere."

"Yes," Terran said, taking the opportunity to throw his

weight around. "Yes, and as king, if I'm not back soon, the armies will be out searching for me. I'm sure you wouldn't want that, now, would you?"

For a moment, the thief stared blankly at him before turning his much more interested gaze towards Ellara. With one dark eyebrow raised, he offered her his full and undivided attention. The sudden shift in status left Terran feeling smaller than he'd ever felt since becoming king.

"My lady, you seem to be the real negotiating party here."

"Yes," she intoned. "You can keep him if you let me go."

"We can keep him?" the thief asked, skepticism coloring his tone.

"Mm-hm. You see, he was *my* capture first, so by the laws of the forest, he belongs to me. You'll have to bargain for him."

"Is that so?"

"Yes. And unless you want everyone to know what a cowardly welch you are, then I'd suggest you take the bargain."

"Well." He sheathed his sword and turned away. "Let me have a think on it."

No sooner had he done so than Ellara began whispering, her voice dancing between excitement and fear.

"Three...two..."

"Oh, wait." The thief spun on the heel of his boot, sarcasm dripping like sweetened wine from his lips as he sneered a smile down upon them. "If I kill you, then you won't be needing your property, will you? Get her on the block."

With that command, everything happened so fast. The thieves who had been keeping their distance approached and scooped Ellara up from the ground. Another thief brought out a large wooden trunk stained with blood. The head of this brigade took out his sword once again. And before Terran realized what all those little pieces added up to, his future wife's head had been placed on the tree trunk, prepared for execution.

"Ellara!" He screamed and tried to fight against the ties holding him in place, but a strong set of arms held him down.

Even if he could get out of the knots and ropes, there was no way he'd be able to escape the strongman pinning him to the wooden floor. His heart hammered in his ears as he watched, helpless, as Ellara was readied for death.

"Wait!"

At the sound of that word, screamed by the woman with her cheek pressed against the wood, the preparation halted.

"What?" the leader asked, sword almost at the ready for chopping.

"One last request?"

"...Fine."

She drank in a breath through red lips, and Terran's stomach clenched. She'd said to trust her. He *had* to trust her.

"Will you move my head up just one more inch?"

"Why?"

"It's a dying wish. You don't get to ask why."

"Fine."

They made quick work of the request. When she had been properly situated and all parties were satisfied, the leader once again raised the axe he'd chosen for the execution, a heavy construction of metal and timber that turned Terran's blood cold. Then he started counting.

"One..."

Terran's heart raced. *Just trust her. Just trust her. You owe it to her to trust her.*

"Two..."

From her place on the block, Ellara winked at him.

"Three."

And then it happened. The blade swung. It struck her neck. And all hell broke loose.

The axe struck a weak spot in the binder around Ellara's neck, shattering it into a million tiny pieces. The reverberation of metal clashing with metal shook the leader back, and in that one fraction of a second, Ellara ripped through the ties around her wrist, freeing her hands and jumping to her feet, where she introduced a new element to this little tea party they'd all been having.

Magic.

With a push of one hand, she sent a flood of energy through the sky, knocking the first group of approaching thieves flat on their backs, disorienting them enough that they weren't a problem any longer.

"Grab a sword!" she called, one hand flitting in his direction as her other shoved a man over the edge of the platform, straight down towards the floor of the forest. At the tiny flutter of magic she sent his way, the ropes around him fell in a great heap, and he scrambled for the first sword he could reach—the one in the sheath of the man holding him down. He pulled it out and held it aloft, which was enough to send the man running for the nearest rope bridge away from this place.

Terran was grateful for that. He didn't want to have to kill anyone.

He glanced over at Ellara, who seemed similarly inclined away from murder. A small miracle. Her two hands worked in perfect synchronicity, grabbing villains by their collars with invisible fingers and lifting them into the branches above, tying them by their laces or belt straps to the bark. Terran used his sword to hold anyone off who tried to approach her, exercising his non-lethal force.

It was difficult to keep from watching her engage her power. It arced through the air with golden light, manipulating the world around her to her will. She was more beautiful than anyone he'd ever seen before.

When the villains were all strung up, cursing their names from the treetops, Ellara reached for his hand and pulled him along. But not towards the rope bridges, which might have provided them passage away from here, and instead towards the tree's central platform. Towards the edge.

"Terran, let's go."

"Yes, I quite agree."

Not that he had any choice. She'd taken his hand and was yanking him along. Even if he wanted to stay, she was holding too tight for him to let go.

"That should hold them for an hour, but we need to get as far away from here as possible."

"Where are we going?"

"It doesn't matter! Just hold on."

"Onto what—?"

They stepped to the edge of the platform, and Ellara's arms encircled him, gripping his body tightly to hers. In the split second before she stepped off the edge, his entire body rose to the challenge of hers against his, memorizing her every curve and inch. She pulled them over the edge, but instead of plummeting, they began a gentle, soft descent.

Magic. They were flying.

Terran's chaotic mind tried to make sense of the experience, but it was only when their feet firmly landed on the ground that words finally reached him. He'd just gone *flying* with a *witch*. Oh, if only his family could see him now.

"That was—"

"No time," she said, as she pulled away from him. "Just follow me."

In a rush of movement, she mounted her mare and tore off towards the far end of the forest. Terran struggled to follow suit.

"But the castle's that way!" he called over the roar of hooves and their heaving breaths.

"I know that. But we're not going that way!"

"Why not?"

"Because I have an idea!"

"Oh, I hate it when you have an idea!"

Maybe there was a part of him that meant it. But there was another part of him, a greater part, that loved her ideas. Because today, the day he was jilted at the altar and kidnapped by thieves, was one of the best days of his life. And he would follow her wherever she led.

CHAPTER ELEVEN

The small village of Elzinior was nestled in the far reaches of the main province of Aulen, a good day's ride from High Court. It was a sleepy place where most of the industry came from manufacturing liquor, and if the stories about the place were true, it was the perfect place to begin the next chapter of their journey. When they finally arrived and their horses' gallops slowed to tired walks, Ellara allowed herself an exhausted sigh of relief. She hadn't used her magic in so long, she'd forgotten what kind of toll it took on her body.

"Are you alright?" Terran asked, pulling up beside her. His exhausted white horse looked nearly as slumped and defeated as she felt, but Terran was as fresh as a morning flower.

"I'm fine."

"You don't look fine."

"I'm just tired. That's all."

Elzinior was a humble place, and even calling it a village was a stretch. As they rode through the main street and the sun threatened to set around them, the sleepy hamlet mostly remained inside of their homes. The smells of rich stews and fresh wine filled the air. This was the kind of place Ellara dreamed of finding if Outerland was ever truly freed. She'd always wanted a quiet life where she could practice her incantations in secret and make a few human friends. She'd wanted nothing like a crown or power, just enough room to live her life.

As she glanced into the window of a nearby house, a pang of jealousy stabbed through her heart as she watched a young couple—no older than she and Terran—kissing at their dinner table.

They'd ridden in silence for most of their journey, so when Terran spoke, the sound nearly spooked her out of her saddle.

"You know, if we were back at the castle, we'd be married by now."

Just beyond the next hill, the sunset was melting into the horizon in a spectacular display of jewel tones. It was like something out of a romantic painting, the kind that would make passersby stop dead in the middle of a gallery in order to stare at it for hours. It would have been the perfect night to marry him. Instead, she'd lured him out to the middle of nowhere so she could convince him to fall in love with her instead. A pang of regret smarted through her.

"Yes." She fiddled with her hair, tucking a stray lock behind her ear, her hand hiding her face. "I guess you're right."

"Who knows? Maybe one day I'll convince you to try it."

"Maybe."

She missed the silence. At least in the silence, he couldn't make her feel like she was the only woman in Aulen. Maybe Briony had been right when she guessed that running away would be the only way to make Terran see how much he needed her, how much he wanted her. But uncertainty mixed in the pit of Ellara's stomach. She'd wanted him to feel something for her, yes, but now that he seemed to be trying, she wasn't sure how to handle the attention.

"I'm going to have to send a raven back with the news.

They've probably already started assembling the armies." He sniffed a laugh. "They'll think you've kidnapped me or something."

"I kind of have, if you think about it."

"Oh, no. After what you did back there, I think I'm safer with you than anywhere else in the kingdom."

"But if it weren't for me, you wouldn't be on a horse in the middle of nowhere."

She would not apologize for that, nor was she going to apologize for running away in the first place. Every one of her reasons was valid, and if it finally got Terran to pay her a compliment—*he thinks he's safer with me than with his armies*—much less got him to talk to her, then she counted the entire thing as a victory. For the first time since their initial meeting, it was as if he actually saw her, and in seeing her, he could finally listen to and understand her. Exhausted as she was, she couldn't help the dizziness of relief that blurred her vision.

"Well, then," he said with a smile, and her knees went weak. "Let's just say I'm a willing victim."

Change the subject before you fall off this horse.

"There's a tavern up ahead. We can stop there for the night."

"So, why have you brought us here?" he asked once they'd begun dismounting for the night. Handsome smile or no, after the hard rides and magic she'd done today, Ellara's legs barely supported her own weight.

"Your Highness—"

"Terran. You really should call me Terran."

"Really? You don't seem very comfortable with it."

"I'm not. But I did promise you I would try."

Reaching for her saddlebag—a nightmare of a task given that her poor mare had driven herself face-first into the nearest bucket of water—Ellara pushed forward. This plan had been swirling around in her head ever since they made their escape, and she could only hope that these newfound attempts would earn her his attention and consideration. After all, besides being knighted, she was basically a no-one. By refusing to marry him today, she'd given up any right she might have had to make demands on him or on his time. So, she just had to hope he would see the wisdom in her idea.

"Alright. *Terran*, you didn't know that we were arguing in a thieves' forest, did you?"

"No."

"And you didn't know that this was once a witches' town?"

"It was?"

He blinked wildly and glanced up and down the village's main thoroughfare, seeing it with fresh eyes. It was almost enough to make her laugh. What did he think a witch town looked like? Humans had so much to learn about her people.

"It was. And the word is there's still some witches who live here today, glamoured so no one knows who they really are."

"And you've brought us here to meet them?"

"No, I've brought us here because I have a better idea than courting at your fancy castle."

Whenever she thought about *courting* Terran, she imagined those cold, lonely days when she'd first been brought to the castle. The most exciting thing she could think of was a ride around the grounds or dinner on a balcony at sunset. High Court was isolated and isolating, away from anything that could be considered an adventure. Maybe the queens she'd read about hadn't killed their husbands because they hated them, but because they'd lost their minds from the boredom of living cloistered inside the high palace walls.

"And what's your idea, then?"

"We'll go on a tour of Aulen, the entire country. You'll meet your people. Learn about them. Understand their plights. See the destruction left from the war and figure out how to help them recover from it. And when it's all over, if you've earned their respect and mine, then I'll be your queen. And theirs."

He raised an eyebrow, but she couldn't tell if he was unconvinced or merely playing with her. "You're changing the terms of our agreement."

"You're their king. Don't you want to get to know them?"

"Of course, but—"

"Then you should want to do this as much as I do."

Ellara had only seen most of the kingdom as a soldier. As a weapon of war. Never as a citizen or one of the people. She'd never sat in their taverns or eaten at their tables, never taken in their landmarks or walked barefoot along their seashores. All she knew was roads and battlefields, sniper's tree branches and sea-vessels. How could she be their queen if she had experienced no part of their lives beyond wartime?

"There are rules," Terran said, taking her saddlebag and shouldering it. Such a casually chivalrous gesture she almost toppled over from the shock of it. "There's the court."

Humans. Always thinking about the *rules,* as if rules weren't arbitrary, easily broken and meant to change with the ages. "Bring the court with you. I'm sure it would thrill some of those ladies to finally escape their sewing."

"I can't just leave High Court. Anything could happen to it while I'm away. Like now, for instance. We have to go back."

"Your armies are at the castle, and so are my witches. Your stronghold is fine, I assure you."

"And who will protect me?"

I'm safer here with you than anywhere else in the kingdom. "Well, I hoped that today I'd proven *I* could do that."

Without another word, she led him straight through the saloon doors of the tavern, raising her hood to cover her face. Word was that the people of Elzinior still held allegiance to the witches, but she could never be too careful, especially when they didn't exactly want to advertise that they were runaway royalty.

The Elzinior tavern was, like the rest of the town, shabby and quiet. Besides the old dog snoring in front of the roaring fireplace, the only living soul on the first floor was the tavern keeper, who leaned heavily against the bar and read from a tome, her wrinkled eyes sagging every few seconds as she tried to keep up with the words.

"Hello, dearie! What can I—" The older woman's face dropped, and her eyes widened. Apparently, the shadows provided by the hood did less to cover Ellara's face than she realized. "Oh, good Fates. It's you."

Her heart hiccupped. Nothing in the woman's tone gave away whether that was a good curse or a bad one. Thankfully, Terran stepped up, and his face—the face of the king, even if Ellara hadn't given him his signet ring back—was enough to distract the woman from Ellara's clear witchiness.

"Hello, miss. We're looking for two rooms for the night."

"Aren't you—"

"Yes," Terran said, the gloss on his words enough to indicate that they weren't to be identified. "We're two weary travelers looking for a place to stay the night."

"Right. Of course." She blinked so many times and so hard Ellara was shocked that all of her eyelashes stayed in place. She took notice of their hands, which wore no marriage bands. "Well, I'm sorry to say it, but there's only one room left."

Ellara swallowed at the news. Her fingers twitched, wanting to magic another room vacant at the woman's words. "Only one?"

"Yes. I'm afraid so."

"I'll sleep in the stables," Terran volunteered, ever the gentleman.

"No stables here. That's why we have the hitching posts out front. The nearest stable is at the edge of town, but the man who owns it doesn't really welcome strangers. I'm sorry for the inconvenience. If I'd known it was the two of you coming..."

The woman trailed off, leaving Ellara's curiosity hanging in the air behind her words. It made perfect sense for her to want to accommodate her future king, but Ellara? A witch? What good would it have done her to keep a room open for her?

Turning her thoughts to more practical matters, Ellara ran through her mental maps of Aulen, tracing every likely route. Where was the nearest town? Would they be able to get there in the dark? What about a nearby forest? Could they manage a night in the cold?

But before she could come up with a back-up plan, Terran had already slapped down a handful of coins, more coins than this woman had probably ever seen at once in her life. Maybe he just didn't know how much a room cost and was overpaying on accident, but Ellara got the distinct sense that he was giving her more than she was due on purpose. She bit back a smile.

"We'll take the room."

Her eyes flashed up to his. "Really?"

He answered her uncertainty with a confident smile. "I'm sure there's a floor I can sleep on. Don't worry."

And for the next hour, she didn't. She didn't worry about *anything*, in fact. Because no sooner had the old woman led her upstairs and out of Terran's presence, she finally answered Ellara's unspoken question about her surprising deference to them both.

"You're that witch, aren't you? The one everyone speaks of? The witch from the battlefields? The one who spared the villages and—"

The woman's voice ran away from her, and Ellara felt her entire body tense at the outpouring of warmth in her tone. She'd been around the court of Aulen for too long, become accustomed to their barbs and insults. But this woman showed her that the small mercies she'd handed out during the war...they hadn't gone unseen or unnoticed. She lifted her lips into the smallest of smiles.

"I'm Ellara. You can call me Ellara."

Tam, the woman who ran the inn, treated her to the works. A hot bath and a hot meal should have invigorated her, but by the time she made it to the tavern's sole room on the top floor and knocked, waiting for Terran to answer, she'd grown unbearably sleepy.

And cold. The hot bath had warmed her, but now her bare feet and thin shift dress—half a size too tight and loaned to her by the keeper—left her shivering. When Terran answered, he ushered her inside and towards the fireplace where she took in their sleeping quarters. The room was barely more than a closet, with a bed that dominated the space. There wasn't even room for a washbasin.

"Small room."

"Yes," Terran agreed, indicating the small patch of floor where he'd already tossed a blanket and a pillow. He'd have to curl himself into a ball to fit. "It's not ideal. But I can probably squeeze."

Ellara's eyes sagged, and she yawned as she helped herself to one side of the bed, turning sideways to fit between the giant frame and the wall before crawling under the covers. "Don't be stupid."

"What?"

"You should sleep in bed with me."

It was a heedless suggestion, one that came out of her half-asleep mind. But she didn't regret it.

"Are you..." He cleared his throat. "Are you sure?"

"Yes. Of course."

As Ellara's eyes drifted closed and her cheek pressed into the soft feather pillow, his footsteps followed, and his weight pressed down the other side of the bed. Slowly, the covers moved back, and the movement settled, but she couldn't feel him. He was too far away. She shivered.

"I'm so cold. You should probably get closer. For warmth."

"Yes, warmth. Of course."

There was that chivalry again. Or was it something else? Ellara was too tired to figure it out, too tired to do anything but relax against him as his body melded against her back and his arm slipped comfortably around her waist.

"Is this alright?"

"Yes. Much better. I'm very warm now."

His breath tickled her neck and coaxed her into a dreaming sleep. "I am too."

CHAPTER TWELVE

There was an immutable fact about war that Terran had learned before he learned anything about death and destruction, one fact that stuck with him longer than anything else. And that was cold. Everything about war was cold. Emotionally, sure, but physically, too. War wasn't conducive to long nights by a warm fire with a full belly and a tankard full of something spicy and mulled. War was frigid steel and armor that had been sitting in the dewy grass all night and too thin tunics. It was burying oneself in leaves to keep out the chill. Wearing a dead man's boots because you'd walked holes in your own.

Even after the war, Terran hadn't been able to shake the cold. Somehow, it had settled into his bones, and despite his best attempts to wrap himself up at night, piling the blankets on until he could barely see past them, he always, always, woke up with a chill.

But when he woke up that next morning, in a cheap tavern inn with his arms hugging Ellara close, her every rippling curve running like warm water across him, he was, for the first time since he could remember, truly warm.

He woke before her, a fact for which he was grateful. The fire that the innkeeper had laid the night before was down to its last embers. The curtains were mostly drawn, but there was just enough light in the room that he could clearly see the woman in his arms.

It had been stupid to think he was incapable of feeling anything for another person, but an understandable stupidity. Because in the great wide reaches of Aulen, which he'd travelled as a boy and with his armies, he'd never met someone quite like her. Besides the magic—which, he had to admit, was... bewitching—she was another kind of person entirely. She was a warrior and a fighter, confident and bold, but she was also compassionate and kind, two qualities that would have marked her as weak to anyone she fought alongside.

That got him the most, truth be told. He'd always been told that to win the game of constant warfare that was most of his life, he'd never be able to show any vulnerabilities. Beliefs were a vulnerability. Morals were a vulnerability. Love was a vulnerability. But Ellara didn't see it that way. She'd confessed her feelings to him. That she was tired of the war. Tired of the fighting.

She put into words what he'd secretly felt for too long. And, in doing so, she opened up parts of him he'd been trying to hide since the first time he took up a sword. He'd tried everything to *stop* being the boy who'd almost gotten killed saving a duckling from a dragon, but she'd had the courage to never shy from being the girl who sacrificed her own flesh to save him.

Even with her vulnerability and openness, with her easy smiles and the friends she'd kept in Outerland, still, she'd made it through. And she was going to be queen. That had to count for something, didn't it? That had to prove at least part of his theory wrong, didn't it?

Maybe they were wrong when they said he had to lock his heart away in a cage and bury it deep underground. Maybe, just maybe, he could feel things, too.

Ellara stirred in his arms. He stiffened, unsure what to do.

"Terran?" she whispered. "Are you awake?"

He didn't know how to answer that without making it seem like he'd been staring at her for the last ten minutes. Yawning, he rustled in place, using the opportunity to return his head to a more natural sleeping position. The last thing he needed was a love-hungry wife who also thought he had been dreamily gazing at her. He certainly didn't need her to know how beautiful he thought she was, resting with the golden sun dancing across her unbothered face.

"Hm?"

"Oh, you can go back to sleep. I was just wondering."

Terran fancied himself the man who saw the field and knew a player's next move. He'd worked hard to say that nothing much surprised him anymore. But Ellara did. Often. And she did it again when, instead of leaving the bed and him behind or demanding he take his human hands off her, she reaffirmed their closeness, leaning back into him. Locks of white-streaked hair fell over her shoulder, exposing her bare neck, which bore some small scars from the binder she'd worn there for so long. A surge of guilt swelled through him. He knew it was wrong to bind her, to hold her captive to the whims and prejudices of his court. But he needed that court. He needed their support to keep the crown his family sacrificed so dearly for.

Hands around her waist, he felt her slip her hand over one of his, and her quick-fire pulse caught his attention.

"Is everything alright?"

"Yeah. Just some nightmares."

"Really?"

"Mm-hm."

Another rush of guilt. He'd never slept better in his entire life than he had in her arms.

"Do you want to talk about them, or—"

Bangbangbangbang! A heavy fist pounded on the door, hard enough to rattle the wood on its hinges.

"Your Majesty! Your Majesty! Are you in there?"

"Yes, I'm—"

Practically throwing himself out of bed, Terran stood to greet the guest who, without another word, opened the door, slamming it against the nearest wall, and strode in. Only a tight hold on his emotions kept him from releasing a groan at the sight of the intruder. Apparently, his message last night *had* reached High Court, because Agis stood there in all his finery, a wild and beleaguered expression on his aging face. Instead of bowing or greeting his king, he turned straight to the bed, where Ellara clung to the covers, trying to cover everything the thin slip of a nightdress didn't.

"You! You kidnapper." He withdrew his sword, turning it on her. "It's alright, Your Majesty. You're safe now."

Placing a hand on the blade, Terran forced him to lower it. "I wasn't unsafe before."

"I knew it. I knew it from the moment you arrived that you were going to be trouble, that you were going to—"

But it seemed the arrival of company would not end with Viceroy Agis' sudden intrusion, as the door opened once again to welcome Madame Bovere, whose wide skirts barely fit through the door.

"Oh, please. Give it a rest, Agis." The ire disappeared from her face as she waved a few fingers in Ellara's direction. "Good morning, dear. You're looking quite well."

"Thank you, Madame Bovere."

He wasn't sure if witches *could* blush, but if they could, he was certain Ellara's face was filled with heat when Madame Bovere shot her a conspiratorial wink. His own stomach twisted at the sight. They certainly had done nothing that was worthy of such a saucy wink, but he'd be lying if he said he hadn't had a dream or two about convincing Ellara to be his wife using more persuasive means than just courtship.

Having never made love himself, Terran's neck flushed at the memory of his own wild dreams, but those thoughts vanished when Agis raised his voice once more.

"I was under the impression we'd find you in some sort of dungeon, having been spirited away. Not canoodling in a love shack."

"We aren't—"

"Oh, Agis. It's harmless young love. Give it a rest. And put that sword down before you hurt yourself."

But, like a comedy of errors, they still weren't finished shoving more people into the tiny room, as Briony appeared in the sliver of doorway over Madame Bovere's shoulder.

"Ellara!"

"Is everyone from court going to show up in our bedroom?"

Briony raised an eyebrow. "Ah, so this is *your* bedroom, collective, is it?"

"Just for one night," Ellara explained, before shrinking back when she realized she'd called the attention of the entire room towards her. "There weren't any other available rooms."

"Really? Because this place looks empty to me."

The skin beneath his collar flushed red again as he realized the old lady downstairs had duped them. Not that he minded so much. Or at all, really. What he *did* mind was that he'd been forced out of bed by a parade of courtiers who seemed to think their bedroom was a place to discuss royal affairs.

"Alright. Everyone. Out."

"But—"

"Out." He directed the brunt of his ire towards Agis, as Briony and Madame Bovere had already begun their escape. "Ellara and I will meet you downstairs for breakfast when we are good and ready and not a moment before. Is that understood?" When the old man moved nothing except his eyes, which flickered back and forth between the two of them, he continued. "That's an order, Agis."

"Yes, Your Majesty."

Terran stood his ground until the door closed behind the old man, but he wasn't satisfied until he locked the door's rusting deadbolt.

"I thought the entire reason for having a Warden was to avoid things like that." He was ready to find Elias and wring the man's neck for allowing such an intrusion, but his sudden tirade died as a tinkling, joyful, and completely unfamiliar sound struck his ears. "Are you laughing?"

When he spun to face her, she had her hands fully covering her mouth, desperately trying to stop the giggles. A useless effort, something Terran was glad for. He'd never heard her laugh before, and never with such abandon, as if she didn't care who heard her or who knew she was happy. He wouldn't trade the sound for anything in the world.

"I'm sorry. I can't help it. You should have seen your face."

"And you should have seen *your* face."

"Oh, no thank you. I know what I look like in the mornings."

Lovely. Absolutely lovely. Especially now, with her eyes lit up, not by the sun, but by little bits of happiness peeking out through her eyes. He opened his mouth to say so, but couldn't form the words. He wasn't sure either of them was ready to say or hear such things. And, if he was going to try and love her, he couldn't afford to rush. Even if he wasn't madly, deeply in love with her yet, as she seemed to want, he didn't want to break her heart. He couldn't bear the thought of her running away again.

"Well, I suppose we'd better get dressed, then. Hadn't we?"

"Yes. And you should probably wear your armor if you're going to tell them we're not going back to court any time soon."

As it turned out, he didn't need the armor, but he did need Ellara at his side. In the discussion with the army leaders who'd followed them all the way to Elzinior and the nobles who'd accompanied them, he found himself watching her in awe more often than speaking up himself. Whether it was from years of practice on the battlefield at getting humans to listen to her despite their prejudices or whether she was a natural-born leader, she had a way of making people listen.

And it had nothing to do with magic.

"I think there's still one matter we need to discuss."

In the main hall of the tavern, pressed close together on benches in front of the fire, they'd been discussing and deliberating and making plans until now, when the sun threatened to go down. Just when Terran had been prepared to call an end to it all and order the necessary movements for their journey across the kingdom to begin, Elias spoke up. He'd not brought much to the discussion, preferring to sit back and listen rather than draw attention to himself, so now that he'd finally made himself known, the silent stares of the assembled parties turned to him.

"What's that?"

Elias gestured to his own neck. The very space where, until just yesterday, Ellara bore the magic-inhibiting necklace she'd worn since she'd agreed to marry Terran. "She's lost her binders. We'll need to get new ones before we travel."

"Hear, hear," Agis added, lifting his nearly empty glass of mead.

From the corner of his eye, Terran glanced at his would-have-been wife. He watched as her shoulders slumped and her chin dipped. She'd resigned herself to a life without magic, to a life without her powers. And that resignation cracked the stone wall around his heart.

"No," he declared.

Elias almost choked. "No?"

"No. She won't be wearing them. I forbid it."

She wasn't an animal who needed to be corralled and punished when she didn't behave exactly as they wanted. All those who fought in the war and killed with their swords still got to keep their swords, and even now wore them in his presence. Why shouldn't she get to have her own version of that sword?

"Your Majesty," his Warden said, dropping his voice down low. "This is for your safety."

"The only reason that I'm still alive and sitting here with you right now is because she used her magic to save my life. She has earned my trust and my respect. That should be enough for you." He turned to the rest of the party, who waited in shocked silence as he continued. "For all of you."

An hour later, he and Ellara sat on their respective sides of the bed. Neither of them had spoken since the end of the meeting. They'd dressed in silence—each turning away so as not to see or be seen by the other party—and prepared for sleep in silence. A million unspoken conversations passed between them, but fear hung in the air, too. Neither of them wanted to be the first to speak, to talk about what he'd done today in the tavern's hall.

When the candle died and the darkness covered them both, he felt gentle fingers reach out for his.

"Terran?" she whispered, the two syllables carrying more emotion than he could ever remember feeling at once.

"Yes?"

"You stood up for me."

"I guess I did."

"Thank you."

"No. Thank you. I'm..." He tightened his grasp around her fingers, glad she couldn't see his face. "You're helping me see the world in a different way. And if we're going to start rebuilding our kingdom, then we have to start by trusting each other."

"I trust you."

"And I trust you."

It wasn't much to go on. It wasn't a declaration of love or a kiss in the rain or saving his life from a dragon. But it *was* a start.

CHAPTER THIRTEEN

B y the time the court's tour left Elzinior, Ellara tried to
enjoy the quiet cessation of hostilities that had fallen
between them. More than cordial, more than friendly,
they were genuine allies.

No, not allies. They were friends.

But, in the black of night, when there was nothing to hear
but the wind and nothing to see but the soft starlight through
the window, when she was certain he was asleep, he would always
find some way to unconsciously pull her closer, holding her to
him like they were more than friends or two people who shared a
bed out of necessity.

And what was worse...she liked it. She wanted more. With
every passing night, when she would wake up to feel his hard
muscles against her soft skin, his hands holding her as if to
protect her against the world, she craved everything from him.
Friendship wasn't enough. It was selfish, yes, but she couldn't
help what her heart—and her body—desired.

It didn't help that her nightmares had subsided. She'd prayed
for them to go away, but now that they'd been replaced with foggy

images of her wrapped in Terran's arms, their breath orchestrated in perfect time, and now that she woke every morning with an ache she couldn't satisfy, she almost wished the nightmares would return. At least then her body wouldn't crackle with distracting sparks every time he so much as brushed past her. In all, when she mounted her horse to begin their cross-kingdom journey, leaving behind the small tavern in Elzinior left her with mixed emotions.

The trouble with asking someone who knew her as well as Briony did to be her Warden and the leader of her court was that Briony understood the subtle shifts in her expressions, and she picked at those shifts once they were riding side-by-side, alone on their horses in a crowd of carriages.

"You and the king seem pretty cozy."

Ellara shrugged, noncommittal. "That happens when you share a bed with somebody."

"Only a bed?"

And about fifty of my wildest and most romantic fantasies. In my dreams, we've shared much, much more than a bed.

"Yes. Only a bed. Stop being so nosy."

"I was bored out of my mind at that stupid castle, Ellara. I need someone to talk to."

This wasn't a conversation Ellara could indulge for much longer. Briony knew exactly what buttons to press to make her confess and confessing her mental sins was *not* going to make matters any better. She scraped her mind for something that would distract her friend long enough to change the subject and found one in the man she assumed to be proud to be Briony's greatest enemy.

"Then why don't you go and talk to Elias? He could use some loosening up."

"That bigot? I wouldn't be caught dead talking to him. And I think you know he doesn't much care for me either."

The sharp tone told Ellara she'd gone too far. "I'm sorry. I just really don't want to talk about Terran right now."

"Why not?"

"I just don't."

Briony raised an eyebrow. Oh, that dreaded eyebrow. "What has he done this time?"

"Nothing."

"Oh, and that's the problem?"

"No. I mean, nothing. He hasn't done anything wrong. He's a perfect gentleman."

Realization dawned on Briony's face, her jaw dropping into a perfect O as her delighted eyes brightened.

"And *that*'s the problem. I see. Sharing a bed with your future husband gave you some ideas, and he's too nice to try them, you wild witch."

"He doesn't know."

Adopting a mockery of a sexy face, Briony wriggled in her saddle as much as she could without disturbing her horse. "Doesn't know that you're burning up with desire for him?"

"Stop talking so loud!"

A peal of giggles answered the command. "Of course he knows. Men always know. Usually, they know before we do."

Was that so? Ellara ran through her memories of the last few days, scanning their interactions for any sign that he might have guessed at her feelings. She'd done her best to store away her thoughts and compartmentalize their relationship. At night, she let her fantasies run free, but once the sun came up and they faced the day, she buried them as deep as she possibly could. No, the longer she thought on it, the more certain she was that he hadn't figured out her secret.

"Well, he's doing a very good job of hiding it."

"Why don't you ask him?"

Right. She could just see how that particular conversation would go.

"Hello, Your Majesty, I know I left you at the altar and almost got you killed and caused rifts between you and your court, but would you like to make passionate love to me? I don't think so."

"Really? I think that's the only sure-fire way to uncover his true feelings."

"Can we please talk about something else? How are the walking groups? Any word from my mother?"

News of the witches reaching their destinations didn't distract her from the heat building beneath Ellara's skin, especially not when Terran moved forward in their group, planting himself firmly in her eye-line. She traced the curve of his body, her mind wandering towards other aerobic pursuits they could try instead of horse riding.

It was unbearable. Wanting him. Not being able to have him. Her body was on fire. When finally they stopped for a rest, she dashed into the forest towards the sound of running water, giving strict instructions to Briony that no one was to follow her. Before she'd even spotted the stream, she'd started peeling off her clothes. A dunk in some cold water would cool her bones and return her to normal. By the time her toes touched the banks of the river, she was completely naked, and she submerged herself in the icy depths, shocking her entire system.

This was the kind of thing humans expected witches to do. They fully believed that free witches would swim naked through the rivers, luring handsome knights to their death with their magical ways. But the truth was rather opposite. Now, it was a human trying to lure *her*. Whether Terran knew it, he'd been drawing her in, with his impossibly gentle embraces and his encouraging smiles, the way he leaned on her for guidance and counsel. Everything about him drove her mad, hot in a way that no icy river could cure.

Even so, she let herself float, feeling the pinpricks of the water dig into her skin. It may not have helped quell her internal fire, but at least it was a distraction, a punishment for all the feelings she couldn't bear to control.

Because that was the real trouble—not wanting him but

feeling for him. It was, she thought, exactly what she wanted. To feel a spark of emotion for the man who'd become her husband. She'd constructed this tour around the kingdom as an opportunity to get to know him, and yet now that she was, every spark he set off inside of her heart, every flicker of warm regard she felt for him, terrified her.

The cold water rippled against the binding scars she'd borne for most of her life, tickling at the affected skin and dredging up reminders of the past. She wanted to put who she was during the war behind her. She wanted to love. But instinct, that desire for self-preservation, kept creeping back in, whispering doubts every time she got a little too comfortable or felt a little too much for him. It reminded her of all the times they had betrayed her, of the promises humans and their armies had made and broken during the war. *You may have changed*, the voice whispered, *but humans cannot.*

"Ellara?"

Terran's voice sent ripples through her, and she dove behind one of the rocks jutting out of the bend in the river to hide her body, dipping down as low as she could without drowning herself.

"Oh!" The second he spotted her—bare shoulders shivering behind a boulder—he spun on his heel, turning away and covering his eyes for good measure. The damn gentleman. The chivalric hero of her dreams who drove her absolutely mad. "I'm so sorry."

"No. It's fine. I should have known better. Briony's a terrible guard."

"She and Elias were nearly in a shouting match when I left."

"Of course they were."

For a moment, the only sound was the rambling of the small river, which swooshed past Ellara's bare skin, teasing her sensitive flesh with its chilly fingers. She searched her mind for something, anything, to say to him, but came up empty. He'd just caught her bathing naked. There wasn't much *to* say. From her place behind the rock, she watched his impressive form as he bounced on his knees and stretched out his hands. Even turned away from her, she could see awkward discomfort written upon every line of his body. The sight shot her with hope and despair in equal, confusing measures: despair if the discomfort was because the sight of her naked flesh disgusted him, hope if it was because his wants were internally battling with his chivalrous nature.

"Do you..." He cleared his throat. "I mean, can I offer you any assistance?"

"Oh, no thank you. I just need..."

She reached out towards the bank where she'd laid her clothes for safekeeping, but her hands only found rocks. She tried again, searching a different spot. And again. And again.

"What do you need?"

"Have you seen my clothes?"

A little sound escaped his throat. "Your..."

That's when she spotted them. Near the edge of the tree-line, way too far from the riverbank to be practical, sat her clothes, folded up perfectly beside her boots, almost mocking her with their distance. Certainty curled in her gut. Only one person in this entire procession would have messed with her things.

"Briony," she groaned, internally cursing her friend.

"What about her?" Terran asked, still facing steadfastly away from her.

"She's moved my clothes over there. On the rock closest to you."

With the slightest tilt of his chin, he glanced behind his shoulder only long enough to spot the articles of clothing before turning right back around. The gesture was so kind, so honest, that Ellara almost wanted to scream at him, almost wanted to tear her hair out and demand that he at least *peek* at her naked form, just to prove that he liked it. But she couldn't. Not when she appreciated his kindness so much.

"Oh," he breathed. "I see the problem."

For a moment, she debated her course of action. Walking the distance wet and naked would undoubtedly lead her to catch her death and might allow someone from their traveling group to stroll up and spot her.

No. He'd have to bring the clothes to her. And maybe, just maybe, he'd finally look at her, quelling some of her internal ache.

"Yes. Um...Would you mind terribly..."

"Not at all."

He said it in almost the same way he always spoke to her, with a polite, upturned lilt to his words, but this time, there was an edge to them, sharp and jagged and unsure. Scooping the clothes into his arms, Terran walked towards her, his eyes perpetually downcast and trained on the ground in front of him. He only rewarded himself with a slight glance in her direction in order to place the clothes on the bank, before immediately spinning to face away once more.

So much for her plan.

"Thank you," Ellara said, pulling herself out of the water and reaching for her clothes. As she began working up her skirts—ignoring her stockings altogether, she'd never manage to get them on while she was wet—she sighed and tried to break the ice with a joke. "She's a terrible friend, setting all of this up."

"Why would she do that?"

Oh, no. She hadn't anticipated him asking any follow-up questions. The answers were supposed to be obvious, unspoken. But by asking the question, he was forcing her to give an explanation.

"I don't know," she lied. And when she knew that lie wouldn't work, she amended, "Maybe it's because some people in our group are believing that you and I...that we're..."

When she couldn't finish the sentence, he offered a conclusion of his own, one less salacious than any word she could have pulled out at random. "Acquainted."

Wanting to see him, to look into his soul and assess his feelings, she spun around with the buttons on her shirt only half done. Terran, hearing the sound of her boots against the rocks, turned, his eyes brushing against her exposed breasts before redirecting firmly upon her face. Somehow, that was even more disarming.

She couldn't remember how they'd gotten so close. She could only hope her voice was stronger and louder than the incessant thundering of her own heart.

"Or rather, that we want to be acquainted, but neither of us has the courage to actually do it."

There was silence. Then, his hand moved to her waist, sending waves of flame through her, even though layers of clothing separated them. "I see."

She stepped forward, letting him pull her in closer, relishing the brush of her chest against his. "Yes."

Tilting her chin up, she gazed into his eyes, allowing her lips to breathe against his. Every coil in her body tightened, waiting to spring the moment he gave her permission.

"No one's ever accused me of being a coward, Ellara," he said, leaning in.

She responded in kind, reaching up to stroke his cheek. "Me either."

CHAPTER FOURTEEN

"**Y**our Majesty?"

If this was how his life was going to be, a constant string of interrupted moments with Ellara, he had half a mind to give up the crown this very moment. Not letting go of her or daring to look away, he responded to the disembodied of his Warden, even though every molecule in his body begged him to ignore the bastard and press his lips to Ellara's with reckless abandon.

"Yes?"

"The group is ready to press on. We're awaiting you and your..." Elias trailed off, and Terran could tell how carefully he weighed her address. "Lady Ellara."

Unconsciously, his hand tightened around Ellara's waist. The moment had been perfect. *She* was perfect. He'd given up everything for his people. Couldn't they give him this?

"Tell them to wait."

"Viceroy Agis is getting impatient. I'd hate for him to stumble upon whatever this is."

Whatever this is. Not for the first time, he reconsidered his choice to make Elias his Warden. If the man couldn't see this embrace for what it was, then maybe he didn't need the responsibility of guarding the king. But just as he opened his mouth to inform him it was *his* job to ensure that neither Agis nor any other member of their party interrupted them, Ellara spun out of his arms, closing the buttons on her top with a flick of her magical wrist.

He'd still not gotten used to such commonplace displays of her power, and every single one dazzled him. Whether she was buttoning a top or stirring a teacup, his jaw always dropped.

But this time, he focused on the sudden chill in his body now that she'd moved away from him, and the new distance in her eyes.

"No, he's right, Terran. We should go," she said.

"Go?"

"Yes."

And without another word, she was gone, disappearing into the dense forest, taking half of Terran with her.

THAT NIGHT, THEY MADE CAMP IN A VAST VALLEY THAT Terran thought he recognized from the war. After a while, most of the plains and greenery looked the same, but as night fell and the stars peeked out, everywhere he looked, he was certain he saw ghosts.

This, paired with his roiling thoughts about the almost-kiss he shared with Ellara, made taking part in the night's affairs almost impossible. He'd never traveled with the court before, but apparently, once the hard day's ride was over and the fires kindled, everyone took to revelry, dancing and drinking, or huddling together under their furs and blankets. The logical side of Terran's mind, the kingly side, told him he needed to put on a brave face and participate. No one wanted to follow a king who thought himself better than them or who isolated himself from his court.

But the man inside of him wanted nothing more than to find some way to be alone with Ellara again, to pull her to a private place under the stars and finally seal their relationship—whatever it was and whatever it was turning into—with a kiss. He needed to know what her lips felt like against his own, needed to know how her fingers would run through his hair or grip his arms, how she would press against him.

The only problem was that Ellara hadn't stopped her crusade to turn the minds and hearts of the human court to her side. He'd always suspected *that* was the real reason she'd agreed to marry him. She may have wanted him to free the witches, but more than that, she wanted to prove to the humans that the witches weren't the monsters from the stories, that they weren't so different.

Tonight, she'd taken the chance at revelry to offer a few magical demonstrations. After she'd done a few party tricks like turning water into a finely aged sweet mead and lighting the fire with little more than a wave of her fingers, she rose to her feet as if she were about to tell a delightful tale, clapping her hands together like some grand entertainer.

"Now, who'd like to see their future?"

The party of courtiers, which had, up until now, been mostly drinking and laughing, collectively balked at the question. No one answered for a long time, and when someone finally did, it was Madame Bovere, the bravest of them all.

"You can do that?"

"We all can," she said, waving to the few witches amongst their party, including Briony, who didn't acknowledge the crowd's attention, choosing instead to down an entire tankard of mead in three large gulps. "To an extent."

Elias smiled a dark smile as he attended to sharpening the blade of his personal dagger. "Then why didn't you win the war?"

"Like I said, everything's limited. Even our magic."

This confession didn't deter Lady Bovere, who sat up in her lounge, the fire and the mead reddening her cheeks.

"I want to try. Tell me, are there great riches in my future?"

"Are you in need of riches, Lady Bovere?" Ellara asked, a teasing edge to her voice as she inspected the woman completely beset by jewels.

"I'm doing fine, but one could always be doing better."

"Let's see." In a smooth motion, Ellara swooped down and collected a handful of red clay dust and offered it to the lady. "Give me your hand."

"This is witchcraft, my lady," Agis pleaded. "Please don't."

Lady Bovere collected the dirt and clenched it. Not even a hint of skepticism colored her actions. "Oh, hush, Agis. You're just jealous because you already know there's no wealth in *your* future."

"Now I'm going to speak an incantation, and when I stop, you and I need to throw the dirt in at the exact same time. Alright?"

"Yes."

Terran leaned forward, hands on his knees, as he watched Ellara through the flickering flames of the roaring fire that separated them. Words came out of her mouth in a language he'd never heard before, her hands calling down beams of golden, spell-bound light as she waved them. The entire circle sat silent, enthralled, as she stopped, threw the dirt into the fire—with Lady Bovere following suit—and a bolt of magic erupted from the flames, shooting upward.

But this wasn't some simple, overactive flicker. No, the flame lifted into the sky, transfiguring into the shape of a bird Terran had never seen before.

A night of firsts.

"What does it mean," Lady Bovere whispered, her eyes never lifting from the flying fire animal.

"It's a species of bird from Outerland. They're known to steal and horde treasure. I see great things in your future, Lady Bovere. You might want to open up some new coffers."

"Delightful! Simply delightful!"

"Me next! Oh, please let me go next!"

From there, she told the fortunes of lady after lady, gentleman after gentleman, until the only holdouts amongst the group were Agis, Elias, and Terran. Several women begged to go a second time, wishing for more information, more good news, or some good to salve the bad they'd gotten before.

But Terran decided he'd had enough of other people's fortunes. He wanted one of his own.

"Lady Ellara?" he asked.

The circle silenced, their gazes flickering between the two parties separated by a ring of fire. He did everything he could to maintain control of his expression, even as Ellara's eyes sparkled while her smile faltered at the sight of him.

"Yes, Your Majesty?"

"I was hoping you might indulge a question of mine."

"Of course," she said, tipping her chin up. A show of defiance in her eyes flashed hotter than the fire. "What is it you wish to know?"

The question was a risky one, one he shouldn't have dared to speak in mixed company. A potential political disaster and morally dubious, he knew better than to ask it out loud. But he wanted an answer. And he would not leave without one.

"Is there any love in *my* future?"

A hush fell over the world. The wind caught its breath. The fire softened its crackling tongues. Even Terran's heartbeat stilled for a brief moment in reverent contemplation before rollicking back to life. Terror gripped Ellara's beautiful features. For a moment, the shadows cast by the flames distorted her features, but just as soon as it happened, the moment was gone, and she took hold of herself and her newfound circle of devotees.

"Are you sure you want to know the answer?" she asked,

fluffing out her skirts and sharing a conspiratorial wink with a group of men who had discovered their futures were *not* with the rich-born ladies of the court. Even with the show of good fun, the air crackled with anticipation and dread, excitement and uncertainty. No one—least of all her—knew what would happen next. "We haven't had the best luck tonight."

"I must take my chances. You're the only one who can answer this question for me."

After their almost-kiss, she'd brushed him off and spent the better part of the day ignoring him and avoiding his gaze. After demanding a marriage with feeling and respect, love and honor, she'd reached out her hand only to snatch it away when he was ready to take it. Only she could tell him if he was going to be loved. Only she could tell him what the future held for them.

The eyes of the crowd were upon her, but the eyes of Agis and Elias were watching him. He felt them staring, judging, questioning his move, a move that he, himself, couldn't help but question. Did he even want to know?

"Alright, Your Majesty," she said. Her body moved in a familiar arc as she scooped clay into her hands. But as she closed the gap between them, carefully picking her way around the fire and the assembled onlookers, her pattern of breathing took on a most unfamiliar, almost erratic, pattern.

Terran rose to his feet to accept the hand of dirt, ready for her fingers to brush against his. He wanted that interaction, needed to know if the lightning bolts he'd felt this morning were a fluke, a trick of his imagination, or a repeatable phenomenon.

She didn't give him the chance. Instead of clutching hands as she'd done with her previous subjects, she clenched her fingers and let the sand slither down into his waiting hands. He quickly closed them to keep the wind from disturbing the magic.

"I'll speak an incantation, and when I stop, you'll throw the dirt into the flames. Do you understand?"

He nodded, and she began. He'd never been in the presence of magic like this, magic that wasn't called in the heat of some adrenaline-filled moment, but deliberate and purposeful. This was the kind of magic his family warned him about, the desire to have something without sacrificing for it. He bit the inside of his mouth as the wind itself seemed to hum, a hum that got louder and louder as she spoke until it reached a fever pitch, then silence.

They both threw the dirt into the fire. And then, two birds of pure light flew from the flames, a sight that caused the assembled circle to clap as if they'd just seen a particularly delightful dance routine.

"Two birds," Terran intoned, his eyes never leaving Ellara's face.

"Yes," she replied. "Lovebirds."

CHAPTER FIFTEEN

The first stop on their tour was Hill Country, a small province where Ellara had spent more than her fair share of the war hiding behind mounds of dirt and fighting for the High Ground. Neither the beauty of the purple leafed Sytranil trees nor the ghosts of her fallen comrades could return her from the spiraling of her distracted thoughts. Yesterday, after her humiliation with Terran at the riverbank and Elias' horrified look at the sight of them together, she'd taken the time to reevaluate her feelings. It wouldn't do her any good wishing she could go back to a time before she felt anything for him—no one had the power to turn back time—but she *had* to be more careful with herself. Terran's people were still suspicious of her, Elias was ready to throw up at the sight of them almost kissing, and unless her magic directly benefited them like some kind of carnival diversion, the court still looked upon her as an outsider, an enemy coming to seduce their oh-so-righteous king. If she wanted to live through this trip with her skull intact and the agreement with Outerland still in place, she needed to play the game.

But then he had to go and ask that *stupid* question. As soon as the lovebirds flew into the sky, their fire-wings entwined, she'd made a beeline for her tent, not bothering to look behind her.

No one, not even Briony, tried to speak to her, but their eyes followed her everywhere she went.

So did their whispers. As much as the people of the court seemed to pride themselves on their ability to conduct gossip anywhere and at any time, they were terrible at keeping their voices low enough for discretion.

She never cared about the whispering. When she was at school, she'd taken everything—beatings and all—with good humor, trying to win them over with kindness and gentility. But now...she couldn't help but care about every overheard conversation and snide remark. This was no longer just about her, something she had to bear in order to try and win friends. Maybe the country was no longer at war, but she knew better than to think the fighting had stopped. Gossip was just another form of warfare, one she had to wield and defend herself against carefully.

She thought Terran, of all people, would have understood that, which was why she couldn't contain her shock when the idiot had asked her about *love* in front of all of those people. It was why she couldn't contain her anger at him now, when she found herself partnered with him during the first of their "cultural exchanges," a dance lesson offered by one of the ladies' societies of Hill Country.

When Ellara had suggested a tour around the kingdom, she hadn't meant that she wanted to spend her days in stuffy halls wearing extravagant dresses and being told how to properly jump on the two and four counts of the music. No, she'd anticipated working with farmers to revitalize ruined crops or starting community child-raising initiatives in a time when every hand was needed to work.

But Lady Isla, who'd been largely responsible for the schedule, assured her that this was *the* best way to get on the people's good side. If there was anything Ellara desperately needed, it was a way to do just that. All day, even when she was at Terran's side, she'd been on the receiving end of cold stares and muttered insults from the people of Hill Country. Their hatred bled through the air, agitating her already crumpled spirit.

"Alright, everyone! Now let's try it with our partners."

For the last hour, the traveling court had been mingling with the merchants and laborers alike in the shabby meeting hall that served as the social center for all of Hill Country's sprawled-out villages. A short stick-figure of a woman in a too-loose dress had been barking orders at them every step of the way. The closeness of the bodies and the thickness of the room's air was more than enough to scratch at Ellara's temper, but given that she hadn't slept last night because she was thinking of Terran and his *stupid* eyes and his *stupid* questions about love, her nerves were at their very frayed ends when the king offered her his hand.

The spark that flew between their skin at the meager contact only inflamed her further.

"And we'll begin without music," the dance instructor called, clapping her hands to keep the rhythm of the simple country dance. "One, two, three, and—begin!"

As best as she could, Ellara focused on her steps instead of the man beside her. The partnered dance began with them facing outwards, moving laterally and then forward to the beat, before eventually coming together for the more complex partnering.

"Ellara?" he asked.

Her name on his lips was almost enough to reignite the fire she'd felt for him yesterday, but recalling the sight of the love-birds flying off into the night's sky was enough to quash it.

"Yes, Your Majesty?" she replied, carefully using his title, putting distance between them even as the dance brought them closer.

"...You seem upset."

If she hadn't been ready to explode, she might have laughed.

But as it was, opening her mouth too wide put her at risk for a full-on rage to escape, so she stuck to letting conversation carefully slip between her lips, though she mostly focused on keeping her face impassive and her hand from crushing his. "Do I?"

"Yes." As they spun into one another, adopting a more traditional dancing pose at the encouragement of the dance master, their noses almost brushed. Ellara's breath caught in her chest. "And I think I'm the one who's caused it."

Turning her face away from him, she raised an eyebrow, unable to help that small display of emotion from passing through. "Your keen powers of deduction have once again served you well."

"I'm sorry, Ellara." He spun her out as they'd been taught, and Ellara's heartbeat kept pace with the pounding feet around her. *I'm sorry.* Such a little thing to say to someone, but in all of her years around humans who wanted her dead, she'd heard it so rarely that its sudden arrival in the conversation made her trip. She flushed as some women behind her snickered. "I shouldn't have called you out like that. I shouldn't have made you—"

"No. You shouldn't have." Righteous anger rose within her. "Now half the court thinks I've bewitched you into falling in love with me, and the other half thinks I'm a terrible tease for leading you on and breaking your heart."

"I was trying—"

"*I* was trying to win them over and to show them that magic isn't all the sinister stuff from their childhood stories. It was working. They were seeing magic as I see it, as a wonderful tool and a gift for connecting the divine and the worldly. And in one little flash, you ruined all of that. They're suspicious of me again."

She voiced her most reasonable concern while hiding the one that really bothered her. Yes, she was furious he'd broken her progress with the court. Yes, she wanted to wring his neck or tie him up from a church spire by his ankles. But if she were being honest with herself, it was that she'd come into this little trip of theirs thinking she was safe from feeling anything for him. After all, *she* was trying to get *him* to fall for her, not the other way around. But her feelings for him had crept up on her slowly, and they'd been brutally, publicly confirmed for all to see last night.

"They aren't all suspicious," Terran said, not so subtly trying to catch her eyes again as they spun into the next musical phrase. "Madame Bovere likes you."

"Have you met the courtiers Madame Bovere is forced to spend her time with? She'd like anyone with more than two pieces of sense in their head."

Determined not to look at him, lest she give into her anger and let him have it in front of all these people, she pursed her lips and tried to keep up with the dance mistress' counting. Organized dancing had never been one of her strong suits, and more humiliation wasn't what she had in mind after last night's disaster.

"I wanted to apologize," Terran said, readjusting his fingers at her waist. She repressed a shiver.

"And now you have. Can we focus on the dance, please?"

"I just..." He struggled for the words, a quirk she noticed he only did around her. It was a small sign of trust, but one she couldn't read into too deeply. "I needed to understand where we stood."

"And you didn't think to just *ask* me?"

"Of course I thought of it, but you wouldn't even look at me. I just...I was so...*You* are so..." As much as she hated him in this moment, there was something to be said for watching Terran, the aloof and proud king, fighting for words. She'd gotten to him, and they both knew it. "You were going to kiss me, and then you ran away like it meant nothing. Did it?"

Her delight at his struggle lasted only until he stopped speaking, when it crumbled into a fine dust. Neither of them needed to hear her answer, at least not out loud. Confessing that the kiss meant everything to her and that walking away had been so painful she'd almost started crying was going to break them both. She focused on that pain. Pain was so much easier to feel than love.

"Did you see the way Elias looked at us? How much I disgusted him? Look around you. It's in the faces of everyone here." Despite dancing in the front of the room, a privilege reserved for the king and his companion, their hatred followed her everywhere she moved. She didn't need to see them to know what was happening. "They hate that you are with me, and they hate that you could ever feel something for someone like me. I'm a symbol of everything they want to despise."

"But you said you wanted—"

"I know what I said." She blinked rapidly, pushing back the heat welling behind her eyes. "And I still do. I still do want..." *Don't say that you want love. He might just give it to you.* "I still want what I asked for. But maybe it's better if we go back to the way things were. Maybe a political marriage is better than whatever we could be. At least then, your people would look at you with a modicum of respect."

"I don't give a damn about them."

This time, she allowed herself to laugh. But it was bitter and brittle, the kind of laugh she hated to hear coming from her own throat. As much as she wanted it to be true, as much as she dreamed that one day he'd stop caring what his people thought of him, she knew it would never happen. There would always be a kingdom-sized gap between her and Terran. Always.

"That's not true. And even if it was, you *do* give a damn about keeping that crown on your head. Don't pretend like that isn't the most important thing to you."

CHAPTER SIXTEEN

Ellara believed that the crown upon his head was the most important thing in the world to him. He knew she was right. For days, as they carefully did the dance of avoiding each other while not seeming they like were *purposefully* avoiding each other, Terran stewed over that truth, a truth that got no easier to swallow no matter how many times he tried.

Even at prayer in the small Fated Temple, which travelled with the court, that truth followed him, echoing against the golden statues and jeweled icons, reminding him of his failures. Like a chant, it repeated over and over again even as he fought for some kind of clarity and freedom from its noise.

Of his family of eleven—two parents, seven brothers, and two sisters—he'd always carried a small portfolio, no bigger than the palm of his hand, of their family portrait, the last to be painted before the war broke out and scattered them all to the winds. He'd never been a particularly religious man. While some of his troops carried lucky charms into battle or prayed all night before they took out their swords, Terran didn't much care for any of that. But coming to the temple and kneeling before his family's icon, surrounded on all sides by candles and incense, wasn't about prayer or meditation for him. It was the belief of the court that he came here to pray to his lost family, to ask them for guidance and wisdom, and that was partly true.

Really, he came because he missed them. And the temple was the only place he felt like he could talk to his family's images without sounding like he'd lost his mind. He couldn't bear the thought of being caught in his tent, talking out loud to a picture of the dead, but something about the temple made even the maddest things look and feel natural. It was a strange quirk of religion, one he often used to clear his head. He didn't know if any of them could hear him. Even if they could, he wasn't sure they would want to listen to anything he had to say. But it *did* make him feel less alone.

Alone.

As he stared at the image of his family, resplendent in their finest colors and stone-faced as if ready for a battle they didn't yet know was coming, that word rattled around in his empty chest, banging at his insides with the force of a marching battle drum. He blinked at the image, barely realizing that when it became blurry, it was from unshed tears pooling in his eyes.

Alone. He was alone. And for the first time since he found out that Arran, his youngest sister and the last of his siblings to be seen alive, had been killed by her husband...he truly felt alone. He had no family. No friends, none he could truly trust or confide in. No allies. Just a crown and a painted image of the family who'd died to give it to him.

He slumped against the hard-backed bench, not caring when his weighted sigh escaped him, and blew out several of the nearby candles. From their place on the altar, his family's painted eyes stared back at him, speechless, unseeing, and unfeeling. Their imagined presence threatened to crush him as he realized that he wasn't just ruling for them. He was doing everything *else* for them, too; he was trying to live on their behalf.

And he was doing it all *alone.*

Behind him, the flaps of the temple's entranceway fluttered, and he spun around just in time to catch Ellara trying to sneak in, a small votive painting of her own clutched in her hand. No sooner had she seen him than she attempted an escape, raising her hands to magic the curtains closed once more.

"Oh, I'm sorry. I'll just—"

"No, please don't go."

The spell hovered, its thin, silvered spots like dust in the sun. Then, she released it and reached to pull the curtain open once more. A reflex made him slap his family's portrait face-down on the altar, a reflex he realized was stupid when a flash of hurt crossed Ellara's face like a shooting star and her shoulders caved in, making her body smaller than he'd ever seen it. The simple gesture made her think he was ashamed of her, that he didn't want even his dead relatives to see that they were alone together in this place. Her green hand clutched at the white sheet opening of the tent. From his place across the temple, he could see the way her shaking hand disturbed the fabric.

"Prayer is a time for reflection and solitude," she said, a note of finality playing in her speech. "I'd only be interrupting."

Reaching for his portrait, he reassembled it on the altar, letting the painted pictures of his family see the woman who vexed and delighted him, the woman he wanted to stand along-side him as Queen of Aulen. He touched the empty bench beside him. "I'd like for you to be here."

When the thought of inviting her to stay popped into his head, he wasn't entirely sure he believed that he wanted it. After all, they hadn't had the warmest of relationships since their botched kiss by the river, and he couldn't afford any more disastrous encounters with her. But when her skirts brushed up against his thigh and her boots tucked themselves beside his own, when he caught the scent of her flowered perfume and heard the quiet hum of her steady breathing, certainty nestled in doubt's place.

The empty, hollow loneliness that had gutted him not two minutes ago filled in at her presence.

Clinging to her own portrait, she nodded in the direction of his. If she noticed the extinguished candles all around them or the shadows that occasionally cut through the golden light around them, she didn't remark on it. "Is that your family?"

"Yes. All of them."

Not brave enough to give her his full face, he glanced sidelong at her. Leaning slightly forward in the pew, she homed in on the faces, surveying them and drinking in the details. The quiet attention she paid to people who'd hated her, to the people in his family who would have rolled over in their graves to see them sitting so close, rattled him. And when she smiled, a softly sardonic smile, he knew that she was better than all of them.

"Ten children. What a family." She whistled, low and as reverent as a whistle could be, considering they were in a temple. "Your parents must have been very fond of each other."

Of all the subjects he wanted to discuss with Ellara—the future of their kingdom and their marriage, the finer points of Tikanian opera, what it would be like to finally kiss her and hold her in his arms without fear of her running away—his parents weren't high on that list. He fought back a wince, even as he told her something he'd never told anyone else about his family: the truth. "They weren't, actually. I didn't think it was possible to share a roof, yet live in completely different worlds, but my parents managed it."

"Then why—"

"Their ambition brought them together. They both wanted to rule Aulen. The more children you have..." He ran the tips of his fingers across the faces of his siblings, the feeling of the raised paint reminding him that they had been real, more than just pawns. No matter what had happened to them in the end, he wasn't going to let his memory of them be tainted by his parents' dreams. "...the more power you can accrue. And my mother had two boys by her first husband before he was killed, so they knew she could produce many, many heirs."

Ellara fell silent for a moment, apparently considering his words. He watched the thin worry lines on her brow move with her thoughts.

"But it must have been a happy childhood, at least. Lots of children running around, lots of fun to be had, I'd imagine."

Even after what she'd been through, after all that she'd seen and done and had done to her, even after the way he'd treated her and the way everyone in his court still treated her, she tried to see the good. Not for the first time, he thought back to that first night they met after the war, when she said she was tired of all the pain. Searching for the moments of light in the otherwise dark world must have been her way of surviving. A shield for her mind against all the trauma.

"We all knew from a very young age what was expected of us. When we did play games, there was usually an imaginary war and actual swords involved."

"Does it hurt you, to talk about them?" she asked, still tracing the paint lines.

"No. I don't think so, at least. Would you..." He swallowed nothing except air, but it slid down his throat and into his stomach like a river-sharpened stone. They'd been close and intimate before. They'd almost *gotten* intimate that day beside the river when she was covered more by water droplets than clothes and they almost kissed. Somehow, this encounter felt different. He never spoke about his family, not to anyone. Sharing them with her felt like opening a door he couldn't walk back through, but one he had to cross if he was going to move forward. "Would you like to hear about them?"

"Yes." She searched his face, but for what, he couldn't possibly begin to guess. Whatever it was she was looking for, he hoped she found it. "I think I would."

Warning an Aulen citizen that his family history was bloody and violent was like telling a siren that the water in the Etrurian

Sea was particularly wet today, so he skipped over the caution and dove straight in. Picking up the portrait, he leaned in closer to her, relishing her warmth, which seeped through their clothes and broke the frost coating his skin. He tried to focus on the story rather than her soft skin so close to his, but it was nearly impossible.

"My father killed my mother's first husband. They met at his funeral, and my father proposed then and there, offering her protection and loyalty if she swore to give him the family he needed."

"Romantic," Ellara joked, her voice frail and brittle.

"Oh, she was happy to accept. She always told us that the day my father proposed to her was the happiest day of her life."

"Even though it was the same day she buried her first husband?"

"That's what she said."

The uncertainty of that answer hung between them, and Terran realized that he'd never thought critically about his own family's history. Ellara, outsider that she was, probed at all the things he'd spent his entire life ignoring.

"Do you think she loved her first husband?"

Terran blinked, trying to clear another blind spot from his vision. "I don't know. I never asked. I never asked if she loved my father either. I never heard either of them say it."

"I see."

Strange, the things he *knew*, but never realized or thought of until now. Some part of him always knew his parents didn't love each other, but now that he was here, glancing at Ellara's all-too serious, all-too beautiful face, with candlelight glinting in her eyes and catching the pink tones in her lips, he understood how abnormal it was. Or, if it was normal in Aulen, then he didn't want that kind of marriage. He didn't want to share a life with someone he didn't love.

Now, Ellara running away from the castle didn't seem so strange. She'd just realized it much, much faster than he had.

He changed the subject, swiftly moving away from the topic of romance and love, or lack thereof.

"My father had lost his brothers in the Treetop Wars, fighting for a king they didn't believe in, so he wanted the throne for himself."

"So he could be the kind of king someone could believe in?"

"No, so he'd be the one men died for instead of the one doing the dying. Not that what he wanted really mattered, anyway. He was the first of my family to die."

She winced. "In battle?"

"No, strangely enough. One day, his heart just gave out. I suppose that happens to some people, doesn't it? They just hoard everything in their chest and one day..." Releasing the grip he hadn't realized he'd had on his own tunic, he fixed his breathing back to something resembling normal and tried his best to continue. "But no, he didn't live to see the War of Seven Kings. Thank the Fates for that. He probably would have killed me rather than see me on the throne."

"Why's that?"

Memories resurfaced, ones he hadn't thought about in years. "He didn't care for me," he answered simply. "I was the second youngest, but I cared the least about war and conquest. I was the kid who'd throw himself at a dragon to try and save a baby duckling, remember? Father didn't approve of me. I would not win him any battles or deliver him the crown. Why would he have wasted time or affection on me?"

Terran didn't enjoy thinking about his father. The man was cruel and unfeeling, as ambitious as he was unethical. And in Terran's worst moments, when he dismissed Ellara or killed on the battlefield, he felt himself becoming more and more like the man. The thought frightened him to his core. It was one reason he'd started softening towards Ellara in the first place. After she ran away from the castle, he could only think of his father, how this was something a woman would have done to him, run away because he was cold and manipulative. He hadn't wanted to become the kind of man who deserved it when women fled in fear or heartbreak.

Turning his thoughts away from the man and their relationship—or lack thereof—he glanced at his picture of the dead. What had once been a proud painting of a noble, prosperous house with enough children to control Aulen through marriage alone now stood as a reminder of everything he'd lost, everything he could never get back.

From there, he told her the end of his family's history. As with everything after the war, it all came back to death. His mother died in the siege of Rosson Keep. One of his sisters had been murdered, while Karri, his other sister, had died on a battlefield somewhere near the center of Etruria. He catalogued the deaths of his brothers as if he were telling the details to a census keeper, before pivoting and trying to tell her the little things. Robert, his younger brother, had been his closest companion. Tyon's favorite color had been blue. Hemarc spent most of his afternoons holding parties with the trees until he turned eight and realized trees couldn't talk back.

Ademar was the second son of his father, and the one everyone believed would one day wear the crown. Terran had followed him throughout the war, fighting at his side, hoping that one day, he'd see that man sitting on the throne and ruling over their kingdom.

It had been his life's mission until Ademar took a sword to the gut at the war's final battle and died in a pool of his own blood.

Ellara's accusation from this morning's dance lesson broke through the image of his brother's dead body. She'd accused him of caring about nothing more than the crown. She'd been right. But for the wrong reasons.

"So you see," Terran said, uselessly waving his hands over the painted faces. For a moment, he considered asking Ellara if her kind could raise the dead like the stories told, but he knew that if she could have saved the kings who'd sworn to protect her kind, she would have done it and seen his family defeated a long time ago. "I wasn't ever meant to be king. And I never wanted it. But when the war was over, and I was crowned...I couldn't say no. My brothers and my sisters and my mother died so that one of us would sit on the throne and rule Aulen. I couldn't let them die in vain. I wanted an alliance with you because I thought the witches would keep my family's legacy alive forever. I care what the court thinks because one wrong move could end my reign. I watched my family die for this. I can't lose it now."

He swallowed and dug his fingernails into his palms repeatedly. All the things he normally did when he tried to prevent himself from publicly displaying any emotions. This time, none of them worked.

Ellara's fingers brushed his hand, the only sign that she'd seen the traitor tear he'd wiped away with his sleeve. "But your heart is telling you something different, isn't it?"

"I thought you didn't want to talk about the heart," he replied, thinking of this morning when romance and matters of the heart were the last things on her mind.

She offered a half-shrug. "I didn't when I thought you were just another ambitious human trying to claw his way to glory on the backs of the dead. I've heard so many human men tell me about their feelings as if they were supposed to mean something to me, as if their feelings weren't just a manipulation. A way to make me believe in their cause. But this..." Her fingertips, painted black in the lacquered style the witches often wore, brushed over the portrait of his family before reaching up to tap her own heart. "This feels real to me. So, what is your heart telling you?"

"It's telling me..." He swallowed hard and tried to speak what was on his heart, an almost impossible feat given how long he'd tried to avoid even thinking about it. "When I sat down tonight to be with them, I realized that you're all I have. In this world, in this life, I don't have anyone except for you."

They'd been so close until now, their bodies near enough that he could count her breaths. He wondered what she was thinking, whether she was as viscerally aware of their closeness as he was. The question answered itself when she moved away. "Terran, you have an entire kingdom, one you just said—"

Turning, he captured her hands in his and held onto them. Her eyes were more difficult to hold on to, but eventually, she relented and focused on him. That one look charged him with lightning and filled him with hope and determination.

"They're my responsibility. Just like my family was." He squeezed her hand. "But you're my choice. And I hope you choose me. But even if you don't, know that I will do everything I can to protect you and make you feel loved and welcomed here." She dropped her gaze, as if she thought what he was proposing was an impossibility. But he'd stopped believing in impossibilities when she saved his life all those years ago. Now he was sure that there wasn't anything the two of them couldn't conquer. "When you were first brought to the castle, you said you wanted to marry me because together, we could change and break the system that kept you and your kind banished. You thought we could change the world. I still believe that. That's what my heart is telling me. The question is...do *you* still believe it?"

Her silence was reply enough, and it gutted him. With a polite smile, he returned her hands to her lap and reached for his portrait before heading for the exit.

"I see. Well. Goodnight, Lady Ellara. And thank you."

He walked away. And with every step, he thanked her for something new. *Thank you for listening. Thank you for being here. Thank you for saving my life so many times. Thank you for saving my soul. Thank you for the you-shaped hole in my heart.*

CHAPTER SEVENTEEN

Every word he spoke in the temple was another small cut, slicing and cutting through her skin until she thought she'd drain out before him entirely. But it wasn't until his farewell, when he'd called her by that made-up title he'd bestowed upon her, that she felt run through.

Sitting in the pew where he'd left her with the portrait of her mother, she counted to ten. Then fifteen. Then twenty.

And then she rose to follow him, her prayers and her devotion forgotten.

She'd used him. Tried to manipulate him into feeling something for her so their alliance might be stronger. So she might live to see a free Outerland. She'd been so terrified of being used that she'd gotten to it first. Without care. Without remorse. She feared the man he was — feared the man he could be.

But...tonight, she'd seen him in a way she'd not seen him before. She glimpsed him in fullness, with all his faults and flaws and fatal promises to the dead. He wasn't an ambitious king who couldn't or didn't love her. He was a lonely man who wanted to love her...and would do anything to try.

When he'd asked if she still believed in their future, her voice died in her throat. Initially, she'd said that to save her own skin and escape the executioner's axe. Now that there wasn't any threat of death, did she still believe they could?

Maybe. But *maybe* was enough to bring her to his tent, and *maybe* was enough to tingle her lips and fill her heart with that same burning desire she'd felt for him the day they'd almost kissed.

Witches didn't really believe in marriage. After all, the human men that some of them used to have children rarely stayed in Outerland. But they did believe that physical love bound the emotional. And if Ellara was going to give herself to him—in marriage, in royalty, in her heart—then she wanted him to give himself right back.

As she walked through the quiet camp, her mind ran over the contours of their relationship. Sometimes it was fraught and uncertain, with jagged edges and sharp teeth. Other times, she sensed his softness.

She couldn't help but wonder which side of him would come out when they were alone.

Gooseflesh erupted across her skin as a rush of wind brushed against her, mirroring the anticipation building in her heart. All their dancing around one another had finally come to a head. There was no avoiding their feelings any longer, no holding up the nation or their people as a shield against their growing affection. It was just the two of them.

At the entrance of his tent, she raised her hand and rapped on the wooden frame three times.

"Elias," the man inside groaned, a pathetic, quivering sound. "Go away. I'm not in the mood."

A thread of guilt wove its way around her heart before painfully tightening the strings. She'd done this to him.

"It's not Elias," she said.

The tent entrance easily gave way, and she let herself into the resplendent king's quarters with a gasp. The gasp wasn't because of his luxurious surroundings, though.

It was because he stood there wearing nothing but a blanket wrapped around his waist, the knot at his hip frightfully close to giving way. A more retiring or shameful woman would have turned away for modesty's sake, but no one ever accused Ellara of having any shame. She'd been the one to jump headfirst into a frigid river because she couldn't get imagined carnal images of him out of her head. Now that she had full, unbridled access to the real thing, she would not waste it.

He was a warrior, and the heavy swings of his sword were written into every line of his form. Muscles cautioned brutality and scars warned of toughness while the set of his shoulders promised tenderness. The muscles in her lower abdomen pulsed as she spotted some life stirring beneath the covering, obscuring the fullness of his body from her view. It seemed he didn't mind being looked at.

When she finally reached his face, that familiar set of features that sent nervous birds fluttering in the pit of her stomach, he shook his head. "No, you certainly aren't Elias."

An unfamiliar fire burned in his eyes, but it would never dare burn her. Maybe the threat was there, but it was the kind of fire she wanted to sit beside forever, the kind of fire that promised never to let the chill touch her again. She gripped her skirts, hovering in the tent's opening.

"Are you disappointed?"

"No. Not at all. Just curious."

Her stomach twisted, but whether it was at his directness, the sight of a droplet of sweat slipping down the planes of his stomach, or from the knowledge of what she was about to do, she couldn't begin to guess. The air hummed as she closed the space between them, moving towards the overly pillowed camp bed in the center of the room. Gripping the cool metal of the far end, wrapping her fingers around the metal embellishments fit for a king, she held on until her knuckles ached from the effort, focusing on the pain instead of the distant coloring of his eyes.

"I came here because you have a question to ask me."

"A question?"

"You told me you would ask again." She braved a glance up at him from under her eyelashes, only to spook and return to her fingers when she caught him licking his lips. "I want you to ask."

"Oh," he breathed, taking a step closer to her. As he moved in, the quality of the surrounding air shifted. It tightened, a coiling spring that threatened to pop at any second. "You want me to..."

"Yes."

There was no doubt in her mind that he could hear her heartbeat, just as she knew that the thrumming of his pulse in his neck was because of her. Heat radiated off of him and invaded her space, sending an array of goosebumps across her flesh. She wanted him to touch her, to hold her, to spend all night and maybe the rest of their lives in her embrace. She wanted to pull him close and know that this was real, that they could change the world, that they belonged to each other, that all those fairy tale dreams she'd given up when she went to war could be real. And more than anything, she wanted to know that he wanted the exact same thing.

So, when he finally spoke, it took all of her strength to keep from melting.

"Ellara Wist of Outerland, will you marry me?"

The question was barely out of his mouth when she reached up to kiss him. Threading her fingers through his hair and pulling him down to meet her, she let the days of pent-up passion flow through her like a river in spring, crashing into him with all the desire and hope she had kept buried for so long.

To her joy, he reciprocated in kind, touching her face with a tenderness she'd never before felt like she was a treasured being he valued over everyone and everything else. But even as his hands were gentle, his lips were aggressors, hungrily exploring her, drinking from her like the spring of all life.

When they finally broke apart, she couldn't help teasing him.

"Does that answer your question?"

"Yes," he breathed, tipping his forehead against hers and closing his eyes even as he smirked. "But I'd still like to hear it."

"Yes, Terran, I would like to marry you. Now kiss your bride."

He didn't need to be asked twice. Capturing her lips once again, he moved a hand to the soft curves of her waist, sending a thrill straight through her pelvis. All her imaginings of this moment hadn't lived up to the magic of reality. When he touched her so intimately, so forcefully, she couldn't help but feel that this was it. This was the moment she'd been dreaming about and fantasizing over for days and days. He wanted her. *She*, the green girl who'd been tormented all of her life, was wanted by this brave, sensitive, captivating man.

She'd never been the kind of woman who found her worth in a man. But there was something to be said for the feeling of being wanted, and that feeling puddled between her thighs and begged for his attention.

Her body begged her not to stop, but when the backs of her knees edged against the bed, she knew they had to. Breaking away, she held his gaze, gripping his bare shoulders for dear life.

"And for the record?"

"Yes?" he asked, panting.

"I do believe in us."

There were few things Ellara liked as much as she enjoyed seeing Terran's smile. There weren't a lot of times he allowed himself to beam freely. His serious expression was part of his kingly uniform, a mask he wore to conceal his true self. But when he allowed himself these brief moments of freedom, she didn't just see it. She *felt* it.

When he smiled at her, the warmth of it struck straight and true at her heart.

His smile was infectious, and she wanted those lips as close to hers as possible. Her weak knees gave way, and she pulled him on top of her, relishing the hard length of his form against her own. Her thin dress hadn't defended her against biting winds ripping their way through the camp, but now that she felt his every muscle and every breath through the thin cotton, she thanked her past self for the choice. Besides, with him atop her body firmly between her legs, lips moving in time with her own, she was almost certain she'd never feel the cold again.

She was also grateful for forgoing underclothes. After a long day of riding, she'd wanted her body to be free, and when Terran's wandering hands met a bare breast and a hard nipple beneath the fabric, his gasp against her lips made an evening's worth of shivering worth it.

Now, when she shivered, it was because of Terran's breath on her bare neck. Or his fingers exploring her breasts. Or his growing length disturbing the place between her legs.

But when she moved to respond, her hand wandering down towards the small knot holding his blanket up, he jumped away from her as if she'd thrown cold water over them both.

"Wait."

"Wait, *what?*"

Throwing himself out of bed, Terran paced the floor of his tent. His free hand ran through messy hair while white teeth bit swollen lips. Ellara's entire body was on fire, but the second he left her, the heat clashed with the frigid air, leaving her a mess of painful contradictions. The conflict raging in Terran's eyes quieted the urge to pull him back into bed and beg him to take her. A conflict she couldn't begin to understand.

For a while, he was quiet, stalking back and forth as if he were trying to plan out a particularly difficult battle strategy. No. Not a battle strategy. It looked like he was trying to gather up the courage to confess a secret. No general on the battlefield— no matter how the odds were stacked against them—would betray the vulnerability Terran held when he finally turned back to her. He gestured uncomfortably, pushing through his words.

"I can't. I mean, I've never—"

Understanding dawned on her. Terran, the son of a high-born house and the king, hadn't ever had sex? Even as hated as she was in the human world, she'd managed to have a few wartime flings. How was it Terran, with his soft icicle eyes and gentle hands, had never found a person to share his body with? She swallowed back her shock, not wanting him to feel any worse about it than he clearly already did.

"Never?"

"No," he breathed, eyes downcast. Turning his attention to the small table at his bedside, he fussed with a stack of already perfectly stacked papers. "Never."

"Oh, I didn't know."

Shame rushed over her, flushing her skin and worsening her current temperature problems. Taking his cue, she stared down at her own hands, the ones that had only a moment ago been threaded through his hair with stupidly reckless abandon. Once again, she'd misjudged the situation and gone for passion when caution would have been wise.

"I don't exactly share it with the world," he said. Every second he spent not looking at her was another knife into her heart. "Do you think half of the people out there would follow me if they knew?"

"I would," she said, hoping the softness she felt in her heart would flow out through her words.

Rolling his shoulders back, he released the knot of tension forming between his shoulder blades and visibly sunk, breaking his perfect posture.

"I wanted it to mean something. I didn't want to blow off steam after a battle or, I don't know, just share skin with some member of court. Those things are fine; they're just not for me. I wanted—"

This was one of those moments when the light from within him shone through the cracks in his facade. In his need to be respected by his subjects, he'd hidden away a part of himself, that romantic side that wanted something more out of sex than a means of exploring his own power. As he spoke, more and more breathy and defensive, Ellara held up a single hand to stop him.

"We don't have to do anything you're not ready to do."

"It's just I never imagined it would be in a tent in the middle of nowhere."

"I understand," she said with a smile.

He glanced up at her, surprise written across his handsome features.

"You do?"

"Yes." Of course she understood. And even if she hadn't, she couldn't bear the thought of pressuring him into something he didn't want yet. When he finally made love to her, it would be all-consuming and life-changing, not rushed and uncomfortable in a camp bed. "I mean, I wish it were different, and we were doing something much more fun than talking right now, but yes, of course. I only want to be with you when you're ready."

The relief that flooded his face, the soft solace he seemed to find in her words, was enough to make her wait ten lifetimes if that's what it took.

"Thank you."

A half-laugh escaped her lips and she pulled herself off the bed. "I feel a little stupid now, running in here all hot and heavy. I should go."

"No, please don't. Please." He captured her hands in his. "Just stay here tonight."

"You know what your court will think."

"Tonight, Ellara..." Raising her hands to his lips, he pressed a kiss to her knuckles, sending a shiver down her spine. "I don't care what they think."

CHAPTER EIGHTEEN

hen Terran woke the next morning, it was to the sound of music. At first, he didn't open his eyes, didn't want to spoil his memories of the night before. He wanted to revel in the sensation, hold on to it for as long as he possibly could. The soft song touched at his ears, playing tricks on his memory. Had he heard that song before? Maybe from Lady Bovere? Yes, he'd certainly heard it somewhere around the castle.

For a few moments, he allowed himself to still feign sleep. Sharing a morning with Ellara—even if they'd only slept in the same bed together, not *slept* together—was something he'd wanted again since the night they'd spent in the tavern. Now that he'd gotten it, he wanted to memorize every detail. The patterns drawn in his skin by the feather-soft pads of her fingertips. The melody of the song she distractedly hummed. The glow of morning sunlight on the bare flesh of his back. The flutter in his heart when she shuffled even closer to him under the blankets and furs.

Being king could wait.

Eventually, he knew he couldn't keep up the ruse. Ellara's fingers, which traced lazy designs along his spine, were going to give him the shivers and reveal him if he didn't reveal himself first. Wanting to hold on to the moment for a little longer, he didn't stir from beneath her hands, nor did he open his eyes. He breathed her janberry and earth scent in and listened to the musical rises and falls of her voice for as long as he could.

"What's that song?" he asked, his voice thick with sleep.

A breath of a laugh told him she'd known he was awake all along. He thanked the Fates that she was good enough not to make fun of him for it.

"It's something we sing in Outerland. Just an old romantic folk song."

That opened his eyes. "Romantic? I didn't know witches believed in romance."

"You don't think I'm romantic?"

"No, it's just that most of our stories are about your kind eating the hearts out of men."

He knew the line of conversation was wrong the minute it came out of his mouth, but there was no taking it back. They were trying to push past all of those old stories and prejudices, but he'd had to go and open his fat mouth, probably reopening old wounds. Sitting up, he arranged himself against the headboard, propping up on the pillows to better watch her. A flash of sadness crossed Ellara's features—just long enough for him to catch sight of it—but it disappeared when she turned a sarcastic glare on him.

"Well, we only do that when they've insulted us, so you'd better be careful, or your heart will be next." She rolled her eyes and let her gaze go distant. "No, we have romantic songs and stories. Many witches love other witches, and some of them magic their children into being with their own kind, but this song is about a witch and a human. They see each other across the Tichal River that separates their worlds, and they fall in love. He leaves the humans and crosses the border to be with her."

"That's a lovely story," Terran said, unable to keep himself from imagining he and Ellara as the song's protagonists.

"That's not the ending. It turns out the human is the son of the Warden, and the Warden shoots him in a rage. The witch is heartbroken at losing her love, so her fellow Outerlanders use their magic to turn him into the wind, so he can always be near her."

The small bubble of joy he'd felt bloom in his heart at the thought of a love song between a witch and a human popped as she told the end of the tale, but strangely, after a moment of silence, a smile stretched across her face. Her eyes caught the early morning light peering in through the flap in the tent, sparking like fresh flames. As dawn broke over their camp, something was dawning over her.

"You know what?"

"What?" Terran asked, afraid to speak above a whisper for fear of shattering the moment.

"That was the story *I* grew up with. But a generation of new witches will grow up with this story. With our story. Can you imagine it? A lifetime of stories about heartbreak and being monsters, then one day, a story where you're a queen."

He couldn't even begin to imagine it. Every story he'd ever read had a man like him or a man like his father and brothers as the hero. Even the stories about women were about women like his sisters. He didn't know what it was like to be a villain, much less a villain in *every* tale. And as he watched her soak in her discovery, he couldn't imagine why millions of bards hadn't already made her their heroine and champion, why they hadn't dedicated forests of paper to the flickers of color in her eyes or the soft rise and fall of her breast or the opera of her laughter. He opened his mouth. It was on the tip of his tongue. *I love you.*

"Your Majesty—"

An intrusion at the opening of his tent ruined the moment and sent Ellara straight out of bed, reaching for the fur cloak she'd discarded last night. The dress she'd been wearing was thin and fairly modest, but Elias' narrowed gaze was enough to make anyone feel naked.

This wasn't the first time Elias had insisted on barging in, and usually Terran welcomed the distraction of his friend. It was lonely being king, and Elias had a habit of breaking up that loneliness with all manner of distractions—great and small, important and frivolous. But with his time with Ellara, the man had a knack for interrupting their most intimate moments.

"Yes, Elias?"

The man focused on Terran, not even bothering to spare a peek in Ellara's direction. Not that it mattered, as Ellara had her back turned on him. "You were missing from breakfast. The council sent me to check on you."

"I will be out directly."

It should have been a dismissal, but Elias took a bold step forward, deeper into the tent, letting the entrance close behind him.

"Actually, Your Majesty. I was hoping we could have a word."

"Alright. Give me a moment and we'll—"

"A word in private." He stressed the last word before finally giving the third member of their party a sliver of his attention. "Lady Ellara, would you mind terribly returning to your court?"

The look on Ellara's face was pointed enough to tell even the far-away stars that she *did* mind terribly, but she collected her things all the same and moved around Elias to make her exit, careful to deliberately shove into him on her way out. Terran bit back a smile as he moved from the bed and dressed. His mind was still a race of thoughts and feelings and hopes and uncertainties. He'd confessed everything there was to confess about himself, won the hand of the woman he was starting to love, and spent the night falling asleep in her arms as they talked about their upcoming marriage. He was completely aware that he'd made himself vulnerable with her, that he'd given her all the power in their relationship. She could run out this very moment and tell the entire nation that their king was a virgin who didn't want the crown. She could kill him in his sleep on their wedding night. Last night, he'd given her unimaginable power over him, and that should have terrified him.

But it didn't. A lifetime of advice and firsthand experience told him that love would be the end of him, but he knew—his very being knew—that Ellara, for all of her threats and powers—would never hurt him. He knew he couldn't hurt her—how could he, when hurting her would hurt him?—so he believed she was the same. She couldn't hurt him without bringing herself pain.

Hiding away his feelings, he constructed his usual mask as Elias addressed him.

"Your Majesty, what was she doing in here?"

Lying would make more sense, but Terran wasn't in the mood to lie. "We were speaking of our wedding last night and fell asleep discussing it. There's so much to plan before we return to High Court and I want everything to be perfect."

Elias might as well have taken a sword to his gut. He spluttered and stammered through his words. "The *wedding*? But I thought she'd refused you."

"She refused me until I could prove myself worthy. And now I have."

There wasn't any doubt in his mind that Ellara would make the perfect queen and the perfect partner. He'd known from the moment she showed up, shackled, in his study at High Court that she could lead the kingdom to great things, but Elias didn't seem to agree.

"What does a witch know about worthiness?"

"What do *you* know about worthiness?"

Impulsive and cruel, he regretted the words as soon as he'd loosed them. Elias exercised self-control, swallowing hard and clutching the hilt of the sword on his hip as if for dear life.

"Your Majesty, if you're going to be in close quarters and if you're going to be..." His skin took on a greenish tint as his eyes flickered to the rumpled bed, clearly getting all sorts of incorrect ideas. "...*Pursuing* this alliance, then I must insist she return to her binders. We have no idea the kind of influence she has over you—"

"I love her. That's the influence. And if you were any kind of friend, then you would find a way to love her, too. Or at least like her."

"Terran." The use of his name instead of his title froze him in place. Ever since he'd become his Warden, Elias refused to operate under anything remotely outside of protocol. The departure from the rule was a shock to Terran's system. "Do you remember the battle of Yabsythe? I was dying, and you carried me out of the way, taking arrows and fighting off raiders with one hand just to see that I got to safety. And that night, when I woke up, and you were in the bed beside me, almost dead from your wounds, I made a vow. Wherever you went, I would follow you and I would protect you like you protected me. I'm trying to do that duty now. This entire exercise with Outerland is an experiment I'm afraid is doomed to fail, and I don't want to see you near death again because of a war I could have prevented. Let me protect you."

Terran remembered the days of Yabsythe, the twisted and gnarled battle that robbed him of so many friends and left him with so many scars. The memories of those long and brutal days resurfaced like blood pouring out of a freshly de-scabbed wound. Still, those memories did the opposite of what Elias wanted them to do. Instead of reminding him that his friend would do anything to repay the favor of saving his life, it reminded him that the real danger in his kingdom didn't come from the witches and certainly not from Ellara. The danger he most feared was from the men who'd spent all those years trying to slaughter him.

"Thank you," he replied, tersely staring into the reflecting glass as he set his crown upon his head. "I'll take your thoughts under advisement. But for now, we have a wedding to plan. We really must focus on that."

Elias' jaw tightened, matching the tension and resignation in the rest of his body. "As you wish, Your Majesty."

CHAPTER NINETEEN

Ellara couldn't stop thinking about him. It was infuriating, really, the way she'd be fully focused on a tour of a grain mill or meeting with local farmers, only to remember the feeling of his hands on her waist or the soft pressure of his lips against hers. Sure, she might not have gotten all she wanted that first night, but she'd gotten enough to make her crave even more of him. Besides, she could be patient.

Especially if he kept kissing her with enough passion to leave her dizzy and holding her in her sleep so she could feel the beating of his heart against her back.

As maddening as it was taking the first steps into being in love, though, the person she currently felt the worst for was Briony. She had to *hear* about every maddening detail about Terran without even the benefit of getting to kiss him.

"And *then*, he took me into his arms—"

A temporary, frustrating lapse in Briony's concentration caused the three quills which she had enchanted to write her daily letters to her friends and family dropped to the floor with a metal-tipped clatter, and she spun on Ellara with a groan. "Are you still going on about this?"

"No, this is different. This was a dream I had last night."

"Great. Just wonderful."

After a lifetime of avoiding humans and human men in particular, Ellara fully understood how annoying she must sound, like a love-struck puppy who wouldn't stop yapping. But she couldn't help it. She'd never felt this way before, never felt as connected to someone or as thrilled to be herself as when Terran held her face in his hands, and she wanted the entire world to feel this happy. Especially her best friend.

"We'll have to find *you* someone, Briony."

Briony returned to her enchanted letters with a scoff. "Don't hold your breath. I'd rather die than be tied down to some human man. They're all monsters."

Monsters. Ellara sometimes thought so too. At least, she thought that about most of them.

"Terran's not a monster. So it stands to reason that maybe we could find *you* one of the non-monstrous types."

"You really believe that?"

"Yes."

"You *really* believe that if things change, if you aren't giving him what he wants or if you disagree or displease him, that he'll still love you and treat you the same as he does now?"

Ellara's own hands stilled, disturbing the pieces of paper she'd enchanted to look like flying birds. They unfolded and fell to the floor in crumpled balls of paper carnage, a complete give-away of her own hesitation. She had to believe that he wouldn't. But a lifetime of bad deals with humans led her to believe that nothing was impossible. Not even Terran's betrayal. Still, she clung to that rope of girlish romanticism, hoping it would be enough to save her.

"...Yes."

"Then you're a fool of a queen." With a wave of her hands, all of Briony's letters found their envelope homes and sealed themselves with the wax seal on a nearby desk. Bitterness coated her words like a thick poison. "All humans are the same."

"Can't you just let me be happy?"

"Not if it ends with your head on a spike somewhere around High Court."

Ellara's heart skipped a beat. "Briony!"

"Be careful. They aren't like us. They don't feel the same way that we do, and they don't protect the way we protect our own." With a heavy sigh, Briony collapsed on Ellara's camp bed, pulled down as if by exhaustion. "You can't lose yourself in this."

"I won't."

But the truth was, she already had. No matter what she said, they both knew any statement to the contrary was a lie. She'd thrown herself into this relationship with everything she had, holding onto the thin, fraying rope of her childhood romanticism for safety. If that rope snapped, she didn't know if anyone could save her.

Lost in her own thoughts, she barely noticed that her friend had gotten up and moved to the opening of their tent, which faced the outside of the camp and a forest far beyond. The night hung around them like heavy damask curtains, but a strange light illuminated Briony's features.

"Ellara."

"Yes?"

"What is that?"

Alarm shot through Ellara at the sound of her friend's voice, brittle and uncertain, and she sprang from her chair to investigate. Over the tall treetops, a column of purple light and smoke spiraled up into the dark night sky. The familiar light filled Ellara with the same terror she'd heard creeping into Briony's voice.

'That's Witches' Fire," she breathed, recognition washing over her. Witches' Fire wasn't the kind of clear, useful magic that Briony and Ellara used every day, the kind that made something out of nothing. Witches' Fire was for changing prophecies and altering the future. Ellara had seen it used only a handful of times in her life—the magic was dangerous and unpredictable, and could bring down a rain of curses if one didn't engage with the magic properly—but the sight was so singular, so unnatural that it burned itself into her memory forever. There was no forgetting Witches' Fire, and there was no mistaking it. Somewhere, out in the forest, there was a powerful, dangerous member of their kind.

She knew her friends in the court well enough to know that none of them were powerful enough conjurers to create Witches' Fire. Or, more precisely, the only one who was even close to capable—and the only one with enough hatred in her heart to even attempt it—was standing right beside her, wearing the same dumbstruck expression Ellara assumed was on her own face.

Briony wrung her hands as she stared into the distance. Had the humans seen what they were seeing now? "I know, but...who could be doing it? I told our court not to perform magic like that out here in the open. The humans would get too suspicious."

A white, translucent foam coiled its way around the column, a sign that another thread of the future was being tugged. The hair on the back of Ellara's neck stood on end. She wouldn't let a rogue witch ruin what she'd built with the humans, tenuous though it was. "I don't know. But I intend to find out. Come on."

Collecting their cloaks and furs, they slipped out of the camp, unseen by the guards as they curled their bodies through the shadows and the dense darkness. The further they moved from the warm fires and the closer they got to the black magic and forest in the distance, the less those furs did to warm the cold uncertainty permeating Ellara's bones. Losing the warmth of the camp wasn't the only source of her discomfort, though. It was the creeping knowledge that she and Briony were about to face the unknown, someone who could likely destroy either of them. Or both. Suddenly, Ellara wished for the company of her old spell books. At least they could give her a little bit of extra protection at a time like this.

"Maybe it's just someone from one of your mother's travel

groups," Briony whispered, wincing as her booted feet cracked some loose twigs. They crept towards the edge of the forest, staying low and keeping their voices to whispers. An invisibility spell would have made matters much easier, but a witch powerful enough to cast the Fire would have been able to sense magic like that. "Maybe she got separated and is trying to signal to them."

"Maybe. How is my mother, by the way? I haven't heard from her."

"I haven't received much word yet, either. There are some whispers and rumblings that I catch wind of every once in a while, but nothing definitive. Have the humans mentioned any disturbances between the new witches in Aulen and their people?"

"No. It's too quiet. It worries me."

For a few moments, they walked in silence, and Ellara considered the possibilities. Everyone could be lying to her about something. The humans could be keeping secrets about the caravans of witches, and Briony could be lying about hearing from her mother. The trouble wasn't that Ellara didn't trust anyone. It was that she *wanted* to trust people. She wanted to believe all of them, to think that they all trusted her enough to give her the truth, which made finding the actual truth even more impossible.

"You don't think they've been captured or anything, do you?" Briony asked.

Ellara sniffed a laugh, a small bit of humor breaking through her cloud of fear and trepidation at what waited for them beyond the wall of trees yawning out in front of them. "I can't imagine anyone who would want to risk the wrath of the future queen. Not even humans are that stupid."

Briony didn't seem to agree with that, but she said nothing. And once they passed the tree-line, the two ended their conversation.

They edged up on the fire, whose purple light bounced through the trees, and waited for the right moment to step through and reveal themselves to the witch. Their quiet reconnaissance rewarded them with a glimpse of a cloaked, hooded woman who chanted in tongues with her back to them, clearly trapped in the middle of her spell. Ellara fingered the jeweled handle of the Witch-Killer, which she'd sheathed and shoved into the oversized pockets of her skirts. She hoped to the Fates she wouldn't have to use it.

"Let me go first," Briony whispered, her back flush with the tree behind her. "I'll sneak up around her and try the element of surprise, see if we can't get an advantage—"

Briony's voice was quiet. But the woman turned. Her hood dropped. And Ellara caught sight of a familiar face.

"Madame Bovere!" she shouted, leaping from behind the tree.

"...There goes the element of surprise," Briony hissed.

But it was too late for regret and too late for scolding, because Ellara was in full view of Madame Bovere, and Madame Bovere showed no signs of surprise. It was as if she'd wanted this to happen. Ellara's stomach filled with sour sick, and she clutched the cold blade-hilt in her pocket to ground her. *Madame Bovere is a witch...That's impossible. She's human. She looks human. She's installed herself at court; that can't just be done...Can it?* Confusion like a cold dump of ice washed over Ellara's entire shaking body.

"Ellara. Briony." Madame Bovere extended her arms to them, almost as if welcoming them to a family party instead of a frigid witch's circle. Her smile was a mixture of relief and joy, of elation and maternal bliss. It wasn't a combination Ellara trusted. Her footsteps towards the older woman were so small she practically shuffled. "You've arrived at last. Please, come closer. There is much to discuss."

Briony blinked and tripped out from behind a nearby tree. "You're a witch."

"Yes. Always have been."

"But you're human."

"Oh. Sorry. Silly me. Force of habit." With a wave of her

hand, she cast a spell on herself, and it worked its magic through her. Like a spoonful of milk dropped into a cup of dark drink, the color green invaded her human skin, transforming her into a familiar witchy look, one she'd been hiding. She *was* a witch. She'd been a witch this entire time, hiding in plain sight as Ellara had been playing politics. "There. Better?"

"But how did you—"

"It's a long story, really. If you want the quick version, I knew I was adept at changing my face as a little girl, but when I was older, old enough to really know my power over the humans, I glamoured myself and jumped in the river between Aulen and Outerland. A little fake drowning was enough to have a few human soldiers save me, and a little fake amnesia and a fake family pendant were enough to convince the House of Mont that I was a long-lost cousin who needed their protection. I've been playing this game for years, my darlings."

And she was clearly proud of herself for it. The deception riddled Ellara with chill-bumps that stubbornly refused to go away, and she held her hands out defensively, ready for whatever was coming next. Someone this adept at deception had an agenda. And now, a powerful witch with an agenda had two of the kingdom's most important witches alone with her in the middle of a desolate, lonely forest.

"What game? Explain yourself."

"Are you threatening me?" Bovere asked, hand on her heart as if this were all quite adorable and amusing.

"Maybe. Are you threatening us?"

"Maybe. If you don't cooperate."

"If you want our cooperation, then I'm afraid you'll have to explain," Briony said, adopting a pose similar to Ellara's. Not for the first time, Ellara thanked the Fates she had a friend as loyal and true as Briony. And she thanked Terran for bringing her to court.

"I don't think you should be making threats, my dear ones.

You're not the one who can glamor herself for half a lifetime and conduct Witches' Fire, are you?"

"Briony, go." No sooner was the word out of her mouth than Briony turned on her heels and headed for the forest entrance. "Find Terran. Tell him—"

"No, Briony. Stay." With a flick of her wrist, Madame Bovere captured Briony in a ball of light-magic, paralyzing her mid-step. A wicked glint in Madame Bovere's eyes matched the purple fire playing in the middle of the woods, a glint that shook Ellara to her core. "We'll need all the help we can if we're going to succeed."

"Succeed at what?"

"Lady Ellara, how would you like to end the reign of men?" The glint in her eye turned into a raging inferno. *"Forever."*

CHAPTER TWENTY

"Something's wrong."

Terran spent the last week of mind-numbing dance lessons and tours of grain refineries planning something just for him and Ellara, a moment for them to get away and spend the evening alone. Once they returned to High Court the following week, everything would change. No longer wandering around the country with hours of free time to spend in one another's company, their lives would be regulated and regimented, outlined by their advisors and planned by the council. Sure, he'd find the time to spend with her, but for now, he wanted a night that the both of them could remember whenever they were apart.

But things hadn't gone exactly to plan, and with every step towards their destination, Terran realized that the mood he'd caught Ellara in wasn't a passing oddity or a fleeting funk, but something more substantial and worrying. Even as she slept in his bed night after night, kissed him with dizzying intensity, and captured his thoughts, he couldn't shake the feeling that he'd done something wrong, that he'd failed her in some way. They had been getting along. Their union seemed so secure. Now...he wasn't sure.

"What do you mean?" she asked, the smile she flashed not quite rising to her eyes.

"You haven't been yourself lately. I'm worried about you."

It was a bold confession, maybe even bolder than the other confession dancing on his tongue. *I love you* seemed an easier thing to say to a woman like Ellara than *I'm worried about you*. She was more than capable of taking care of herself, and he feared she would see his concern as an insult.

"Oh, was that what this is about?" She snorted and pulled at the high grass they were walking through, ripping some of it out of the ground. If she knew they were on protected king's land, she clearly didn't care about the penalties for destroying it. Not that he cared either. "You've pulled me into the forest to tell me I'm not acting the part of the queen?"

"No, of course not. I'm *worried* about you."

He repeated the charge even though he knew it was the wrong thing to say. It was liberating, actually, that confession of caring about her. He enjoyed knowing that he could care about someone again, that the war and the crown hadn't completely robbed him of his ability to feel something for another person.

"Well, don't. Don't worry about me. It'll all be over soon," she muttered.

"What will?"

Carefully dodging the question, Ellara shivered against the night air, a delightful motion that sent Terran's mind racing. She was so effortlessly alluring, drawing him in at nearly every opportunity, even when he couldn't be sure she realized what she was doing. There was something about the effortless grace with which she walked, the confident slide of her hips and the proud tilt of her chin that often left him hot under the collar and covered with chill-bumps all at once.

"Where are we going?" she asked, and he allowed himself to

be led away from the subject at hand. After all, now there was a small smile on her lips, one of those dreamy smiles she occasionally let slip when she thought no one was looking.

"It wouldn't be a surprise if I told you, would it?"

"Maybe I don't like surprises."

"I don't either, but humor me."

They walked another few steps before she inevitably asked, "Can I have a hint?"

"It's the most beautiful place in all of Aulen."

"You're taking me to my bed?"

"Very funny."

When their nighttime hike—illuminated by a pink glowing orb Ellara had enchanted to move before them—took them straight up the side of a steep hill, Terran gave a quiet prayer of thanks for all the walking and hiking he'd had to do during the war. His younger self from before the war wouldn't have been able to survive the steep climb. He just kept reminding himself of the paintings he'd seen of this place, of the wonders it supposedly held. Wonders he wanted to share with her.

When they finally reached the top, they both let out a collective gasp, a shared moment of awe that clenched at Terran's chest. They were so different, and yet so similar. They understood each other and saw the world in the same way.

Above them, in the dark night's sky, was a swirling sea of pastel color, an effect of stars thousands of light years away moving too fast for their eyes to comprehend. It was fitting that Terran had seen them first in a painting, because that was what the Royal Lights reminded him of—a blind man's painting done in ultraviolet pastels against an impossibly black backdrop.

He tore his gaze away for the briefest of seconds, just long enough to catch Ellara pressing a hand to her heart. Her green skin flooded with the colors of the sky, brightening at their sight.

Perfectly beautiful. Perfectly kissable. Perfectly perfect. And now, despite the natural wonder hovering above them, he couldn't take his eyes off her.

"Oh, Terran," she whispered. "It's beautiful."

"Do you like it?"

"Yes. Of course. It's..." Straightening, she turned to him. Suspicion colored her gaze. Part of him couldn't blame her. They were up in the mountains with no one around for miles, surrounded by darkness on all sides. If this had been the war years, and if they didn't love each other—even though they hadn't said it yet—he would have completely understood her skepticism. "But why are we up here?"

"Can't a man just share a beautiful sky with his betrothed?"

"A man can, but a king wouldn't."

She said it gently enough, but he heard the words as a subtle dig, one he accepted. Reaching out for her waist, he let his fingers dig into her soft curves and pull her close enough to count the handful of dark freckles peeking through her green skin.

"Maybe tonight, I don't want to be a king," he whispered against her neck as he moved to kiss his favorite spot just at the base.

"There's something going on here," she gently admonished, pulling away from his touch. "And I want to know what it is."

He hadn't come up here to assassinate her or anything that he might have done during the war, but he *did* have an ulterior motive. Of course, Ellara recognized that. Another reason she'd make a great queen. He was incapable of outsmarting her.

"I was wondering, hoping, really, that you would show me some magic."

Her magic was as much a part of her as the warmth of her palms or the softness of her lips, but he understood those pieces of her with better clarity. She was a witch, and sometimes he forgot that. He wanted to be incapable of forgetting. He wanted to know every part of her, even the parts that other people hated and feared. He wanted to love those parts especially, so she'd never feel the sting of harsh words or cruel gestures ever again.

She tugged at the ends of her hair, her gaze returning to the sky above them.

"You've seen my magic."

"I've watched you stir your cup of tea without touching it, and I've seen you write letters without a quill, but I've never seen—"

"You saw me divine your future."

A blush threatened his cheeks, and he was suddenly grateful for her lack of direct attention. He'd been such an idiot that night, demanding in public that she give him affection and promises he hadn't even wanted.

"And it came true," he reminded her. "I want more. I want to know you."

For a moment, he worried she'd deny him, but soon, she removed her cloak, dropping it in a heap at her feet, and rolled up her sleeves. Apparently, performing magic made her impervious to the cold. Either that or she was preparing to work up a sweat. The promise of seeing her natural abilities filled him with uncontrollable anticipation.

"What do you want to see?" she asked.

The question caught him off-guard. It was probably wrong to assume she had a few tricks up her sleeve, party tricks that she could pull out any time a nosey human asked her to display her powers, but that had been his assumption. Truth be told, he didn't know the first thing about witchy powers. Everything he knew was from storybooks and his limited firsthand experience with Ellara, and he assumed that the horrible curses from storybooks wouldn't be the least bit accurate.

"I don't know. What can you do? I'm afraid my knowledge is a touch limited here."

She placed her hands on her hips in a mockery of an agitated pose. Not that he would have minded agitation. No, he found it sexy in her, like she was going to order him about. "What if I told you the answer was nothing else? What if you've seen everything I can do?"

He bit back a laugh. "I wouldn't believe you."

"Why not?"

"Because you *are* magic. There's no way you've shown me everything."

Picking up her skirts, she positioned herself on a flat-topped boulder as if she were a dancer rising upon a stage. He had to fight back lurid images of her dancing in much less than her full skirts and bodice, an urge that proved incredibly difficult.

"There is something I used to like to do. But you'll think it's silly."

"What is it?"

Nothing she could pull straight out of the air would ever be something he considered silly.

With that small encouragement, she rubbed her hands together. "Watch this."

Palms out and eyes closed, she began a slow, whistling song, but with every movement of her hands in an intricate—and he was certain, precise—weaving pattern, the whistle grew louder and louder, until it picked up and carried on the wind. The song swirled and moved with the air until he realized that the air and the song were feeding each other.

When there was movement in the sky, he realized that it wasn't the air moving at all. Or rather, it wasn't the song moving it, but the beating of dozens of tiny wings. Immediately, he jumped to the defensive position, only to balk and return his sword to its sheath when small, scaly creatures began landing around their feet and grazing at the tall grass, calm as cattle.

He'd never seen one this close. And he never could have predicted that the fearsome creature who'd almost killed him as a boy could have grown from something so adorable.

"Baby dragons," he marveled.

One, a black creature with a white star in the center of its muzzle, landed on Ellara's shoulder, nuzzling into her neck as if it was always meant to be there. Ellara brushed the creature's nose with her own.

"They're very good familiars."

"Then why don't you have one?"

"We aren't allowed to have them in Outerland. And it didn't seem fair to chain one to me during a war. But maybe someday," she said, staring at the small creatures wistfully. A pang of unbidden guilt struck at Terran's stomach. He hadn't been responsible for the witches' oppression, but that didn't make him any less responsible for what happened to them. He'd fought a war to defeat them, after all. For so long, he'd wanted to rob them of these creatures, of their magic, of their humanity. He was complicit in the destruction of beauty like this.

Extending his shaking hand, he glanced up at the apparent dragon expert in his midst. The last thing he needed was a face full of tiny dragon fire. Returning to court and explaining how he'd lost his eyebrows to a creature barely bigger than his hand wouldn't give off the regal persona he reached for. "May I...?"

Ellara waved a hand as if to say, "try it if you dare," or "your funeral," but given that the only dragon Terran had ever seen up close had tried to kill him, the small, cat-like creature curled up all snug on her shoulder intrigued him. And besides, its teeth were far too small to pierce his gut. He took the cautious step of extending his fingers out for it, and after a moment of hesitant sniffing, the small dragon pressed its scales against his hand.

Strange though it was, the creature almost reminded him of Ellara. Cold on the outside at first, but fire-warm on the inside and engaging once you got to know her. A sand-paper tongue licked his palm, and he barely fought down a laugh.

"She likes me."

Shrugging as best as she could with a small dragon on her shoulder, Ellara's eyes sparkled. "She has good taste."

That was something else she had in common with the dragons. Her eyes were hypnotic. Barely a day went by when he didn't find himself lost in her depths, trying to puzzle out the woman he'd been falling deeper and deeper in love with.

The thought of falling in love with her was more dangerous than the creature currently cooing at his touch.

Dragging his hands away from the tiny dragon—who huffed at the sudden loss of contact and burrowed her head into Ellara's hair, a clear sign that she was *not* pleased—he turned back to their earlier conversation about her magic.

"What about snow? Or fire? Or can you pull down the sky and bring it closer to us?"

She winced. "Remember the battle of Aroncourt?"

"Yes. I almost lost three toes. My boots were ruined. Why?"

"Let's just say that yes, I can make it snow. I just don't like to. Fire, too. But I kept that a secret."

"Why?"

Gently—so gently he had to wonder where she kept such softness hidden—she coaxed the dragon from her shoulder and returned it to the small flock grazing at her ankles. When she was free, she retired to the flat-topped rock and stared up at the sky as if it could reflect the past or held some hints about the future.

Or, maybe, as if she could take to it and fly away at any moment, which, he supposed, she could.

Why hadn't she? Why was she still here? If she could fly off and use her magic to create any life she wanted, why was she still here beside him? It had to mean something, didn't it?

Yes, he decided. It had to mean something. It had to mean love.

His heart lifted in his chest.

"I wanted to win a war and my freedom, not raze the entire kingdom to the ground. If they'd known I had that kind of power, there wouldn't have been a non-burning building left in this entire kingdom."

A memory flooded back to him from their first encounter in the castle, when she'd told him about the moment she knew he was a good man. She'd said that his willingness to save a duckling proved he wasn't anything like the other humans she'd come to know. He'd known ever since that night, the night that she saved him, that she wasn't like the witches in his storybooks or from the stories told around campfires, but hearing firsthand about the way she'd manipulated humans into letting her keep hold of just a slice of her humanity...It shattered whatever was left of the walls around his heart.

He'd long and secretly suspected that she was the legendary Good Witch of Aulen, the same one the villagers whispered about as the armies passed through their muddy streets, but he'd never had the courage to ask.

"Ah. So," Terran began, helping himself to the seat beside her. "*You* were the Good Witch of Aulen, then?"

Ellara blinked. "Was that what they called me?"

"By those who didn't have to face your axe or your magic, yes."

"Well, I'm ready for a lifetime of being the Good Witch of Aulen. No more fire or snow or axes. Just a little dragon and a bed of my own."

A bed of her own. The muscles in Terran's stomach tightened as he imagined a lifetime in a bed of *his* own. No. He couldn't have that. She'd just have to share. Leaning in, he caught a loose strand of her hair between his fingers and tucked it behind her ear.

"And me," he reminded her, leaning in for a kiss. "You'll have me. Forever."

"And you'll have me," she breathed against his lips.

It was as close to an *I love you* as he could ever hope to get, and he took it. Pressing the words tightly against his heart, he pressed his lips to hers, relishing the way she moved against him. It was another tiny sign, a giveaway that she felt a reflection of what he felt for her.

A voice from the hill below snapped him out of his entranced stupor.

"Your Majesty! Your Majesty, please!"

He pulled away and shot to his feet, ready to destroy

whoever had come here to interrupt him. How tired he was of being interrupted. "I'm busy! Can't you *see* that I'm busy?"

"Your Majesty, this cannot wait."

"What is it, then?"

The uniformed sentry fought his racing breath, struggling to sound out the words. "High Court has been invaded."

CHAPTER TWENTY-ONE

It was all part of the plan. A plan that had been set in motion before Ellara was captured. A plan that took shape when she was. A plan that was solidified the moment she'd been announced as Terran's bride. Originally, it had been more complicated, with a horde of witches strong enough to make Witches' Fire collaborating to take down the barriers between Aulen and Outerland, then marching on the castle at High Court. With so many dead after the War of Seven Kings, there was no better time to attack. But once Ellara's mother heard of her daughter's engagement, her plan changed. Drastically.

That was when she organized the marches. That was when Lady Bovere began manipulating the king. And that was when Ellara—stupid, stupid Ellara who her mother knew so very well —decided she didn't want to be trapped in the castle anymore.

The plan was simple. Distract the king. March on the kingdom. Take the castle. Steal the crown. With the defenses of High Court protecting the king on his little jaunt around the far reaches of the kingdom, the witches were free to march right into the keep and hold it for as long as they needed to. The typical issues of holing up—food supply, water, ammunitions—didn't apply to the witches. Anything they needed, they could magic. And if Lady Bovere was to be believed, Terran would crumble and the kingdom would belong to the witches in a matter of days. Better still, once they had the power, they could do some banishing of their own, sending the race of men to the craggy rocks of Outerland. They would have to bear the frozen winters and the springtime hurricanes off the northern oceans. And they'd have to do it without magic. A fitting punishment for one hundred years of exile.

Ellara's mother was the mastermind of the fall of Aulen, and if Ellara played her cards right, she'd be queen of her own. She wouldn't need Terran. She wouldn't need anyone.

That was…If she'd played her cards right. Which…she hadn't. Not in that conversation with Madame Bovere, the witch in human's clothing.

"End the reign of men? What do you mean?"

She knew exactly what Madame Bovere meant, but she needed context, needed more puzzle pieces to understand it in fullness. There was a plan here, something at work that Ellara couldn't clearly see. Her pulse thrummed, and the long sleeves of her furs chafed against her skin. The clouds above threatened snow, but the timber of fire broke them up. Now, the sky looked filled more with ash than cloud.

"You've played your part valiantly, dear. Beautifully. And you didn't even know what you were doing. You've distracted the king just long enough for your mother to take High Court."

"Take High Court?"

The words were simple. Even a child would have understood what they meant, but Ellara understood them more keenly than most. In fact, she'd heard that same phrase countless times during the war. All plans—stupid and brilliant, well-laid and foolhardy—led directly to that phrase. Take High Court. It was the crown jewel of the kingdom, the seat of power. Anyone who wanted to control Aulen couldn't even imagine themselves there without first capturing High Court. Ellara's mind flashed to the days she'd spent there, wandering the castle halls and trying to earn Terran's affections. She had no love for the place, but if someone was going to take High Court, it meant they were going to take Terran's crown with it.

"Yes. What? You thought our people were traveling just to find a scrap of land in Aulen that they could call their own? No. We aren't content with that. We will have the Kingdom and you've emptied High Court of anyone who could stop them." The already dark world turned darker around Ellara as the older woman—green-skinned and luminous in the purple light—half-giggled to herself. "In a matter of days, they'll make it to the keep, where they'll capture a stronghold and begin making their demands."

"And what demands would those be?" Briony asked when Ellara's words failed her.

"The end of the reign of men." Madame Bovere turned, reaching out to grasp Ellara's face. Her fingers were ice cold. "And the beginning of our reign."

Her eyes were soft and gentle, the kind of maternal gaze that promised sweetness and love forever. It was the kind of gaze that held everything Ellara ever wanted. For the first time in her life, she wouldn't have to bow and scrape to the humans. She wouldn't have to rely on them for help or salvation. She would be the leader of her people. She, not Terran and certainly not his lords and viceroys and ladies and madames and advisors, would be the one who saved the witches and punished the humans for their years of cruelty.

She would have everything she ever wanted, everything she ever dreamed of having, everything she'd promised herself she would one day have. Freedom. Real freedom.

"End it," she whispered, pulling her face from Madame Bovere's hand and turning her back on the woman. She swallowed back the urge to vomit.

"End it? My dear, it's already been done."

She'd suffered at the hands of the humans. Been manipulated. Abused.

Beaten. Nearly slaughtered. Imprisoned. Assaulted and violated in every way a person could be. But she wouldn't—couldn't—allow her people to become like them. Even if it meant losing.

"End it or I will tell Terran to reverse his decision to end the banishment. His armies will find every witch and send them right back to Outerland."

"You would do that to your own people?"

The accusation was laughable, but Ellara didn't have the strength to laugh. And even though she wanted to walk away and leave this woman, she remained rooted to the spot.

"I have been doing nothing but working for my people."

"No, you have been falling in love with a human. You haven't done anything for us."

"I gave up my life to free them."

"You gave up your life to save yourself from a hangman's noose. You are no martyr, darling."

There was nothing but truth in Madame Bovere's words. Lies would have stung less. She had lost sight of the reason she was here. She had let herself fall in love with the most dangerous human in the entire kingdom. She had leveraged her position to save her own neck and only fought for her people when she was sure she'd live. She had forgotten herself, as both Madame Bovere and Briony attested. But if anyone thought she would admit that out loud, then they were living in a fantasyland.

"And what about you, Madame Bovere? Hm? How was it, glamouring yourself as a human and abandoning your cause, your people?"

"I haven't abandoned anyone. I have never stopped working from the inside."

"Yes, in a lord's warm bed with coffers overflowing and enough food in your stores to feed all of Outerland for three lifetimes," Ellara snapped.

"We must do what we can now. Not focus on the past."

But Madame Bovere's brittle voice told her that they were equally weak in their self-defenses. The Witches' Fire towering above them was starting to flicker and falter, a sure sign that the user who crafted it was losing her control.

Even in the middle of an argument, Ellara's mind wandered. A few weeks ago, she might not have thought twice about destroying these people. Yes, she was tired of war and tired of suffering, but what better way to end war and suffering than to end humans and their reign over Aulen?

Now...She'd seen their cruelty and their capacity for kindness first-hand. Someone like Elias told her how terrible they could be, while Terran showed her they might be worth saving. And if there was even one of them worth saving, then the witches didn't need to become monsters and defeat them. Maybe there was another way. Ellara turned and squared her shoulders, using her position on the upward slope of the forest to look down on her opposition. Briony watched from the sidelines, her concerned face colored by purple light.

"Yes. I agree. Which is why you must end it. If we keep fighting this war, it will never end. It will always be the humans and the witches, killing each other until the end of time. Is that what you really want? You loved a human, Lady Bovere. You had human children. You survived their wars. How could you hate them enough to want to see them sentenced to a fate worse than death?"

Determination pinched the woman's expression.

"I want the power," she hissed.

"And we'll have it. A witch will be queen, and she will one day have daughters who will be queen. An unending line of witches on the throne of Aulen, ensuring our safety forever. Isn't that what we want? Isn't that better than becoming monsters like them?"

"We have set this plan in motion—"

"Then stop it. Everything can be stopped." This time, it was Ellara who reached out for Madame Bovere, taking up her hands and squeezing them. "Let's start with this plan instead."

Silence reigned. Then, resignation. The Witches' Fire broke, plunging them all into darkness.

"I will send word to your mother."

"No. I'll send word to her myself. If I'm going to be queen, I need to get used to giving orders."

She hadn't played her cards right to become the one and only ruler of an all-witch Aulen. She hadn't had the courage to take up arms against the man she loved. She hadn't had the strength to punish the humans for a hundred years of cruelty and exile. Maybe they all deserved it, but she wasn't the one who could give it to them.

But...she *also* hadn't told Terran. She couldn't. Besides, what was there *to* tell him? By the time they all returned to camp, Madame Bovere was once again the milk-skinned human woman that everyone knew her to be. If Ellara told Terran what happened, he wouldn't have believed her.

There was no reason to cause panic. At the moment, she had the situation under control. Any further worries about the witches would only inflame the members of the court and cause further damage to the validity of Terran's leadership.

Her decision was also selfish. She knew that. She was desperate to keep him and the sliver of happiness that being with him gave her. And that desperation might have just doomed them all.

As they walked through the camp, the air was thick and quiet. Too quiet, too still, too filled with uncertainty and trepidation. Even the soft sound of Terran's boots on the dirt ground resounded like war drums in Ellara's ears, threatening to send waves of nervous shivers up and down her spine. Then, at the far end of the camp, Ellara caught sight of the only illuminated structure in the area: the council tent, the tallest and most grand of the quarters here, the one used for the biggest emergencies and most important discussions of state. They apparently only brought it on journeys like this one *just in case*, but she'd never seen it illuminated, much less in use.

A stone sunk in her stomach.

"What's happened?" Terran asked, hot on the heels of the young advisor who'd gone out into the fields to reach them.

"I'm afraid I can't exactly say, Your Majesty."

No...but Ellara could. And even as the words swirled around her head—*the witches have done this and it's all my fault*—she couldn't find the strength to formulate the words herself.

Maybe...Maybe she could fix this. Maybe she could avert disaster and talk the witches and her mother down. Maybe she could save them all and keep Terran at the same time.

Maybe. But she doubted it. And with every step she took closer to the council, her resolve faltered.

"You're shaking," Terran muttered.

"I know."

She fell a few steps behind him and slowed to a death march. Finally, the steward tipped the curtain of the council tent open.

"Your Majesty. If you will."

Terran stepped into the puddle of light revealed by the tent, leaving her behind. Through the small flap, she watched as viceroys and hands and wardens rose to their feet in a hushed *swish* of fabric, but it was another swish that caught Ellara's ears. The swish of a too-sharp knife slipping through her cloak so the tip of the blade pricked into the skin of her back, drawing blood.

"Don't move," a familiar voice whispered from behind her. "Not even a breath."

A searing pain dug into her skin, and Ellara realized she hadn't checked her bag for the Witch Killer blade. So, she wasn't just going to lose Terran and her place at his side as his queen. She was probably going to lose her life as well.

"Ellara?" Terran asked, turning back to face her with concern in his eyes.

She didn't need another prick from the blade to tell her what to say. The words were strained from the poisoned burning in her skin, but she choked out, "You go ahead. I'll meet you back in our tent."

With the knife in her back and the poison beginning its dangerous path through her body, she watched as Terran disappeared through the tent. In moments, he would know about the witch's betrayal. And he would probably think she'd orchestrated it all. All because she'd been too selfish to tell him the truth.

"So, you thought you could betray Aulen? Betray Terran and fool me?" Elias, her captor, sunk the knife in deeper, filling her blood with more of the poison. The world blurred before her. "I know what you've done. And now you're going to die for it."

CHAPTER TWENTY-TWO

A s Terran stepped into the make-shift council chambers, he noticed two things: one, this room, though only a tent, was more resplendent and ornate than any room back in the castle. The rich fabric walls were sewn with jewels that caught the light of the gold candlesticks and bounced back. In contrast to where he had just been—out in the lush wilds of nature with Ellara by his side—this place reeked of gaudy excess, of superficiality, of falseness. The lords and viceroys and wardens were assembled in large, carved, wing-backed chairs arranged in a circle, and they watched his every step as he moved towards the last empty seat at the far end of the room. He wasn't on trial here—at least, he didn't think he was—but he couldn't help but feel like a criminal walking to his death.

And that led to his second discovery. For the first time in his life, certainly for the first time since they had crowned him as their king, the entire ruling class of Aulen was completely silent. Agis didn't insert himself into the middle of a conversation to which he clearly hadn't been invited. Madame Bovere didn't play peacemaker. Bickering and raised voices gave way to quiet.

It was a battlefield silence, one that Terran recognized.

When he finally took his place in the seat of honor, his body a knot of anxiety and his mind rushing with questions he didn't have the courage to ask, his right hand twitched out for Ellara's, only to remember that she wasn't there. His palm burned from needing her here, from *wanting* her here. It was truly baffling. He'd been so ready to do all of this on his own, but now that he had someone, he couldn't fathom facing the expectant, staring faces of his peerage without her.

He affixed his expression to match the mood of the room. He'd hoped it would help him feel brave, but it only made him feel as superficial and false as the walls that corralled them.

But this was what a king did. No matter that he felt he was pretending to these people. What mattered was the people. And they were all looking to him now.

"Is someone going to tell me what's happened?"

No one stirred. Gazes moved back and forth, back and forth, and it was then that Terran realized Elias wasn't in the tent. Strange. Normally, it would be his job to speak and brief them.

When Agis finally stood to speak, his face pale and withdrawn and without a trace of hope or victory written in the lines there, Terran's chest clenched. He'd never seen the man look entirely selfless, entirely absent of self-interest or ego. Even if he hadn't known about the invasion, even if he hadn't seen these advisors terrified out of their minds, that alone was enough to shake him.

"We have all been duped, Your Majesty. We have all been taken in by magic and our longest, cruelest enemy." He took in a breath. "The witches have taken High Court."

He didn't need to repeat the words or examine their meaning to bark out a reply. "You're lying."

"I'm not. We've received their demands."

Black parchment bleeding gold ink moved into the air, delivered for the king's inspection by Agis' own hand. His own shaking hand. Wordlessly, knowing that every eye in this room watched their every move, Terran locked eyes with the old man and saw his own fear reflected back to him. The expression was strange and foreign on both of them, like they'd tried to fit their hands into a pair of gloves two sizes too small. He took the black paper into his hands and read the glowing words, written in the familiar gold ink he'd once written his marriage decree with. Breaking the black seal of the king, he took in the message, bracing himself.

Whatever they wanted, he reasoned, he could give. As long as they didn't want Ellara. Ellara was all he had left.

Terran of Rosson House:

We have dispensed with the title of king as you no longer are one. As of this moment, Aulen belongs to the witches. You may choose to surrender, or you may choose to fight and find yourself utterly defeated.

Resist us and you will die. Surrender, and the ones you have cast out will rule over you forever. A terrifying prospect, is it not?

Yours in the Fates,

Allecta of Outerland, Mother of the Future Queen.

It wasn't so much a list of demands as it was a death warrant. And it wasn't so much an offer of terms as it was a letter-shaped hangman's noose. And it wasn't so much a kind letter from the woman who would have been his mother-in-law as it was a threat to everything Terran held dear.

It was everything he couldn't accept.

"Your Majesty," one viceroy asked, his voice low enough Terran could barely hear the crack in it, "What does it say?"

Mother of the Future Queen. The words, simple as they were, fragmented in his mind, their shards digging into his skull. "What happened?"

"We need to know—"

"I asked you a question, Agis," he spat dangerously. "I expect it to be answered without delay."

The room's energy shifted uncomfortably, but Terran didn't look up from the black-and-gold paper in his hands. He wasn't brave enough to face any of them, not when all of his thoughts ended with question marks.

How had he been so happy fifteen minutes ago? How was it possible to fall so low so quickly, to have joy stripped from one's hands as easily as leaves tripping on the wind? His jaw ached from locking it.

"It was an ambush, sir. The witch settlers entering the kingdom weren't coming to join Aulen, but to take it over. They broke up into smaller groups so we wouldn't notice them marching straight for High Court. With most of our armies dispatched to the borderlands and to accompany us on this journey, it was barely a contest. They took the keep within an hour of their first strike. Now, what are their demands?"

"There aren't any demands. I've been deposed."

A roar came over the crowd, shattering the tension, and they broke out into small snaps of conversation, none of which Terran bothered to break up or listen to. He kept returning to that send-off. Mother of the Future Queen. It couldn't mean what he dreaded. He didn't want Ellara to be a part of this. He couldn't bear it.

It was only when Agis spoke again, his firm and authoritative voice returning, that Terran bothered to pay attention to anything but his own thoughts. "What is your plan, Your Majesty?"

A stupid, laughable question from a stupid, laughable man. Bitterness seeped into every inch of Terran's body. "What do you suggest that I do? Hm? With our armies scattered to the winds and barely enough manpower to mount a basic assault on a chicken farm, much less the most fortified keep in all of Aulen?" He barked out a laugh and returned to the first plan he had devised, seeing no other way forward from this disaster. "We will regroup with our troops at Castle Moch and plan our next steps from there."

Again, silence. Then Agis spoke once more, timid but determined.

"Your Majesty. We have a hold of witches in our midst. One is their leader's daughter. That gives us leverage."

Future Queen. Mother of the Future Queen. What did it mean? And why did it stab him straight through the heart every time he thought about it? Shoving the feeling aside, he focused on the rage welling up.

"You would ransom your queen?"

"She is not my queen."

"Not yet, she isn't. But she will be."

There was no way Ellara could be party to a coup. There was no way she could betray him in such a manner, no way she could have been playing him the fool. They loved each other. And one day, when all of this was settled and there was peace once more in a unified Aulen, then they would be married, and he would have the perfect queen and partner at his side.

The witch sitting in High Court was trying to manipulate him. And he would not fall for it. Not let it tear him apart. Word of his love for Ellara must have spread, despite how hard he tried to shield it from the world. He wouldn't let anyone take advantage of this weakness.

That's how they saw it. A weakness. And maybe it was.

"This—"

"Matter is settled. We will depart for Castle Moch at first light. I suggest everyone rest because the journey will be long. Agis, send missives to all of our troop holdings and tell them of the plan."

He was already at the mouth of the tent before anyone objected, and he barely replied before escaping into the dark, cold night.

"But—"

"You are dismissed."

No one dared to follow him. No one dared to call out after him. And for the first time in this chapter of his life, Terran almost wished that someone would. Because at least if someone had followed him, he'd have something to distract him. Somewhere to focus his directionless thoughts and his frantic energy. Once in the dark of the starless night, he paced between the tents, unable to decide where to go next. His heart told him he had to see Ellara, had to tell her what had happened. But his mind—the voice in his head that sounded so much like his father—told him he couldn't face her right now. Terrible questions and doubts whispered in the back of his mind, always returning to the same swirling script... *Mother of the Future Queen.*

"You don't want to see her, do you?"

Terran spooked and spun on his heel, barely able to see the profile of the vicereine standing just a few feet away from him.

"Madame Bovere." He cleared his throat, collecting himself. "I'm not sure what you mean."

"You know she had something to do with this. And you can't face it."

The woman's confident, hushed tone sent scratching shivers down his spine. Someone had voiced out loud his first and worst fears he'd been denying ever since he read the letter. *Mother of the Future Queen.* The rage returned, swelling inside him, demanding to defend the honor of the woman he loved...and his own. Maybe if he denied it strongly enough, it wouldn't be true. "How dare you. Ellara is your future queen, and you are accusing her—"

"I'm an old woman," Madame Bovere scoffed. "I can afford to accuse *my queen* of treason. No one will hang me, and if they do, they aren't costing me much time. I don't have much of it left."

"We will find a solution. Ellara and I together—"

"Why would Ellara want a solution to a problem she caused? Or, if she wanted a solution, why would she want one that benefits the person she wants to destroy?"

"You don't know what you're talking about," he said, though he couldn't force his legs to move, to leave her and her spurious accusations about the woman he loved behind.

"Your Majesty, whose idea was it? This little *union* between you and our future queen. Who first suggested it?"

His lack of response didn't disturb her, and with every word she spoke, her heavy flowered perfume grew closer and closer.

"Well, for the sake of argument, let's just say it was Ellara's idea. And, after that, whose idea was it to travel away from High Court? Whose idea was it to leave the keep virtually unguarded? How has she manipulated you? Has she told you sad details of her past? Hm? Maybe saved your life a time or two? Accidentally let you see her without her clothes on? Kissed you just like you always dreamed of being kissed?"

Madame Bovere was circling him now. Close. Too close. Too close to him and too close to a truth he couldn't accept.

"Stop."

"Why? You can't bear the truth? That you allowed yourself to be taken in by the one creature in this kingdom you thought you could trust? That you believed every one of her lies?"

The marriage had been Ellara's idea. She *had* saved his life. It had been her idea to tour the kingdom. She had shown herself to him oh-so accidentally. But she also spoke to him like he was the only person who understood her, like he was the only person who could help her find the peace she so desperately wanted.

"She wants to unify Aulen. She's tired of war."

"And what better way to end war than to get rid of the humans, the only beings the witches have ever fought?"

"She loves me," he whispered, more prayer than promise.

"No, Your Majesty. She used you." A hand laid upon his shoulder and squeezed twice. A cloud of flowered perfume engulfed him. Her breath was cold on his ear as she leaned in closer and closer. "But you can use her back."

"What?"

"If you don't defeat this invasion, you're going to lose your kingdom *and* your crown. What would your father think? Your brothers? They died so you could rule."

"Then what do you suggest?" It was his turn to scoff. A miracle, really, considering how numb he felt. "I have no army."

"No, but you have the witch leader's daughter. And she

would do anything to get her back. Use her as bait. Use her just like she used you. And you'll have your kingdom."

Not even the Fates themselves could take you from the throne. Ellara's words rang in his ears as though he'd been punched. Pain peered through the numbness, pressing like a knife against his heart.

"But I love her."

"I know. Anyone with eyes knows. But she doesn't love you."

She doesn't love you. She used you. She made you believe that everything could be different, that you could love, and now...You have to punish her.

"After all," Madame Bovere whispered, her skirts swishing as she disappeared into the darkness. "How could she love you when she's spent every minute plotting to end you?"

CHAPTER
TWENTY-
THREE

Somewhere between the Witch Killer piercing her skin and her first steps into the shadowed darkness away from Terran, she'd lost consciousness. Her body didn't know what to do with itself. There had never been a pain her magic couldn't stop, never a wound it couldn't stitch. But now it just shut down, bringing her mind into darkness with it. And when she awoke, everything hurt. It wasn't any kind of hurt she'd encountered before: not the raw ache of sore muscles after swinging an axe for hours, nor the burning singe of a fresh wound her magic hadn't yet managed to heal.

This was fire raging through every one of her pores. This was drowning under frigid waters. This was a thousand cuts digging into her very soul, an inescapable hurt that never offered an ounce of relief.

It was agony.

Everything was agony. And she deserved it.

Between her screaming and convulsing, she struggled to take in her surroundings. There was straw beneath her. The smell of horse dung and saddle wax. A lantern light was close enough and hot enough to make her sweat. A barn? Yes, it must have been a barn.

She couldn't help but twitch. She couldn't help but move. Yet, every movement and breath and blink and every moment of wakefulness sent wave after wave after wave of shattering agony through her. No, not waves. Waves implied a break, an ebb, a disruption. There was no escape from it, no escape from the poison razing her from the inside out.

And then...It was gone. One moment, there was nothing but pain, and the next, there wasn't any pain at all.

"Good morning, *my lady*."

A swift kick cracked her ribs, and the familiar tickle of magic itched her fingers. A broken rib was nothing against her magic.

"I don't think you'll want to be using magic," Elias said, lording above her, his shadow crossing her face. His boot kicked a long and heavy chain into her sightline. He'd brought back the binders. "Wouldn't want to add any more scars to those pretty wrists of yours, would we?"

"Where's Terran?" Ellara asked, relaxing her hands and letting the magic ebb inside of her. She bit the inside of her cheek to distract from the pain in her side.

"Why? Do you think he's coming to your rescue?"

"No."

He was far too smart to try and save her. If the witches had invaded High Court, then keeping her at his side was a death sentence for his reign as king. Despite everything they'd been through, the words they'd exchanged and kisses they'd shared and the parts of him she'd won back from the darkness, she knew he would always, *always* care about his crown more than he could ever care about her.

But she did wish it. She wished with all her heart that he'd storm in here on a noble steed and rescue her from this man, this *thing* who'd tormented her and locked away her magic, this monster who would kill her and her entire court if given half the chance.

As Elias rested upon a hay bale and cleaned his sword, she thought once again about Terran. What were they telling him about the invasion? What did he know that she didn't? And what would he do when he found out she knew it had been a possibility?

It would break his heart to know she'd kept a secret from him. And that knowledge was more painful than a million kicks to the ribs.

Yes, she deserved this pain. If she'd just swallowed her fear and her pride, there wouldn't be another war brewing on the horizon. She would be in Terran's arms instead of on the hard ground. They would be together, facing the world.

She swallowed against the headache forming directly at the center of her skull and resisted the urge to smash her head against the ground beneath her.

"Do you want to know a secret, witch?"

"Always."

"Ah, so excited for someone who's going to die soon. You know you can't use my secrets against me if you're dead."

She licked her lips and tasted blood. Elias must have had fun with her while she was unconscious. Even the pain from being beaten was nothing compared to the witch killing blade he'd stuck her with. "Yes, I know I'm going to die." She smiled up at him, making sure he caught sight of the blood between her teeth. Death always spooked humans, by not fearing it. If he was going to kill her, she wanted to make sure she left an impression. Maybe she couldn't hurt him, but she could slither inside of his mind and lay seeds of fear there. "That's why I'm excited."

It worked. He returned to working with his sword, picking up a flint and running it along the edge of the blade. The noise sent shivers up and down Ellara's spine, but she ignored the sensation and focused on the man's eyes. They were distant. Lost. Desperately trying to grasp onto reality. And they never once looked back at her.

"I'm not the son of a noble house. I'm the son of a witch."

Ellara tried to keep her heart from stutter-stepping, but it was no use. He'd hated something that was part of him, rejected her and her court because they were a reminder of himself. Killing her would be like killing the part of himself he most hated. She felt like she could almost understand him. "My mother, the one who raised me, was in love with a witch from Outerland and couldn't have a child by her husband. Together, my mother and the witch made me. I'm only half-human, you see. Half-human, half magic. And when the war began, my mother tried to flee to Outerland, to her lover, and my father killed them both."

She wanted to hit him where it hurt, flinging out curses she didn't quite mean. "Then why did he keep you, his half-breed bastard?"

"Because he knew I would survive the war. And look." With a flourish, he stood and pressed the tip of the knife into her throat. Without the poison, the pierce into her skin only smarted. His smile was triumphant, but those eyes never returned from wherever they'd wandered back into the past. Any chance of reminding him of his humanity, of reasoning with him, was well and truly gone, if it had ever been there to begin with. "He was right."

"In my experience, the worst men always survive war." She spit out a mouthful of blood, no longer able to take the salty taste just for the visual effect. "So it makes sense that you'd still be standing."

"What does that say about you?"

Visions of the war, of her first days with Terran, played inside her mind, unfurling like distorted paintings of death and destruction. She'd had a code back then, but it hadn't stopped her from killing and destroying humans whenever she saw fit. She had been a monster, just like they were. And concealing the truth of the invasion from Terran—even if she'd thought she was protecting him, even if she thought she'd handled it—was proof that she hadn't changed nearly as much as she thought she had.

She was all self-interest. Part of her had hidden the news to keep their love intact. Part of her had hidden the news so he wouldn't send his armies after the witches. All of her had done it to benefit herself.

She leaned into the blade against her neck. She deserved this pain. If Terran ever wanted to see her again, she'd show him the wounds as part of her penance walk. They'd be signs of her guilt.

But no...that was just selfish thinking again, wasn't it?

Fates, she hated herself.

"Oh, I've always known I was the worst," she breathed wryly, rolling onto her back as his sword left her neck. He loomed large in her vision now, like a god overseeing some poor, pathetic creature he wanted to torture for fun. "And you never let me forget it."

"So, you admit it, then? You betrayed Aulen. You betrayed Terran."

"I would rather die," she hissed.

"Don't worry." He sheathed his sword and placed his hand on the dagger at his hip. "You'll get your wish."

"I won't lie. Not even to save my life."

How could she possibly say she'd betrayed Terran, the man she loved, and Aulen, the kingdom she wanted so desperately to be a part of that she'd given it everything she had to offer, including herself?

Elias knelt down to her, clucking his tongue as though he'd caught her in some sort of trap. "But that was a lie, wasn't it? Saying you'd never lie *was* the lie. I don't believe you've told the truth once over the course of our entire acquaintance." He slapped her shoulder, disturbing an open wound she didn't realize she had until a wave of pain rippled down her flesh. "Don't beat yourself up too much. You can't help but lie. It's in your blood. All witches are liars."

"I never lied to Terran. Not once."

"If you don't stop breaking your promise, I'm going to have to punish you." He slid the jewel-hilted dagger from his hip, and its slightly green blade glinted. It wasn't some magical property that had turned it green. Bits of her flesh had done that. Vomit rose in her throat. "Do you want the Witch Killer again?"

"You're a monster," she spat.

He was going to kill her, right here on this barn floor. There wouldn't be any tearful, apologetic reunion with Terran. There wouldn't be any begging for forgiveness or collapsing into his arms as her wounds took her. She'd never have the chance to finally tell him she loved him. She'd never be able to confess the way he'd changed her life, the way he'd altered her very soul and set her free from all the poisonous want she'd had her entire life. This was it. And if this moment was all she had, then she would tell the only two truths she still had to cling to. That Elias was a monster. And Terran was the only man she had ever loved...the only man she would ever love.

"My kingdom is all I have left. I will protect it as I always have and always will." Elias weighed the Witch Killer in his hands, letting its cold metal balance against his palm. Disjointed rage covered his impossibly light blue eyes in a haze. "He loved you, you know."

"And I love him."

He brought the dagger to her throat, a promise of what was to come.

"Don't lie," he hissed.

"I love him," she said, obeying his command.

"Say it again. I dare you."

"I love him." The dagger pressed into her skin. The agony returned. But she forced herself to speak through the heaving sobs and to tell the truth with her last breaths. "I love him. I love Terran of Rosson House, King of all Aulen, my best friend, and all I have left in this world. I love him."

Elias' smile, devious and cruel, would be the last thing she saw. She slammed her eyes shut and tried to conjure an image of Terran instead. The blade moved at her throat, preparing to slit it. "I don't believe you."

Just think of Terran. The ice in his eyes that you shattered. The little dimple in his left cheek when he smiles that smile that only you bring out of him. The way he slips his hand around your waist when-

As the pain of the poisoned blade threatened her vision and made the imagining almost impossible, she was certain she was hallucinating when the voice of the man himself broke through the haze.

"Elias?"

Her body unceremoniously fell to the floor. The blade disappeared. The pain did, too. She blinked against a fog towards the lip of the tent where he stood without looking at her.

"Yes, Your Majesty?" Elias said, scrambling to his feet to stand at full attention.

Hope replaced the ravaging pain. He had come to save her. He had come to rescue her from this monster. He *was* the hero of the stories she'd always dreamed him to be. Better still, he was *her* hero.

"Have the prisoner brought to the council chambers. I want her in binders. And bring the Witch Killer."

"As you wish, Your Majesty."

CHAPTER
Twenty-
Four

H e heard her before he saw her, and it broke his heart.
No. It didn't break his heart. One couldn't break
what didn't exist anymore.

He steeled himself against her cries, her struggling against
Elias' hold as he, no doubt, dragged her through the camp by her
hair. What had only a few days ago been his worst nightmare was
now done on his order, a horrible action committed under his
command.

Twitches of guilt occasionally tweaked at him, disturbing his
otherwise calm, resigned disposition, but he could answer every
doubt with a single question: *do you think Ellara would have done
the same thing?* Thoughts of her betrayal, of the invisible knife
she'd drawn the moment he'd shown her the slightest of his
vulnerabilities, cured him of any softness that threatened to
break free.

What he'd failed to realize when he'd first been in this
council chamber this evening was that the golden threads sewn
into the tents weren't monochromatic. When viewed from a
distance, they appeared so, but when viewed up close, they were

tapestries sewn of different shades of gold. Terran inspected them now, looking to the old rulers for any sign of help, any wisdom. He certainly needed it. The one person he'd relied upon to tell him the truth and guide him through this wretched world was now lost to him forever. It was time he sought out new assistance.

But the figures sewn in gold didn't move their mouths to answer his silent questions, and by the time his reverie was disturbed, he was no clearer on the future than he had been the moment he opened that letter from Ellara's mother.

"Terran."

Since his coronation, he'd only heard Elias use his given name a handful of times, and never over anything good. But this time, when he called his name across the now-empty council tent, it rang with the same golden tones that he had used to tell Terran they had won the war. A shiver of familiarity ran down Terran's spine.

"Bring her in," he commanded.

More protestations. More struggling. Then, finally, quiet.

Well, quiet except for the hammering of his revolting heart. It slammed against his chest with all the force of a rioting prisoner, threatening to beat its way out. His hand ghosted up to his chest, pressing down as if he could still it through the bone.

His heart wanted to go to her. It wanted nothing more than for him to run across the room and take her up in his arms, to hold her and never let her go. His heart wanted to clutch her to him and give her the world she'd been denied, to run away with her into the forest—away from evil and politics and war and everyone who threatened to destroy them. His heart wanted to spirit her away so they could finally, *finally* rest.

Which was exactly why he couldn't move.

He stared at the old kings, their stitched, emotionless faces matching his own. He knew better than to ask them what to do now that he had his once-almost-wife as his prisoner, merciless at his feet. Instead, he counted the plodding steps that Elias took to cross the tent's circular floor and waited for the cold kiss of steel to singe his hand.

"Terran," Elias began, whispering as he relinquished the blade to Terran's care. "Remember when I told you why I followed you into this service?"

"Yes."

"It wasn't because you saved my life. But I couldn't tell you the truth. Not back then, not when you were under her spell. I followed you because I always believed that you would be the one to save Aulen."

"Thank you for your confidence," Terran said, voice as flat and lifeless as he felt. There wasn't any room left in him for conflict or rage, just a blank, unfeeling emptiness. He didn't even have the energy to consider what kind of man he must have been during the war for Elias to believe he would be the one to rid Aulen of the witch scourge Elias hated so much. "I'd like to be alone with the prisoner."

"Are you sure that's wise? Her magic—"

"You've put the binders on, haven't you? And besides, I don't think I'm weak enough to fall for the same trick twice."

"Of course not. I'll join the preparations for our departure."

"Good man."

And with that, Elias departed, leaving Ellara and Terran completely alone. The still eyes of the tapestries were the only ones left to witness their reunion. The tent kept out the wind and the sounds of the outside world. Here, between them, there was nothing but stillness.

It would have been so easy to turn around and face her, to see the brutality done to her by Elias and revel in it, to bask in her pain and know that it was only a fraction of what he felt when he'd discovered her betrayal. So easy to lean in close, memorizing the bruises and welts and bleeding cuts left behind by a man with more brute force than sense.

His father's words in his head stopped him from making that simple gesture. The man at the head of Rosson House never had much faith in Terran, but the thing he despised most about his youngest son was his weakness. After all, only a defiantly stupid weakling would attempt to take on a dragon just to save a duckling's life.

Terran remembered that night at the Academy with vivid clarity. The poor little bird flapping its wings, desperate to escape the monster who'd grabbed it by the tail. His heart had bled for the creature, and he'd known in that moment he'd be as monstrous as the dragon if he turned around and walked away without trying to save it.

The reason he didn't turn around to face Ellara was because he knew, in his heart of hearts, that examining her destroyed body wouldn't make him feel better. It would only make things immeasurably worse. She would be the duckling, and he would want nothing more than to save her.

No, moving wasn't an option. Not if he wanted to cling to the pain and the rage that had turned his insides into a white void.

"Are you alright?"

The voice, so familiar and so foreign all at once, was so soft he wondered at first if he hadn't dreamed it. When he didn't respond, she spoke again.

"Terran, are you alright?"

"You'll address me as *Your Majesty*."

It seemed as if just being in her presence brought back more memories than he knew what to do with. He remembered when he'd begged her to call him Terran. What a stupid, emotional fool he'd been, thinking that she could actually want affection and friendship from him instead of power.

He should have known better. The only thing anyone wanted in this world was power.

"Are you alright, then, Your Majesty?"

The genuine worry in her voice gutted him. Or rather, it sounded like genuine worry, and *that* gutted him. How many times had he fallen for her oh-so-innocent and caring act?

Humiliation flooded him, coloring the white void inside of him with splotches of sickly, bitter yellow.

"You're very good at it, you know."

"Good at what?"

"Pretending to care for me."

"I'm not pretending."

He had to give her credit where credit was due. If she was trying to play the love-sick puppy concerned with nothing but him and his well-being, if she was still pushing the line that she was in love with him, if she still believed that feigning innocence would save her life...she was doing an incredible job.

But her being brilliant at the act only made it more painful. The reminder of what he'd fallen for—the trap and her—cut through his wall of emotionlessness. He opened and closed his free fist once, twice, letting the tight leather stretch over his skin. He was grateful for the gloves; he never wanted to touch her again.

"The charade is over, Ellara. I know who you are and what you've done. I understand your plan. There won't be any fooling me a second time."

"...What do you think happened?"

"I *know* what happened," he snapped, but regained control over himself. It wouldn't do to show emotions in front of her. She'd only use them to manipulate him further. "You convinced me I was worthy of love, that love was real, and used me so you could become queen. The invasion of High Court was all your doing, and I was just your willing pawn."

"That's not true."

"It was a clever scheme, to be sure. Lure me away from High Court with all of your promises of romance and making the world a better place, then sending your armies to the empty castle."

"I didn't do any of that."

"Oh, really?" he said, his voice dry and sarcastic "Then this has all been a terrible mistake. I must restore you to the court immediately."

"Terran, you have to listen to me—"

That, of all her other protestations, was the final straw that forced him to turn and face her. He'd done nothing but listen to her and deny his own instincts these past few months. He'd fallen for her against his better judgment and the better judgment of everyone who advised him. He betrayed the memories of the dead to be with her, and there was no betrayal as bitter as that. Listening to her had been the beginning of the end of everything, a sweet poison he had to stop drinking. Turning on her, the veil separating her from his emotions snapped cleanly in half, and he didn't allow himself the opportunity to stagger back at the sight of her.

She was so small, dumped on the ground of the tent. Her body, which he had always thought of as larger-than-life, imposing and entrancing all at once, now crumbled in on itself defensively. Wounds covered every visible inch of her skin, accompanied by the telltale yellowing of bruises. Dirt and mud caked at her hairline. Her perfectly kissable lips bore a split right down the middle. She'd never looked worse. And if he allowed himself to dwell on that, he might have been tempted to take pity on her. But he couldn't, not when he had so much righteous rage begging to be flung straight in her direction.

"No, I don't. I'm your king. You are my subject. Worse than that, you're my prisoner. I don't owe you anything. And you are nothing to me."

A lie. She wasn't nothing to him. He'd fallen too deeply in love with her for anything to shatter their bond. Forever, whether he lived to see himself reseated on the throne of Aulen or dead at the hands of her witch armies, he would always feel a rushing wave of love every time he looked at her or thought about her. But she couldn't know that.

At his tone, she winced, reopening one of the fresh wounds over her left eye. Blood trickled down her face, drawing a line through the dirt on her skin. His fingers twitched for the hand-kerchief in his pocket, but he tightened his grip around the Witch Killer instead. The gems of the hilt rested easy and cool in his grip, a reassuring presence against the oppressive, flicker-ing, candle-fueled heat of the room.

A voice like his father's rang out in the back of his head, loud and clear as bells calling him to prayer. It would be so easy to kill her, to rid the world and himself of her. If she was dead, he wouldn't feel this way, like a man who'd already lost another war.

He pocketed the blade. His father was right. He'd always been too much of a coward to make the right decisions, espe-cially when it came to his heart.

"Don't you want to know the truth?" she asked, barely louder than a whisper. He couldn't look back at her. He didn't have the strength.

"I *do* know the truth, Ellara. I finally know the truth. And it's that you are exactly who they always said you were." Something like a strangled sob came from her throat. The sound shot straight to his heart, a muscle he fought to deaden. "The Good Witch of Aulen was a lie. This, what you've done to Aulen, to me..." He swallowed hard as he reflected on his own failure. Yes, she was a deceiver. But he'd allowed himself to be deceived for some nice words and a pair of soft lips. "That's the truth."

No more sobs. No more strangled protests.

"What?" He glanced up to see that she'd pulled herself up from the ground. Now, she knelt on uneasy knees, her head downcast like the king's subject that she was. "Nothing to say in your defense?"

"You've already decided, Your Majesty." She sniffled, but with her head down, he couldn't tell if she was crying or laughing. "Our love doesn't mean anything to you."

"It meant everything to me," he hissed.

"No, it couldn't have." It was then that she looked up, capturing his gaze, refusing to let it go. Her eyes burned like impenetrable walls of fire as blood made tear-tracks down her dirty skin. It gleamed black in the candlelight. "Real love wouldn't crumble so easily."

A challenge. In her eyes, she held all of their memories and whispered promises, all of their arguments and agreements. Her words held a promise and a threat of a future he so desperately wanted but could never, *never* have. No matter how badly he wanted it.

And in spite of everything she had done, all of her lies, he *did* still want it.

"Guards!" he shouted, turning his back on her and letting them flood the room with their clanking swords and scuffling armor.

"Yes, Your Majesty?" one called out when they were settled.

"Get her out of my sight. Have her chained and prepared for transport in the morning. There's been a change of plans."

From the sounds of struggle and moving metal, he could only assume they were following his orders when Ellara's voice once again reached out to him, brushing against him like the dead wind.

"Where are we going?"

"We're going to take High Court," he said, his hand adjusting over the handle of the Witch Killer. Bitterness flooded him. "And then I'm going to destroy every witch I can get my hands on."

CHAPTER
TWENTY-FIVE

The road to High Court was easier to trek on the back of a horse than walking with chained ankles and boots half a size too small, but the hours of walking and tuning out the verbal abuse flung at her by the court gave her plenty of time, time she desperately needed to plan her escape.

Ellara had been used as bait before. During the war, her green skin was like honey to men who desperately clawed at power, and so she found herself dangled on the end of many sprung traps, calling to their intended targets like aged cheese called to mice. Those various traps had, in turn, seen her dunked, imprisoned, chained to a tree, nearly killed by a poisoned arrow, nearly killed by a poisoned chalice of water, nearly killed by strangulation, and switching allegiances when her captors offered her a better alliance than the ones who'd put her in the trap in the first place.

What she didn't realize was that she'd been the bait in a much larger trap all along. Her mother had been using her to lure the King of Aulen right into her grasp, never caring what Ellara might have wanted.

She was so tired of being bait. She was so tired of having zero control over her destiny. Her mother had betrayed her. And Terran believed everyone who said she had betrayed him. No, when Ellara of Outerland made good on her escape, she would not run to the witches and join their cause. She would not stay in High Court and try to plead her case.

Once she escaped this caravan, this walking death in which she was currently trapped, she was going to run into the distance and never look back. She was going to escape it all, everything that had ever kept her captive. She'd catch a ship and go to one of the kingdoms across the sea. She'd work on a farm in the north until her hands bled, where no one knew her name. She'd run to the mountains and play games with the snow until no one could track her footsteps across it. Little by little, the world would forget her, and she would forget the world until they were strangers to each other forever.

No amount of time could ever erase Terran. Or the way he made her feel. But everything else, she was more than ready to forget.

She just had to escape first, and that was the trick of it all. They bound her magic. A four-man troop of soldiers guarded her at every second. The caravan stretched on for miles. She didn't even have the foggiest clue where Briony and her court were or what had happened to them, so they couldn't be of any use to her and she couldn't be of any use to them.

For the first time in months, she was utterly and completely alone. It brought her back to the days of the war when no one could be trusted, and something as stupid as love hadn't dulled her instincts. Back then, she made escapes like this for breakfast. They were the entertaining cakewalks of war, the adventures she used to love indulging in whenever the opportunity presented itself. Prisoner escapes were puzzles to be managed, puzzles to break up the monotony of battlefields and marches through the woods.

Today, a prison break would be a fitting distraction from thoughts of Terran and her mother.

Her mind raced with the possibilities. *We are marching north, which means we will need to cross the Yahari River. The same river that my traitor mother told me she'd take me to swim in one day. No, focus, Ellara, focus. If you can get into the river, then you should be able to let the fast tide take you far enough away that you can get to a place where you can break the binders. Of course, I wouldn't need the binders if Terran had just given up his stupid pride and listened to me.*

But that was the problem with this particular escape attempt. During the war, the only person she had to think about was herself. Staying alive then had been her only priority. But today, she was torn between the two people she loved and hated most in this entire world. Neither of them was ever far from her thoughts, no matter how strongly she vowed to never see either of them again.

"Oi, witchy!"

One of the soldiers called out to her from atop his horse, leering down at her from his position of power. She ignored him.

"Not so high and mighty now, are you? What do you think the king will do to you once he's taken you back to High Court? You're too pretty and wicked for killing right away."

His compatriots laughed and slapped each other with their metal gauntlets, thinking his insults oh-so amusing. She'd almost successfully tuned them all out when she heard the soldier call out again.

"What? Too big to talk to us? Or did the king cut your pretty little tongue out?"

She didn't have magic. She didn't have spells or incantations or curses. But she had her spit.

Throwing her head back, she projected a mouthful straight at his face, relishing the splatter against his splotchy skin and the way it dangled from his too-thick mustache.

Not exactly the best thing she could have done or the wisest, but there was no overselling the satisfaction that rolled through her body as he reeled back and tried to wipe her spit away with his indelicate sausage fingers.

"Why, you little—"

And that's when her plan came together. She'd need a lot of luck and would probably have to put herself through a bit of pain, but if she was going to get out of here, she'd have to be willing to do anything.

The beefy soldier leapt off his horse and his compatriots tightened their circle around her, their feet still moving in time with the marching caravan. Everything was happening so fast that Ellara struggled to keep up, but the fight for her life was one she knew like the back of her hand. It was mechanical, it was instinctual, it was a daring escape she'd made countless times, and one she knew she could make again.

She just had to time it right.

The man lunged for her, sending his friends scattering out of formation to avoid his vast form, disturbing the ranks of the entire caravan. Horses spooked, dragging carriages slightly off their path, a dangerous proposition considering the upcoming bridge. She dodged his approach, a dodge only made possible by the sudden chaos.

It only worked because she knew something that her attacker didn't. She was faster than him.

Ducking his arm, she lithely moved through the bucking horses and confused guards, her attacker's voice not heard over the distressed cries of various courtiers. She lost herself in the crowd, slipping between them, faster and faster and faster until she reached the center of the caravan—and the beginning of the bridge.

There wasn't any time to think or to gauge the depths of the river beneath her. There was only time to jump.

She propelled herself towards the water, going limp in the air and letting the wind carry her down to the icy depths below. At first, she could have sworn she heard a familiar voice—Terran's voice—call out behind her, but she must have confused it with the smashing sound of water against her body.

The nearly frozen water penetrated her skin, paralyzing her movements and keeping her from swimming to safety, but in a split second, she realized the truth: her body was protecting her. If she played dead and let herself wash down the river like a discarded petal, she'd be halfway across Aulen before any of them could even trip down the ravine towards the riverbanks.

But there was something else, too, about the cold, a trick of the binders she'd never realized. They couldn't handle the freezing temperatures. The further she slipped down the river, the more brittle they became, flaking off piece by piece until finally, she was free.

Free. For the first time in her life, she really *was* free. She'd escaped from her mother. She'd fled her betrothed.

Now, she just had to figure out what to do with that freedom.

CHAPTER
TWENTY-
SIX

Terran could see the keep of High Court from their camp's position on the high hill, only miles away from the defensive walls of the castle. It was no doubt that the witches knew of their presence. No matter how hard he'd tried to keep the tents and the troops hidden in the belly of the forest, he knew better than to underestimate how much these insidious, all-seeing creatures knew. But if his suspicion was correct, and they knew about their location, they'd sent no emissary or armies to greet them. The lantern light of High Court flickered in the distance, filling the keep with light and reflecting the white stone even into the black night. It called out to him, a beacon in the darkness, begging him to return home.

His stomach twisted as he thought of the daydreams he'd had of his return to High Court. Only a few days ago, he'd laid awake in bed, imagining he and Ellara arriving hand-in-hand, their plans for the nation secured and their hopes for the future placed in their marriage. What would that ceremony have been like? How beautiful would she have looked in a wedding gown, bearing the crown of Aulen as she approached him for their vows?

And what would she have done with him if they'd gone through with it? Surely, she would have killed him in his sleep just as Elias tried to convince Terran to do on their first attempt at a wedding night.

He hadn't slept since she made her escape. And, of course, it was an escape. For a moment, he'd believed what his eyes told him, that she'd rather jump to her death than walk with him as a prisoner, but his heart knew better. Ellara of Outerland wasn't dead. His heart would have known if she was gone.

Every time he tried to close his eyes, a new wave of rage or hurt would well up, shooting him through with adrenaline. Sleep was impossible, especially when he saw her shadow everywhere he looked.

She was a monster. But dammit, he missed her. Every so often, he would think he saw her in a crowd or moving through the tree-line towards him, coming to apologize or wrap him in her arms, or to beg him to run away and leave all of this behind. It was never her, but that didn't stop his brain from conjuring up fanciful daydreams of everything he couldn't be and couldn't have.

After giving orders to his soldiers about their prisoners—keep them warm, keep them in binders, and don't touch so much as a hair on any of their heads—he'd taken up a post in the tree-tops, watching the keep for any signs of the witches' preparations or movements, a fruitless position seeing as they appeared content to let the human armies come to them. At least up here in the trees, there were fewer places for him to imagine her. The downside was the memories. From up here, he could see the road they'd taken through the Thieves' Forest. He could see High Court, where he'd re-met her and found his feelings for her. Each memory was a freshly scabbed-over wound, one he couldn't stop picking at.

Emotionally, he hadn't been able to stop the bleeding since the moment he uncovered her plot. He would have to give Madame Bovere a medal one of these days for helping him realize the truth. She hadn't been afraid to speak plainly and honestly with him. That kind of courage and foresight deserved reward, one he would happily grant when they returned to High Court and he was crowned king once again.

He was uncertain if the witches knew of their leader's disappearance. If they knew, he would have to destroy them; he would make the witches sorry they'd ever attempted this little revolution of theirs.

These were the thoughts that kept him from sleeping, that fueled his constant gaze at the keep in the distance. And it was in these thoughts that Elias found him.

"You must sleep," he called from a few branches below, grunting as he made his way up towards the top branch where Terran had situated himself.

"Can't sleep," Terran replied.

"Then you must eat something."

"Not hungry. And we must save the rations for the soldiers."

Over the days he spent perched like a bird in this tree, he'd practiced this exchange dozens of times. He'd known that Elias would eventually arrive. His mind was too preoccupied and distant to focus any energy on keeping up a proper conversation with his combative Warden, so he played the lines he'd rehearsed rather than offering anything authentic.

Elias sighed, settling down on the branch opposite him. From the corner of his eye, Terran examined the man with his heavy-bagged eyes and his sickly skin. He wondered if he looked half as bad.

"You can't lead any army like this."

"I can and I will. You don't need to worry about me."

There was no question in Terran's mind that he would succeed. Nothing could break his steadfast determination to reclaim his future. He would not let his family down as he had before. He would not let Aulen down. He would defeat the witches and reclaim the throne. It was his destiny. No one need worry about him.

"But I do. What if this is a side effect of her magic being broken? What if there's no cure for this sickness of yours?"

He wasn't unwell. He was heartbroken. And it was high time Elias understood the difference. Turning away from the castle for the first time in days, Terran focused all his energy on making him see the truth. He spoke in an even, unbroken tenor, flat as a board and twice as unforgiving.

"Elias. She didn't bewitch me. I fell in love with her. There was no magic. She was kind and gentle and funny and strong and wonderful and everything I'd ever dreamed that I could want in another soul." He stopped himself before he drowned in the happy, tainted, poisoned memories. Breathing always became a little too difficult when he thought about her for too long, and he didn't want to give her the power of leaving him breathless even after she'd left him. "I was a fool, but I was an honest one. No tricks. No magic. Just...love."

Elias' face crinkled in disgust. "But how could you really love that thing?"

Hadn't he been listening? Hadn't he seen them together? He would have thought the answer to that was obvious by now.

"Because when I was with her, for the first time, I felt like a king. But more than that, I felt like the man I'd always wanted to be."

"And what kind of man was that?"

"A good one."

For so long, he'd believed that the possibility to be good was no longer open to him. He'd murdered—no, slaughtered—in the fields of battle and played every cruel trick in the book to win his crown and title. But Ellara made him believe not only in love, but in himself. And in her. He thought that goodness was within his grasp. He only had to reach out and accept it.

Now he knew better.

"I'm..." Elias opened and closed his mouth several times, genuine remorse washing over his face. For the first time in months, it felt as if they were two friends again speaking about real things, rather than a king and his advisor speaking only of power and how to attain it. "I'm sorry, Terran. I can't imagine what it must have been like, losing someone like that."

"You were right about her all along. I should have listened to you."

His stomach filled with sick. His mouth smacked with the taste of bile. If he hadn't been so stubborn and blinded by emotion, he would have known better than to ignore his friend's counsel. He chose Elias for a reason. He should have trusted in that choice.

"There may have been some wisdom in not listening to me," Elias muttered.

"Oh, really? And in possibly losing my crown?"

"That's not ideal, but we'll win this fight just as we've won many others. I just think that maybe this was worth it if it means you were happy, even if for a short while."

Terran didn't know if he agreed with that assessment. He'd forever be marked as the king who let his heart almost lose the kingdom. Was such trauma worth it to spend a few weeks happier than he'd ever been? And did that happiness even matter if it had all been a lie?

No one else cared about his happiness. Why should he?

"You really should try to sleep," Elias said, breaking up his chain of thoughts. "I can keep watch tonight."

"You're right. I'll see you in the morning."

Climbing down that tree was one of the most difficult things Terran had ever done. It was an admission of his weakness that he couldn't fix this mistake on his own. This war that he'd been tricked into would have to be won with the help of his allies, with blood, with steel and sweat and death.

The camp at the base of the forest bustled with activity, illuminated by thousands of lanterns and dozens of campfires. The dinner bell rang while he was on his way down. And now the camp was full of laughing and drinking and eating, the hallmarks of an army preparing to face the enemies with their swords and lives in hand. He hadn't yet slept in his tent at the encampment, but he moved towards it, praying with each step that no one would disturb him.

His prayers were in vain. Just as he reached his temporary home, a hand reached out, desperately clawing at his shoulder.

"Your Majesty, I must speak with you."

He spun, retrieving his sword and leveling it before coming face-to-face with Briony, Ellara's best friend and Warden. The taste of acid filled his mouth. She was just as responsible for all of this as Ellara was. No one became that close with another without learning their secrets.

"I'm afraid I'm busy, witch," he said, blade still outstretched.

Chaos erupted at the sight of a chained witch facing off with the king. Soldiers and guards approached her, grabbing around her waist and pulling her out of his reach.

"She didn't know anything about this," she screamed, her tormented voice echoing through the trees and reverberating in Terran's ears. "You have a traitor in your court, and she's the one pulling the strings! You have to believe me!"

Kicking and screaming the entire way, she was dragged off by the guards assigned to protect her. But even after she was gone and the night was quiet, Terran still heard her voice in his head, screaming out those words. *You have a traitor in your court.*

They teased him until the morning when he woke to the news that the entire imprisoned witch court was gone.

CHAPTER TWENTY-SEVEN

T he Forest of Thieves was actually rather nice, once
Ellara had magicked away all of the spiders and bats
who liked to crawl around at night. The temporary
shelter she'd conjured in the trees at the castle's edge of the
forest wouldn't do for a permanent home—that, she decided,
would be at the seaside—but it would do for now.

Maybe she didn't want to see Terran or her mother ever
again. They were cruel and heartless, and both had abandoned
her when she needed them most, using her as a pawn in their
games for power. But she wanted to make sure they were both
okay. Monsters or not, she loved them. From her house in the
trees, she could see the keep with perfect clarity, and she was
able to enchant the evening dew into a watery spyglass that
allowed her to adjust and see the finer details—faces, uniforms,
weapons. This would be the place where she'd watch the war.

This wasn't what she meant when she said she wanted peace,
but it would have to do for now. Every time she tried to run for
the seaside, her feet found her back here, heading towards the
castle and her loved ones. She just couldn't leave without seeing

them first, without making certain that they both still lived. Once that was assured, then she would leave, and *she* would live.

But tonight, there was a rustle in the trees.

It should have been impossible. She'd cloaked this place in magic so no one could see her. No one should have been able to pierce this world she'd built for herself. Grabbing at the bow and arrows she'd carved—she'd been looking for anything to do with her hands these days, anything to stop thinking about him—she approached the window in her box of a treehouse and peered down.

No one there. She must have been hearing things.

Crack.

No, but there it was again. She waited behind her doorframe, bow in hand, waiting for the intruder to make themselves known. She wouldn't be going back. Not for anything in the world. No one could make her, and they would die if they tried.

"Ellara?"

The hairs on the back of her neck stood, but she didn't move. That was Briony's voice. No, it couldn't be Briony. It had to be some kind of trick, a way to lure her out. Or, if it was really her, she was being used as pathetic bait. Ellara exercised caution, counting her breaths as she pressed herself tighter into the wall of her makeshift house. Her fingers shook on the bow.

"Ellara, I know you're up here. And this is a really terrible welcome." There was grunting through her words, as if she were staggering up the tree. Not a trick of sound, then. If they were using Briony, then she was really there, climbing up this tree. "No wonder the humans didn't want to make you their queen. You're a terrible hostess."

With that, the door smacked open, revealing the long shadow of Briony as she stepped into the treehouse's single room. If she was surprised by Ellara's raised bow, she made no mention of it.

"There you are. I've been looking everywhere for you."

Ellara couldn't stop from letting her shock drag her jaw down and widen her eyes. Suspicion rose within her, and she peered out of her slat windows and down the trees, her hands still clenched around her bow. *Fates, what she wouldn't give for an axe.* But, when she saw no Aulen soldiers hiding between the branches, she finally spoke, loosening her hold on the weapon.

"What are you doing here?"

"I escaped, obviously," Briony said, blowing hair out of her face and revealing a black eye and a few healed-over scrapes, which Ellara immediately set about healing. The escape hadn't been easy on her, just as it hadn't been easy on Ellara. The humans could be cruel when they wanted to keep their witches on leashes; she knew that firsthand. Briony hissed as the magic worked its way through her wounds, but downplayed it with a self-deprecating smile. "Couldn't let you have all of the fun."

Ellara gave another glance down below. Sure, there weren't any human soldiers, but there also weren't any witches. Her heart stutter-stepped.

"But where are the others?"

"Safely stashed in Elzinior. I left because I had to find you, to talk to you."

With her wounds healed over, Briony stepped away from Ellara's hands. Ellara considered what this new information meant. The witches had made a daring escape, refused to return to the castle and join her mother, and now... Hope filled her chest. She wasn't alone anymore.

"Everyone's safe?"

"Safe and alive." Briony smiled, then lifted the chains wrapped around her neck and wrists. "I could really use your help with these, though."

Ellara hesitated. Taking off the magical bindings of another witch was punishable by immediate death, but it wasn't the law she was worried about. It was the pain she might cause her friend. Binders rejected magic, even outside magic, which meant removing them by non-human means could cause some trauma.

"This might sting a little."

Briony cracked her neck and prepared for whatever was coming next. "I handled being around Warden Elias. I can handle a little bit of sting."

Harnessing her magic through her fingertips, Ellara traced the circlets around her friend's wrists, drawing magical, glowing white lines around the metal, tracing the runes of her ancestors that replaced a spoken spell. The lines flattened and spread, infecting the binders until they cracked and fell, useless, to the floor. Briony rubbed at her sore wrists and neck, but Ellara knew that the red rawness would eventually subside. Briony was much smarter than Ellara ever was; she hadn't used her magic to stupidly save humans, thus landing her with permanent scars like those Ellara had.

The lights of the High Court keep burned in the distance. The temptation to peer through her enchanted spyglass was nearly too much to bear, but Ellara turned her back on the sight.

"Why have you come here, Briony?" she asked.

Briony helped herself to a sip from Ellara's canteen and shrugged, as if it were the most simple thing in the world, as if her friend was stupid for not figuring it out in the first place.

"Because you have to stop this war."

The bitter taste of blood filled Ellara's mouth. "I don't have to do anything."

All traces of humor and nonchalance evaporated from Briony, turning instead into thick, heady distress and determination. "Yes, you do. This war, this battle, whatever it is...It will destroy everyone. This war is destruction."

Ellara scoffed and deposited herself onto one of the benches she'd used her magic to build. "All war is destruction. And you know what? I am so tired of everyone telling me what I have to do. I want my own power. I want control over my own life. Can't any of you people see that?"

"You don't care about anyone but yourself. That's what I'm hearing."

Swallowing hard, Ellara tried not to think about how many

times she'd pinned the same accusation on Terran. Now she knew it was true. But why in the Fates' name would she possibly care about the world when it didn't seem to give a damn about her? They didn't deserve her. They didn't deserve her magic. And above all, they didn't deserve her help.

"I care about you." She nodded to Briony, her face a cool mask of indifference. "You and the rest of my court are pretty much all I have left."

"You're going to let your traitorous mother and one bad relationship ruin you? You're going to let them steal away who you are?"

Who she was? Ellara wasn't sure she knew the answer to that question any longer.

"And who is that, exactly?"

"The Good Witch of Aulen. You are the one who can save us." Briony took her hand and laced their fingers together, a common sign of togetherness in Outerland. As much as Ellara wanted to smile at the familiar gesture, she couldn't gather the energy. "And I'm going to help you."

Terran's words rushed back to her, the curses he threw at her during their last moment together. She winced, removing her hand from Briony's.

"The Good Witch of Aulen was a fiction."

"Maybe," Briony conceded. "But a useful one. And you can save our people and theirs if you become her for real."

Emotion spoke for her instead of reason, hissing from between her teeth like a spell gone wrong. Briony and her court were the only people in the world who hadn't betrayed her, the only people she felt even remotely inclined to save. The rest...? Tightening her arms around her chest, hugging herself close, she shivered as she stared back out at High Court. "I don't want to save them. I hate them both so much."

"You don't hate them."

"Yes, I do."

"Then why the hell are you here?"

She didn't have an answer for that. Because no matter how she tried to deny it to herself, Briony was right.

"You just want them to learn a lesson." Briony came up behind her and pressed a hand to her shoulder. "And I think I know how to go about it."

"Really?"

"Yes. I tried to explain it to Terran, but he wouldn't listen to me. Now, it's up to us. We have to end this war."

As Briony set to work pulling out papers and quills and bewitching the candles to burn stronger and brighter than ever, Ellara beheld her dear friend, the one who'd been at her side ever since they began this entire life in High Court. Her best friend. Her confidant. And now, the woman who woke some sense into her. Briony worked with clarity and focus, speaking with all the grace and gravitas of a military leader...or something else.

"You would make an incredible queen, Briony."

"I've known that for years. It's nice of you to finally catch up, though."

CHAPTER
TWENTY-
EIGHT

The darkness around High Court was as thick and impenetrable as its walls. This close to the stone surrounding the city and the keep beyond, none of the city's light bled out into his path, but Terran pressed forward, letting his eyes adjust. This was the endgame of the war that had only just begun, the risky gambit he'd have to play if he wanted a chance at saving his people.

He knew the walls of this castle as though they were the walls of his own bedroom at Rosson House. During his reign as king, he hadn't lived here long, but in the last few days, he'd done nothing but stare at them. He could count the exact number of bricks around the base and the precise timing of the guard rotation. His knowledge meant that sneaking in would have been relatively easy. It was a simple matter of slipping between the guards, into the sewers, and back up through the servants' quarters until he reached the belly of the beast.

It would have been easy, but it wouldn't have been successful. The humans still inside the small city would have helped him all that they could, but he was certain he'd be caught before he could take out the Witch Killer and end Ellara's mother and her reign of terror for good.

No, he'd have to be let in willingly. And he knew he was the only one that they would allow entrance. No emissaries, no envoys, no stewards or knights. They wouldn't see him or his bargain as genuine if he didn't put his own skin in the game.

There were only two potential flaws in his plan. One, the witches could kill him the moment they saw him and declare victory before he'd even had a chance to open his mouth. Or two, he could have overestimated Allecta's affection and love for her daughter, ending with her killing him and damning Ellara.

He bowed under the weight of the heavy, white flag of negotiation he carried. Under Aulen law, anyone entering an enemy's house while bearing the flag couldn't be harmed. It was a sign of momentary truce, of a hope for peace.

Oh, Fates, please let them want peace as much as I do.

When he finally reached the base of the castle walls, he approached the guards' station, where a heavily fortified door greeted him, and a brass bell awaited him. He rang it. Once, twice, three, four times. The slat in the door opened and the eyes of a green-skinned witch stared out from inside. At the sight of him, those eyes widened in surprise, then narrowed. He waved the flag in his hands.

"I've come to see the Queen of Aulen."

It took time to climb the thousands of steps between the doorway to the base of High Court and the highest rooms of the keep. It wasn't a route Terran had ever taken on foot before, and by the time he arrived in the queen's throne room and was pushed to the ground by his witch escorts, he almost welcomed the sweet rest that laying on the ground gave him.

But when the creeping voice of a witch struck his ears, he knew that there was no time for rest.

"Ah, Terran of House Rosson. Or, should I say, Terran of Nowhere? Rosson House has been quite destroyed, you know."

A pang struck through him. He'd had no great attachment to Rosson House, but it was all he had left of his family. Was it really destroyed? Or was she bluffing?

Rising to his feet, he presented himself, not caring that the assembled witches circling the room were seeing him with sweat on his brow and knots in his hair. Once at his full height, he could stare down Allecta for the first time, the witch who'd given birth to the woman who broke his heart, the woman who had helped to orchestrate this entire scenario, the woman with whom he'd have to broker peace.

And, if peace didn't work, then she was the woman he'd have to kill if he wanted his throne back.

Terran cleared his throat. "I have come to strike a bargain with you, to broker peace between our people."

Laughter rang out from the assembled witches, bouncing around the walls in a torturous, mocking echo.

"There will be no peace."

"No?" he asked.

"No. There will be humans marching to Outerland, to their own exile."

"Humans won't take to exile."

"Neither did our ancestors a hundred years ago."

The muscles in his face tightened involuntarily. He thought of Ellara's stories of Outerland, the broken pieces of their lives there. It still hurt—a dull ache, one he hated—to think of her there. No matter how he hated her now. "Of course. But you have to know that we will fight it."

"You may fight it, but there won't be any choice. Our new queen will command your exile, and thus, you will be exiled."

"Funny thing, that. I have your queen."

"I know you have my queen."

"I do."

"And she did not escape?"

"You know even the strongest witch can be contained with enough chains."

Something shifted in the witch's face. Her nostrils flared, the slightest hint that she was losing patience with the conversation. "Let me see her."

"I'm afraid I can't do that."

"Why not?"

"You're more powerful than me, aren't you? And I hear you witches are more powerful when you're all together, in close quarters like this. If I show her here and now, then you'll over-power me in a minute, won't you?"

"If you *don't* show her to me, I'll overpower you."

"I propose a deal. The crown for your daughter. Don't worry. She's still in mint condition."

"You expect me to give up and return to Outerland?"

"Yes, or I'll kill her."

"Oh, little king. You think I don't know? You think I haven't heard all about your magnificent love affair, your runaway romance? You think I believe you could ever kill the love of your life?"

"She isn't the love of my life."

"That's not what I've heard. I've heard that the two of you are quite the match."

Quite the match. How else could Allecta have possibly known about Ellara's magical prophecy of love in his future if she hadn't told her mother herself? His stomach turned. He couldn't throw up right now. He wouldn't. Gripping onto the handle of the Witch Killer with enough strength to make his hand shake, he leveled his gaze at the beautiful old crone. It was impossible to read her face; every muscle was drawn with supreme confidence. She was a mask of non-feeling.

"Then I'm afraid you have a terrible intelligence network," he said, his voice thin even to his own ears.

"But not worse than yours. Tell me, how long did it take you to realize my plan?"

He swallowed, his mind torn between two realities: on the one hand, by now, his armies were ambushing High Court from all sides, preparing to battle the witches who would be too distracted by this meeting to do any real damage. He needed to keep his mind sharp and focused if he was going to keep up the facade for them. But on the other hand, her question choked him.

"Your plan?"

"My daughter," she said with a devil's smile and an angel's eyes as she turned to lounge across the throne instead of sitting in it. Terran tried not to think of all the times he'd imagined another green-skinned woman sitting in that seat of power, ruling at his side. Now, it seemed he might get half of his wish. "My daughter was the cause of your undoing. And it was my plan all along. Place her in your prison. Know she's clever enough to talk to the one human boy she always loved. And from there...It was all too easy."

The war brewing outside of the tall stained-glass windows was forgotten, and the world warped around Terran as if it was bending in on itself. Briony had been telling the truth. And if this witch was also telling the truth, then that meant...

Oh, no. His throat tightened, and breathing became an impossible chore.

"So," he exhaled. It took every ounce of his energy to keep himself in the regal posture he'd walked in with rather than crumbling to the floor under the weight of every stolen opportunity. He and Ellara could have saved Aulen and Outerland together. He'd ruined it by not believing her. "She was really in love with me?"

"I can only assume so. But now that she's seen who you really are, there's no chance she'll still love you."

The words resonated with truth, echoing in the empty chamber of his chest that once held his heart. If he ever saw Ellara again, if she ever sat on that throne and stared down at him from it, he knew there wouldn't be space for love amongst all the hatred.

He'd practically fed her to Elias. He'd threatened her with

death, with the blade of the Witch Killer. He'd been right all along, of course. The war had ruined him for love. He'd had it in his grasp, and he'd thrown it away the second his power was even the slightest bit threatened.

"I knew from the start," he lied, vomit rising higher and higher in his throat with every word he spoke. "That's why I didn't fall in love with your daughter. No matter how well she played the game, I was always one step ahead of her. You think a king would be duped by a teary-eyed witch begging for her life? I wouldn't have touched your daughter, much less loved her, if she was the only creature left in this kingdom."

He felt the oppressive air of magic cloister in around him, pushing in from all sides as the witches stepped in closer, their magic and spells clearly at the ready. A shadow crossed the would-be queen's face, as if all the surrounding candles had suddenly flickered out.

A thrill of fear rippled through him, one quelled only by the sounds of battle roaring outside and the sudden racing of witches from the main chamber.

"Be careful how you talk about her."

"Why? You don't care about her either. You're just using her as a pawn."

The throne room was now chaos, the alarm sounding as she waved a single hand and dragged him across the room without moving from her seat.

"I'm going to place her on the throne of Aulen. Something you never did."

"I would have given her everything."

"So, you admit it. You did love her."

Yes. With everything in me, yes.

"No, I admit that we had a deal. Her life for our marriage, for the unification of all of Aulen. Clearly, you didn't care about that as much as she did."

She threw her hand up in annoyance, dropping the cursed

link between them and releasing him into a pile on the cold stone floor.

"My daughter is a stupid girl who needs guidance. And I will be the one to guide her."

He leveled his gaze in Allecta's direction, issuing the strongest challenge he'd ever given. Allecta would understand he would not give her up. He knew that meant he'd rather die than see the woman he loved—the woman he loved and sacrificed for a chance for some power in this destructive world—fall back into the hands of her mother. Truth be told, he didn't want her falling back into his hands either. She didn't deserve either of them, either of their worlds. She deserved the clean air of the ocean and the sky above her and a bed of her own and a host of dragons to keep her company. She didn't deserve this broken life anymore. That is, if she ever deserved it in the first place. "If you can find her, of course."

"Then it is war."

The noise in the chamber echoed painfully against the walls. Terran's head throbbed. "You don't want her back?"

"I do. But I cannot pay the price you want. I will win her back, human. And you will be sorry." She waved a hand and a small set of witch-guards moved towards him. "Bring him to the dungeon."

His stomach plummeted. He couldn't join the fight from there. Reaching down, he grasped the heavy flag of peace, turning it upside down so he could use the blunt end as a weapon against the onslaught of approaching witches. "But I come under the banners of—"

"We are witches, Terran of Nothing and Nowhere. We don't respect your rules. We are the monsters you have made us."

The flag disappeared, magicked out of existence, and a pair of cold hands clamped around his wrists. A dizziness settled over him, one as heady and as clouded as a drunken stupor. But then, a voice from the gallery far above them stopped all the room's movement. All the battle preparations. All the talking.

It was Ellara's voice.

"Yes, we are witches. And I am your queen. And as your queen, I will make the grand pronouncements around here."

CHAPTER
TWENTY-NINE

There was a taste to war. Not the taste of blood in the mouth or sweat trickling down the skin, nor the taste of shattered teeth or bitten tongues. There was a taste in the air that always told Ellara that war was near, that the future held the promise of bloodshed and sacrifice. It was a contradictory mixture—a metallic taste, a bitter taste, a heady, sweet, whisky taste that coated the inside of her mouth and made everything from the palest water to the gamiest meats taste of war.

And when the attention of the entire throne room turned to her, their faces gazing up in abject shock, that familiar taste flooded her mouth.

She'd come here to avert a war. But she might have just started one.

Outside of the walls of the now silent, now still room, a battle raged. From her place high above the throne room, Ellara could easily peer through the windows and see flashes of magical light striking human swords. She could hear the screams. Smell the blood.

She had to work quickly.

"Ellara! My daughter! Welcome home."

The taste sickened her stomach like cheap wine. Her mother had betrayed her. Her mother had used her. Her mother had just announced to a court of their friends, their people, that she was a stupid girl who was only queen because she could be easily manipulated.

"Hello, Mother," she returned the pleasantry even as it clawed its way up her throat.

"Come. Take your place on the throne. And give this human the punishment he deserves."

Yes, this was exactly what she wanted, exactly what the plan called for. She and her mother were more alike than Ellara wanted to admit. They were both masters at playing each other, at manipulating the chessboard of war once they decided where all the pieces should be placed. Activating her magic, Ellara flew down to the gallery.

The moment her boots hit the ground, the small sea of witches fell to their knees, bowing their bodies and their heads before her in some kind of twisted display of loyalty. Only...she didn't want their loyalty.

Well, maybe she did. But only because she wanted them to have their freedom as much as they wanted it for themselves. And with their loyalty, she could give it to them.

Her mother vacated the throne, standing beside it so Ellara could take her place. Even during her time in the palace, she'd never been seated in this place of power, never before taken over the mantel in this way. Yet, when her mother placed the crown on her head, it wasn't power or control she was thinking of. It was the man kneeling before her, the man who'd knelt the moment he saw her.

"Ellara."

"Terran."

From under his long eyelashes, he glanced up at her,

breathing words from his lips that she'd always wanted to hear from him.

"I always knew you would look beautiful in a crown."

"I never wanted one."

"I know. That's why I always thought you'd look beautiful in one."

Sickness roiled in her stomach. She hated them both so much, hated her mother for using her, and hated Terran for not loving her enough to believe her, to fight at her side like he'd always promised, to work with her to find that better world they'd both said they'd wanted. She hated him for not being the man she wanted him to be, hated him for getting her hopes up just before dashing them against the rocks like little more than a toy sailboat.

She hated him because she'd loved him so, so much. Because she *still* loved him. And if she didn't focus on the hate, then she'd never be able to let go of that love completely.

"I won't save your life, you know," she whispered, her voice barely carrying past her lips, a secret just for the two of them. He closed his eyes and swallowed hard, sharing with her the vulnerability that had swept her off her feet so many times before.

"I know."

Sitting rod-straight in her throne—*her* throne...she almost laughed at the thought, considering her plan, considering the war raging outside, considering what would happen if all that she and Briony planned actually came to pass—she let the dagger of his acceptance stab through her chest. Her breath came in quick gasps, but she held fast to her expression, not letting her face slip and give anything away. All the eyes of the new court of witches were upon her. She could feel their stares.

"What shall it be, then, daughter?" her mother asked, voice rising and echoing them.

"Exile."

She didn't have to look at the woman to hear the triumph in her voice. "Well done."

Ellara swallowed hard and said what she had to say. Peace was just one sentence away. "Exile for you all."

A ripple of disquiet ran through the room and her mother moved in close to her, leaning down for private counsel. Ellara couldn't take her eyes off of Terran, who kept his head down and his breathing even as if he hadn't heard her at all.

"What? You can't exile me. I am your mother," she hissed.

"And I am the queen."

"I put you on that throne, little girl. I can just as quickly take you down from it."

Ah, there it was. The truth her mother wasn't trying to hide any longer. Ellara snorted a laugh, short and harsh as the true weight of her own power flowed through her veins. It wasn't a sensation she particularly enjoyed—it burned hot like fire and itched for more—but she *did* enjoy the flicker of fear in her mother's eyes.

"Yes, well, that's where you're wrong, Mother. You can't take me off this throne. No one can."

"And why is that? Where is your army?"

"I don't need an army. I have dragons."

With a wave of her hands, the glass dome above the throne shattered, and a sea of the creatures flocked over the newly emptied space, breathing their fire and snapping their jaws, their ire only held in place by Ellara's magical guidance.

Disquiet turned to panic, fear turned to awe, and she caught the first flicker of a smile on Terran's face.

"I..." Her mother couldn't take her eyes off the dragons, their glistening teeth, their menacing scales. "How did you..."

"You may leave," Ellara said, brushing an imaginary speck of dust from her skirts. "I will give you a head start."

"Ellara." Her mother's eyes softened, and she knelt down before her, the very picture of desperation and sickening sweetness, the same combination that brought them both to this place. "Sweetheart. Be reasonable."

"I have been reasonable, Mother. That is why I was betrayed and used by everyone I ever knew. I am done being reasonable. I am done waiting for someone to give me peace. Now, I am *making* the peace." She ripped her skirts from her mother's hands. "Get out."

"Ellara—"

"Go."

Ellara's control on her magic started to slip, and the first of the dragons poked its head through the empty space in the ceiling. Ellara's mother ran faster than Ellara had ever seen her run before. Many of her witches followed her.

Their departure was a welcome victory, the beginning of the great change Ellara wanted to see in this nation, but it wasn't enough. Reaching for the staff waiting for her, she banged it twice on the ground, its heavy golden weight scraping against the marble each time. This was the beginning of the new world. She didn't have time to so much as glance down at Terran, not if she wanted to keep her nerve.

"Bring in Madame Bovere."

"*What?*"

Terran's hissed question went unanswered as Briony led the struggling woman forward, pulling on her unwilling arm before throwing her at Terran's side. The man Ellara had loved stared at their newest guest with wide, disbelieving eyes, his mouth opening and closing repeatedly as he fought to form words. Not that Ellara gave him the chance. The sooner she was free of this obligation, the better.

"Madame Bovere. You are charged with crimes against both Aulen and Outerland. How do you plead?"

"I am not guilty of these crimes. Don't be a fool."

The woman's gaze was desperate and threatening, vacillating between the power she once had and the power she now held, kneeling before the queen who controlled an army of swarming dragons.

"Madame Bovere," Ellara commanded. "Reveal your true form."

The woman laughed weakly. "...What are you talking about?"

Ellara raised a single hand, a threat she didn't know if she could make good on, but a threat Madame Bovere wouldn't risk. "Reveal it, or I shall do it for you."

The silent hall rustled with whispering voices as the woman worked her magic, threading it through her body and washing away her human disguise, taking on her full witch form. There were gasps. There were cries of *traitor*. There were whimpers of fear and doubt. But it was Ellara's voice that rang out over all of them.

"Tell them what you've done."

"I haven't—"

"Tell them," she growled, reaching for the woman's arm and turning her around to face her people.

It was this betrayal that had scarred Ellara the most, the one that had convinced her to take on this mantel she didn't want, this world saving she wanted no part of. Her entire life had been ruled by the exile of the witches, determined and shaped by it. Now she understood it in fullness.

When Madame Bovere made no move to speak, Ellara worked her magic through the woman, forcing the confession, which she spat out from between unwilling teeth.

"I cursed the land of Outerland so that nothing would grow. I sowed the seeds of discontent within our people and then fled to stoke the hatred on this side of the war. I have watched and waited and played your strings until you all fell right into my plan."

Ellara threw Madame Bovere back to the floor, too disgusted to touch her any longer. The eyes of the witches in the crowd turned murderous, pained, and they closed in. Closer and closer, stepping towards the betrayer as waves of hatred rolled off them like walls of harsh, heavy rain.

"Why?"

"Because we are more powerful," Madame Bovere cried, no longer needing Ellara's influence for honesty. She believed every word she said without reservation. She believed her own propaganda. "We deserve the power."

"The war is a lie? Outerland is a lie?"

"This is what Outerland looked like in the days of our ancestors," Briony said, stepping forward and conjuring a mist-like image she'd pulled from the woman's own records. The land was lush and green, overrun with clean water and bright sunshine, far removed from the cracked, rocky wasteland of Ellara's childhood. Horrified gasps rang out. "Madame Bovere is the only one old enough to remember. Because she killed all the others who might remember."

"It can't be true," one witch whispered, her knees shaking as she held onto another for support.

"Test her magic. I know it's true."

"How did you...How did you know?"

"You really shouldn't leave your diaries lying around, Madame. Take her away."

The mob needed no asking twice. Nor did the dragons circling the shattered dome above them. At Ellara's direction, the creatures swooped, all talons and teeth. With the magic of the surrounding witches and the monsters from the sky, Madame Bovere had no choice. She was pulled into the crowd, disappearing as they took her outside to face justice.

Soon, Ellara, her small contingent of witches, and a few human prisoners were all that remained behind.

Outside of the chamber walls, the dragons flew from Ellara's control. The battle slowed. The bloodshed stopped. The world seemed to turn backwards as Ellara projected her voice and her image to every corner of the kingdom, as she brought herself into the closeness of homes and the vastness of war. It was more magic than she'd ever used in her life, more exertion than she'd ever put forth.

She was powerful. And it was a power she was ready to give up.

"There will be no war. There will be peace. Briony of Outerland, step forward."

Briony blinked. "Why?"

Ellara extended the scepter to her friend, one of the few people she trusted with the future. "Briony, will you faithfully and with all of your power protect Outerland as its queen?"

Briony gasped. She struggled for the words, but eventually whispered with reverent awe, "I will."

"And will you foster peace with the humans of Aulen, nurturing a friendship that will last forever?"

Briony glanced at Terran, who glanced right back, both of them sharing a sudden dawning of understanding of Ellara's plan. Two nations, but two nations that shared an alliance, a promise of a peaceful future. "I will."

"And will you rule as a just and fair ruler, never asking your people to rise up against another unless the cause is just?"

"I will."

And as Briony said the words, Ellara knew them to be true.

"Then rise, Your Majesty, Briony of Outerland." Extending her hand, she pulled her friend to her feet. "We will restore Outerland. We will come together to heal it and make it the prosperous kingdom that it once was. It will be a land for peace." She turned to Terran, who stared up at her with silent confusion as she took the crown off of her own head and handed it to him, handing him her heart along with it. "That is, if our brothers in Aulen will accept. Terran of Nowhere and Nothing. Will you be the King of Aulen once again?"

He was as blank and as uncertain as a man who'd been stolen away from the hands of death. "Why?"

Since she'd come up with this plan, she'd asked herself that same question many times. Why was she willing to trust her peace and her kingdom in the hands of a man who'd broken her heart? The answer was simple, and it came down to an extremely simple explanation.

"Because you saved the bird from the dragon. And I believe you would do it again, despite everything."

Tears pooled in his eyes. She wanted nothing more than to reach down and wipe them away. "But I didn't save you."

"Which is why you will have the kingdom instead of my heart."

She placed the crown on his head and released the magic that cast their images out into the world before vacating the throne and leaving them all behind.

"Wait," he called after her. "Where are you going?"

"I've done my part in this story. There's nothing left for me now."

"Ellara."

"Yes?"

Say you love me. Ask me again to be your queen. Say you'll run with me. Anything, anything, anything.

"I'm so sorry."

"I know you are. Which is why I know you'll never let it happen again."

CHAPTER
TWENTY-
THIRTY

I t was amazing, Terran thought, how fast the world moved both towards and away from chaos. Just yesterday, the entire city was a sea of flames and battle cries, of magic spells and flying arrows. But today, fretting viceroys and newly appointed members of the witches' council stalked through the halls of the court—or what remained of the walls... there would need to be a serious conversation on the subject of reconstruction—sniping and bickering about what they would call this nationwide spat...The Wedding War? The Civil Conflict? An Addendum to the Seven Kings' War? No one could agree.

For Terran's money, he would have gone with *The Last War*. Not because he believed that it would be the last one. No, he'd certainly not found that much faith in people or witches, but because he wanted it to be the last. Last night, in the few hours, when he'd managed to shut his eyes between discussions of state and arguments about the future, he'd dreamed of it. A world where swords were used for slicing down too tall wheat, and magic was used to make tea sweeter without adding sugar. In that world, he sat beside Ellara, holding her hand in his, and they watched from a perch over High Court as a festival took place beneath them. The people were dancing, and the music was so loud that it hurt their ears even with the distance.

He'd never had a happier dream. Not in his entire life.

But that's all it was, he reminded himself. A dream. A dream and nothing more. The happiest dream of his life emptied him, hollowed him, so that when he woke, he wanted nothing more than to crawl back into sleep and never wake up.

The ministers and viceroys and councils finally disbanded when the first yawning colors of sunlight broke through the darkness of night. Despite only a few collective hours of sleep in the last two days, his feet didn't carry him to his chambers or to the nearest bed, but rather out of doors. He needed to be outside of the castle walls, away from everyone who looked to him for answers and approval, away from the pressing questions about choosing a new bride.

He needed fresh air. And space to think. Running away would have been preferable to staying, but he'd made a vow. And since he couldn't take off to start a new life in the hills, he settled for a walk at sunrise.

Stepping out from the keep, he moved along the high walls of the castle, taking in the distant sights of his kingdom. High Court wasn't chosen only because it was a stronghold, but because its central location gave one a full view out into the far reaches of the country. Mountains and rivers. Prairie and grassland.

The only thing he couldn't spot was Outerland. But perhaps that was for the best, considering how often his hand reached to take Ellara's, which was no longer there, and how often he opened his mouth to speak to her, only to remember she'd returned home.

Home. This was his home now, now and forever. He'd made a promise to the woman he loved that he would protect this place and her people, and he would do it with his very last breath. Even if doing so meant ripping out his own heart in the process.

The smoking embers of the fires had died with last night's rain, and a fresh wind from the east filled the air with the sweet scent from the holiday trees and the clean notes from the snaking Boxian River. As he walked, the rain slowed to a shaking mist, washing the horizon with dew. It was as if everything were beginning anew before his eyes, as if the country were cleansing itself in a kind of baptism. His boots carried him over the slick stones beneath his feet with ease.

It was the sight of a green woman in a warrior's gown, sitting on the edge of the castle wall, staring out at the first blinking eyes of sunrise, that made him slip.

Ellara. He couldn't even speak her name. He was too terrified to, as if speaking it out loud would make her disappear into the mist. He blinked. He held his breath. He dug his fingernails into the palm of his hands, anything to wake him up if this was a dream or to break the vision if this was some kind of miserable delusion.

But no matter how much pain he inflicted upon himself or how many times he wiped the water from his eyes, she didn't vanish. She just sat there, shoulders slumped, eyes to the horizon, hands folded in her lap.

She was drenched. The fabric of her dress clung to her every inch, and her hair hung around her face like too long moss. If she heard him approach, she didn't bother looking away from the distant clouds hiding the rising sun. Instead, she focused on it, as if she were trying to pull it up with only the strength of her stare.

Questions and hope, like uncaged birds, loosed themselves from the confines of his chest, where he'd been hiding them away since she left him with that last, blistering kiss, but he held them back. Maybe it didn't matter why she was here or what she was doing or if she missed him. After being convinced he'd never see her again...here she was. He swallowed back his questions but let hope flutter inside of him.

"Ellara?" he asked, not because he wanted confirmation that

it was her, but because he wanted to feel her name roll off his tongue once again.

"Terran."

He didn't miss the way he'd phrased her name as a question, but she phrased his like a statement. It was as if he'd asked a million of his questions—*Are you back to stay? Did you come back for me? Do you...do you love me? Could you still love me? Do you love me again as if it were the first time?*—and she'd answered *yes*.

But even so, she didn't turn to look at him. She focused on her patch of starlight, of night sky, of cloud where the moon should be. He didn't dare to approach her.

"Can I tell you something?" she finally asked.

"Please do," he replied.

"When I was a little girl, I believed that the weather followed me around. Can you believe that?"

Sensing it wasn't actually an invitation to speak, he stayed silent, listening intently not just to the words she spoke, but the spaces in between them and the breaths she welcomed into her chest, searching every note for some kind of meaning or explanation, for some confirmation of the hope he'd allowed himself.

"I thought that when the sun shined, it was shining just for me, that it was telling me everything was going to be alright. And that when the rains came, it was a sign that I'd done something wrong or I needed to change my path. Snow was more confusing. Sometimes I thought it was a gift, and sometimes, if it killed one of my flowers or gave me a cold, I thought it was a curse. I let the weather dictate my life. The weather told me to lie my way into the Academy, and the weather told me to take a walk the night I saved you from that dragon."

In all their time together, she'd carefully avoided talking too much about her childhood or what it was like to grow up in Outerland. In this moment, when he was so certain she could run away again and take half of his heart with her, such a confession about who she was before they met at the Academy calmed him, even if only slightly. It meant she trusted him with this information, information he wasn't sure she'd ever spoken aloud to anyone before.

"So," he asked, his voice barely audible above the rain, "Do you still believe that?"

For the first time, she awarded him a quick peek out of the corner of her eyes. His stomach knotted, but she patted the wet wall beside her. Careful of the rain, he followed her unspoken instructions and sat beside her. Another leap of faith. A small one, but a leap nonetheless. He was afraid of heights, and she knew it. When he was settled, he gripped the edge of the stone to keep from reaching out to take her hand.

"One year, I went home, and my mother and I were fighting."

"About what?"

"You, actually. She saw the scars I'd gotten, and I told her what I did. I was proud of it. I thought I was doing what the universe wanted from me." Unconsciously or not, Ellara rubbed her wrists. Not for the first time, Terran wanted nothing more than the ability to go back and save her from ever suffering the pain she'd gone through for him, not just the pain the binders caused that night, but every pain he'd dealt her over their time together. Guilt covered his skin in gooseflesh. "I told her. It was stupid, I know, but I told her why I did what I did and that the weather believed in me. The weather was trying to push me to greater things. And you know what she did?"

"What?"

"She slapped me. It wasn't the first time I'd been hit. Girls at the Academy practically used me as a punching bag when they realized I couldn't fight back, but that was the only time my mother ever hit me. And it's the one time I remember the most clearly."

The urge to take her hand and hold her was so strong Terran almost couldn't avoid it. But he pooled all his inner strength and made a noble attempt. The last thing he wanted was to scare her away.

"That was when I learned the truth. I wasn't special. The

weather didn't care about me. It rained because the clouds were heavy, and it snowed because the temperature dropped. It had nothing to do with me. No witch is that powerful. No person is that important. It was a hard lesson to learn, but for most of my life, I was glad I'd learned it, especially during the war. I can't imagine how many troops I would have gotten killed if I'd relied on the weather instead of strategy and intel."

She smiled then, but it was one of those he'd gotten used to seeing on her, the one sort of smile he desperately wished he could wipe from her vocabulary of expressions forever. That was the smile she gave when she hated herself, when she was trying to win someone—maybe even herself—over with self-deprecation. Hugging her arms to herself, she shivered in the cold. Terran went back to unleash his coat, but when his fingers reached the fur, he realized he was now as soaked through as she was. He fought off a shiver of his own.

"I mean, you can't go through this life thinking you're special when you're not. You can't think that you'll change the world. Or anyone's mind. You can't let yourself daydream that you'll be anyone, much less the queen. In this world, in this life, you can't let yourself imagine that the weather is trying to guide you. You just have to accept that you're the only one who cares about you. You don't matter." She tilted her face up to the dark sky, but it wasn't because she was seeking answers or cursing the sky for her fate. It was a pose of acceptance. "You just don't matter. Not even to the rain."

"You matter—"

What was meant to be the beginning of an impassioned defense of her honor halted in his mouth with a wave of her hand. It wasn't magic that stopped him from speaking, but it might as well have been.

"And then...I was walking last night. Walking away from this castle. Walking away from you. It didn't start all at once, but slowly, drop by drop, with every step I took away from you, it started to rain. And it rained and rained and rained until I couldn't see the ground in front of me, until the rivers over-flowed, and...and...and for the first time since I was fifteen, I felt like the weather believed in me. That the weather was speaking to me. And it was saying..."

She trailed off, her voice dissolving as the rain around them did the same. It was slow, at first, but little by little, the thick mist softened and the clouds before them split apart in the sky like two discordant dance partners. The sky was still dark, of course, and there were still droplets hitting Terran's eyelashes and hands, but for the first time, rays of golden sunlight found their way back into the sky. For the first time, it actually looked like morning.

He'd never thought of himself as superstitious, but as a warm beam of light hit his cheek, he was almost certain he heard the weather whispering, too. The echoes were faint, but strong enough that he knew *exactly* what they were saying.

"Come back home," he supplied.

"Yes. It said that everything I wanted, everything I needed was right here."

Her hand reached for his. Their fingers locked. And some-thing inside of Terran awoke with a cry of victory. He knew that the future was stretching out before them, ready to be molded and made into a better one. One that they would face and shape together, hand in hand.

The warmth from her hands worked its way into his heart, filling him with soft courage, the kind he'd never needed on the battlefield but the kind he needed now most of all. With his free hand, he removed the gold circlet from his head and placed it to the side. In that moment, he didn't want to be a king beside her. He wanted to be just a man.

"And what is it saying now?" he asked.

She squeezed him tighter.

"It's saying that their job here is done. I don't need the weather to care about me." Then, finally, she turned to him. The sunlight caught every perfect imperfection in her beautiful, lovable face. She spoke with a certainty they'd both earned, one they'd fought against the world to win. "Because I've got you."

"And I've got you."

The words were better than wedding vows, more honest and more meaningful than anything they could have declared before the Fates and their country. After a moment of being lost in his eyes, Ellara tore herself away and stared down at the land before them.

"There is so much work to be done."

"Yes," Terran agreed, unable to keep his admiration out of his voice. The woman he'd fallen for—the woman who'd given him her heart and stolen his right out from under him—didn't sit still for long.

"And the future is uncertain. We'll need to work with Outerland and we'll need to find Briony a consort and we'll need—"

Catching her chin, he halted her stream of consciousness, capturing her eyes once again. His heart thundered in his chest.

"We'll need to do all of that. Yes. But all of it can wait for thirty seconds."

"What happens in thirty seconds?"

"This."

Their lips met. The rains stopped. And he held her closer— with his body and in his heart—than he'd ever held anyone before.

They were a king and a queen, sitting atop a castle, over-looking their kingdom. But as they kissed in the growing warmth of the newfound sunshine, they were just Terran and Ellara, two very hopeful people who'd found love when it should have been impossible.

EPILOGUE

Lady Ellara Wist, formerly of the now Free State of Outerland, didn't want a coronation. In fact, whenever the phrase was brought up in her presence, she sniffed at the word as if it were a handful of pepper thrown directly at her face. This was much to the chagrin of the new council, a group of newly selected viceroys and hands, each of whom had come through the war or from Outerland to start anew. After the battle of High Court, Ellara and Terran took their time rebuilding the new ruling class of the nation, selecting those who they thought would be fair and just, rather than those whose coffers could most help the crown. Because of the new perspectives in the castle—from witches to former peasants to retired soldiers with missing limbs and nervous eyes—conversations about a new future abounded.

With the old ways gone, perhaps they could start afresh. Perhaps they could rebuild a kingdom that would never again fall to war, one that would never force another generation to endure what they'd endured all those years.

But all of that started with Lady Ellara Wist becoming their queen, and Terran of a now-destroyed house becoming her husband.

And in that spirit, Ellara shook off the words coronation and wedding, since they were old words, words that had no meaning or importance anymore. Instead, she decided to call it the Aulen Festival of Unity, a sign that this wasn't just about her and Terran coming together or some of the old witches of Outerland coming together with the Aulenian people, but about the unification of the entire kingdom.

No more war. No more fighting. Just a future stretching out far before them, a million possibilities waiting on the horizon.

And when Lady Ellara Wist walked out of her palace bedroom on the morning of the first Aulen Festival of Unity, she did so wearing her old binders, those she'd been shackled with during her captivity in High Court, and she wore the tattered war-clothes she'd been imprisoned in. She'd first rescued them from the incinerator out of instinct—what if she needed to escape with them one day, or what if she needed a disguise?—but today, she knew that the real reason she saved them was so she could wear them now.

Today was all about symbolism. Maybe she'd gone a bit heavy-handed with it, but if she was going to stand before the kingdom and make a statement, she wanted everyone—*everyone*—to hear it.

With her court behind her—even the new Queen of Outerland, Briony, who humbled herself to wear her old courtly clothes instead of her royal garments—she walked through the quiet stone halls and out into the main body of the keep, where the gates had been left open for the people.

And...*wow*. Had the people arrived. If she didn't know any better, she would have thought the entire population of Aulen had shown up with their banners and their cheers. The green faces of witches smiled alongside the cheering humans, all watching as she crossed to the center of the keep, where her king—and theirs—stood.

They'd spent days choreographing this entire thing, this mass of humanity and the ritual they would perform here. He didn't turn to meet her, just as they'd planned, and she came up behind him with her bound wrists lifted towards him.

"Your Majesty, I ask you to free the people of Outerland. I ask you to free me."

"You have freed yourself, Lady Ellara of Outerland. And you have freed the people of Outerland. From now on, they are a sovereign nation, and the curses upon their world are now freed."

Hope welled up in her heart, blossoming like new flowers in the spring sun. She smiled, not as part of the choreography but a genuine, beaming smile.

"We will be your great allies, Your Majesty."

"And you, Lady Ellara? What will you be?"

"Queen of all Aulen, Your Majesty. Queen of the people."

"And what shall I be?"

"King of Aulen, Your Majesty. King of the people." He pulled her in close, taking both of her hands in his, and she couldn't help whispering a private declaration, just for the two of them. "And king of my heart."

"As you shall be queen of mine," he said, his voice rising. "Soldiers, put down your weapons. If anyone objects to this union, to this new Aulen, to this new Outerland, speak now and face me."

The yard was silent. Green faces mingled with the human crowd, all breathless in their anticipation of this new future, of an Aulen and Outerland forever at peace.

"Then it is settled. This is a new day for Aulen. A new sun is rising."

"A new sun is rising!"

The crowds cheered and moved forward, pressing them into the waiting temple where they would be married. Where they would, at last, be truly united.

ABOUT THE AUTHOR

Alys Murray is a New Orleans native and graduate of New York University and Kings College London. A screenwriter and novelist in her professional life, she can often be found in her off time testing out new recipes in the kitchen or traveling with her husband.

facebook.com/alysmurrayauthor

twitter.com/writeralys

instagram.com/writeralys

ALSO BY ALYS MURRAY

Small Town Secrets

Villain Lover

Home at Summer's End

The Perfect Hideaway

Sweet Pea Summer

The Magnolia Sisters

Love Spells for the End of the World

Society Girl

Tea and a Cowboy

The Christmas Company

A SPECIAL THANK YOU TO OUR KICKSTARTER BACKERS

Alexa James, Mary Beth Case, Jasmine, Morgan, Elayorna, Brynn, Lane R, Rhiannon Raphael, Sara Collins, Tabitha Clancy, Erica L Frank, Jen Schultz, Tao Neuendorffer, Kyle "kaz409" Kelly, Patrick Lofgren, Rebecca Fischer, Bridh Blanchard, William Spreadbury, Wm Chamberlainq, Adam Bertocci, Susan Hamm, Paula Rosenberg, Morgan Rider, Elizabeth Sargent, Greg Jayson, Jamie Kramer, Karen Gemin, Jonathan Rice, Bonnie Lechner, Katherine Pocock, Mary Anne Hinkle, Marlena Frank, Melissa Goldman, Stacy Psaros, Meghan Sommers, Marisa Greenfield, Anne-Sophie Sicotte, S. L. Puma, Jenn Thresher, Caley, Jim Cox, Kris McCormick, Jamie Provencher, Melody Hall, Ara James, Leigh W. Stuart, Sarah Lampkin, Stuart Chaplin, Amanda Le, Rae Alley, Arec Rain, Megan Van Dyke, Hannah Clement, Kathleen MacKinnon, Paul Senatillaka, Christine Kayser, Jennifer Crymes, Christa McDonald, Debra Goelz, Amber Hodges, Thuy M Nguyen, Jess Scott, Ella Burt, Sarah Ziemer, Mel Young, and Claire Jenkins.

NEXT FROM SWORD AND SILK BOOKS

Coming December 2021
Mind Like a Diamond
By: Amanda Pavlov

Coming February 2022
Unravel
By: Amelia Loken

Coming June 2022
Beneath the Starlit Sea
By: Nicole Bea

CPSIA information can be obtained
at www.ICGtesting.com
Printed in the USA
BVHW071201051021
618194BV00001B/31